WHAT
Lovers
DO

JEWEL E. ANN

WHAT LOVERS DO

JEWEL E. ANN

To every person who has been kind to a fault, you are not weak. You are the light illuminating everyone around you.

"A woman's heart is a deep ocean of secrets."
~Rose DeWitt Bukater, *Titanic*

CHAPTER *One*

SOPHIE

THE NEIGHBORS CALLED 9-1-1. They thought my dad whacked off my finger with the weed eater because of my blood-curdling scream coupled with the dripping crimson from my hand. Minutes later, an officer arrived at our house only to discover an injured garter snake. I called him Hercules—the snake, not the officer. We kept him in a plastic container with newspapers on the bottom, small holes in the lid, a dish of water, and a steady diet of guppies and earthworms.

He recovered weeks later, and we released him back into the wild. Dad promised to be more careful when using the mower and weed eater.

Hercules wasn't the first snake I rescued, but to this day, I believe he was the most grateful one.

"I'm running down to CVS to get some condoms." Jimmy shoves his bare feet into his grungy white high-tops while rifling through my handbag.

His shoes should be burned. When he removes them, the repulsive blackened insoles exude an odor akin to meat that's been left on the counter for three days. He lost his job two months ago, and now he showers every three to four days.

"For what?" I ask, my last nerve frayed and inflamed. At this point, he could sneeze and I'd likely stab him fifty times with the butcher knife he got me for my birthday. I can already hear the prosecution making their case and including that little nugget of information.

"Wow, Sophie. You've forgotten what condoms are used for. Understandable, since we haven't had sex in over a month."

He's right. We had sex a month ago, on *his* birthday. And I know what condoms are for—they're for people who want to have sex with each other and don't want to get pregnant.

I don't want to have sex with Jimmy. And ... I'm already pregnant. It's not his baby. It's not mine either.

"You can't afford condoms." I inspect the last clean plate that he partially dried while making a cringe-worthy attempt at seducing me. His tongue was doing some serpent-like thing while he waggled his brows at me, which has me reminiscing with a certain amount of fondness about Hercules the garter snake.

"Funny, babe." He clicks his tongue like he's on a horse and ready to go. "Good thing *you* have a job."

"I'm not paying for sex anymore." I finish drying the plate and slide it into the vertical slat above the sink.

Jimmy cackles as any carefree, unemployed twenty-nine-year-old would do and runs his hand through his long, greasy hair. It used to be blond, but now it's just nasty. Nasty: the official color of my biggest mistakes.

"You don't have to pay me for sex, just the condoms ... unless you're thinking we should make a baby. I'd crush the stay-at-home-dad gig, don't ya think?"

I bite my lips together until it hurts while padding my bare feet toward him, my hand clenching the invisible knife. "Jimmy ..." I snag my handbag before he manages to rob money from my wallet. "This isn't working for me anymore. I feel like an enabler, not your girlfriend." If I were completely honest with him, I haven't been his girlfriend in over two months—despite the pity sex ... I mean *birthday* sex. What were the chances that he'd lose his job on the very day I planned on breaking up with him?

100%.

I couldn't do it. I told myself I'd wait until he found a new job, assuming it would take maybe a week or two. I was wrong. So very wrong.

He parks a hand on his hip. "I'm not following."

Jimmy was smarter when I met him. Quicker to the draw.

Wasn't he?

Was I that blind? Is a guy with a job and routine hygiene the definition of sexy? I think it might be.

In Jimmy's case, it's one hundred percent true. I think I knew he wasn't going to keep his job for long. He's ... complicated.

His mother has health issues, and he was previously living with her, helping take care of her. *That* Jimmy was easy to love. Jimmy went to college for two years, but he hasn't been able decide on a true direction. When he could no longer take care of his mom, he put her into assisted living and had to sell the house to pay for it. I offered to let him live with me because we were together, and it seemed like the right thing to do in the moment. I thought he'd rebound and find his own place.

He didn't. Instead, he seemed to spiral downward into a mess of resentment toward his dad for leaving them while grappling with feeling like *he* failed his mom.

"I think it's time for you to move out, Jimmy. I'm sorry. It's just over." What am I apologizing for? Being nice? Too generous? I should be apologizing for having the spine of a gummy bear and letting yet another man step all over me and my generosity.

"Sophie, it's time to let Hercules free. Little button noses like you don't need to live with snakes."

I'm a magnet for charming men who just ... flip. Unravel. Lose their way. I honestly don't know what to call it. I've been burned, taken to the cleaners, hood-winked, duped ... more times than I care to admit.

I'm in love with the idea of love.

After my last boyfriend stole my purse and my car, I promised my family and friends that I would be more discerning. I would not rush into my next relationship. I would not open my door to the next sexy guy who needed to "crash at my place for a few nights."

And when I let Jimmy move in with me, and my

family and friends wanted to bitch slap me fifty times, I promised ... *promised* he was different.

Fuck my life.

He's not different.

"What do you mean?" Jimmy furrows his brow.

Yeah, he was *definitely* smarter when I met him. The mind is not exempt from the "If You Don't Use It, You Lose It" law. Jimmy is decomposing in my house, but he's not actually dead. He needs more than a bedding of newspapers, a dish of water, and an endless supply of guppies.

I might have to kill him, put him down. It's the humane thing to do.

Where'd I set that butcher knife?

"You need to get a job. And I fear you won't do that if I let you keep living here with me. If I keep paying for your food. Your clothes. Your condoms."

"*Our* condoms, babe. Really, they're more for you than me. I don't like the damn things. It never feels as good."

I nod slowly. "Our condoms ..." I whisper, trailing off with my thoughts as I struggle to remember what was going through my mind when I decided he was magically different than the others. Really, where will I dispose of his body if he doesn't move out soon?

"It's going to be pretty hard for me to move out if I don't have a job. And right now I can't find anything that pays better than my current unemployment check which I *need* because we didn't clear that much after selling my mom's house. And you know that assisted living facility is stupid expensive."

We are not married. Why is this my problem?

"Jimmy, I'm *breaking up with you*." I adjust my pink-framed glasses on my nose and tip my chin up. A direct and confident approach is best. Rip off the Band-Aid.

"Bye, Hercules. You'll be fine. You no longer need me."

His greasy head and unshaven face jut backward, blue eyes narrowed. "What? No. I don't accept your breakup proposal."

Again, I mentally thumb back through the pages of my life and look for the scene where I suggested Jimmy move in with me. Was I intoxicated? Where was the intervention?

Oh, that's right ... I didn't tell anyone until it was too late. And that's when I swore on a stack of Bibles and my grandparents' graves that Jimmy was different. He took care of his mom. He would get back on his feet quickly. Find a place of his own. Go back to school and make something of himself.

We would marry.

Have a few kids.

And my dreamy love story would be a big fat "I told you so" to the naysayers who had lost all faith in my judgment.

It bears repeating ... fuck my life.

"Breakup *proposal*?" I chuckle. "I don't even know what that is. It's not a suggestion. It's a statement. A declaration. I just broke up with you. Now you move out. Your acceptance, or lack thereof, doesn't change reality. I'm—" I catch my words and swallow them back down. I was about to say, "I'm sorry" again, but why? I didn't screw up and get myself fired. I didn't lose every ounce of ambition because someone offered me shelter and an unemployment check.

He brushes past me and plops his ass onto the sofa in the exact same spot it's been residing for the past two months. There's an actual divot, the outline of his ass. I'm going to need a new sofa after he moves out of here.

"Why don't you wait until you're done with your next cycle, and we'll revisit this conversation?"

Cersei, my poodle, jumps up next to him.

"My cycle? Cycle of what?"

Jimmy turns on the TV and flips the channel, making me dizzy with his incessant surfing. "Your period."

"What does that have to do with anything?"

He lands on some sci-fi show. "You start in two days. You're hormonal and impulsive. I don't want you to regret the things you say today that are clearly just your hormones talking."

I plant myself between him and the television. "You keep track of my cycle?"

He lifts one shoulder in a shrug just before leaning to the far right to see past me. "Of course."

"Why?"

"To know when you're going to be all moody like you are now."

The nerve ...

"Since when did breaking up with my deadbeat boyfriend constitute being moody?"

"Sophie, see ... it's like you're answering your own question. Do you hear the tightness in your voice? The way you're trying to restrain yourself? Happens every month. Last month you ragged about me not putting dishes in the dishwasher and leaving my socks on the coffee table."

"I'm not—" I pause to reel it in, keeping my emotions in check to avoid feeding his ridiculous point. I didn't have a period last month. He can't track anything. "Jimmy, I've felt this way for a while now. I just thought you'd get yourself together, and it wouldn't have to end like this. You were this great guy taking care of his mom, and it inspired me to help you. Temporarily. But I'm done. It's been long enough, and you're not making any effort to change your situation in life. I don't have the same feelings for you. It doesn't have to be personal. We can just go our separate ways. Okay?"

"Sophie, my mom always made me wait thirty days before she'd buy me anything expensive. She said it takes thirty days to distinguish between impulse and true desire. You're trying to break up with me on impulse. Wait thirty days, and I'll consider your proposal." He doesn't give me a single glance. It's irritatingly dismissive.

I'm ... speechless. Really, where does he come up with this stuff? This isn't a divorce. It's a breakup. It's non-negotiable.

"I'll give you a week."

He chuckles. "It's thirty days, Sophie. Call my mom if you don't believe me."

"Fine. I'll call your mom in the morning and tell her we're breaking up and you're a week away from being homeless. Maybe she'll come up with a seven-day plan for you instead of a thirty-day plan. But ... I'm out. Come, Cersei." I march toward the bedroom.

"Have you completely forgotten my mom has MS?"

I bite my tongue. I know his mom has MS. And no money, like her son. I lock the door behind me. "Stupid," I whisper, pressing the palm of my hand against my head.

I'm so stupid. This is the third time I've ended up with a freeloader for a boyfriend. I can't save all the snakes. It ends *now* ... or in a week.

CHAPTER *Two*

SHEP

"Julia's been licking herself. Should we be concerned?" Millie shoos me out the door along with George and Julia. "Sorry. I have a client coming in five minutes. I don't want to have to explain this."

"This?" I walk backward to my car as the dogs run circles around me.

She waves her hand in the air. "You. Our arrangement ..."

"I'm your ex-husband. These are our dogs. What was that? Seven words and two seconds?"

She frowns. "Just make sure you talk to the vet."

"I brought it up to Dr. Stanley at the last visit. She said Julia's fine; she just enjoys licking herself there. It must feel good. You used to like it too."

"Don't be crude, Shep."

"Factual. Not crude."

Truth? I've never hated anyone, but I might hate my ex-wife. To hide my growing detest, I humor her. Or maybe I humor myself to stay on the right side of sanity.

"Listen..." she checks her watch "...how would you feel about us getting on the same dating app?"

"I wasn't into role-playing when we were married. What makes you think I'd want to do it now that we're divorced?"

"Shep ... just ..." She sighs. "I hate when you don't take anything seriously."

I open the backdoor and let the dogs jump in. "Oh, I'm serious, Millie. No role-playing."

"I don't want to date *you*. I want to check out my competition in the area. And let's be honest, you could use a date. If you reject all dating apps, you'll never find anyone. And don't forget, that's how you found me."

"I feel like you're on to something with that statement. An aha moment?"

Once upon a time, I thought Millie was the one for me. No doubt whatsoever. We clicked. Then she did something that felt pretty unforgivable, yet I forgave her. Then she had a fucking epiphany. No-fault divorce, my ass. It was her. All her.

"You divorced me." I scrounge a toothy grin, my grin of choice for her because I can keep my teeth gritted. "If you want me back, just ask. The answer is hell no, but just ask. I don't need to be on a dating app to give you a hard swipe left regardless of *the competition*."

"Not competition for you. I want to know what women in this area are my competition for *other* guys."

"I'm not on any dating apps." I shrug and shut the back door.

"But you could be."

"I'm not setting up a profile on a dating app, again, as a favor to you."

She gives me her poutiest face. To think ... at one point I found it cute. "I thought we ended things amicably."

"We did. That's why I'm saying, 'Thanks for the offer, but no thanks.' I could have said, 'Are you out of your fucking mind, bitch?' But I didn't because we ended things amicably." Doubling down on my condescending, toothy grin, I get into my car. I'm perfectly capable of finding someone without the help of a dating app. Backing out of the driveway, I wave. A wave with all five fingers, not just my middle one because ... "amicable."

CHAPTER *THREE*

SOPHIE

SATURDAY MORNING, I sneak past Jimmy snoring and drooling on my sofa and leave him a note.

Taking Cersei for a walk. Look for a job and an apartment.

No X's or O's.

No smiley faces or hearts.

Not even a dash and my name.

Jimmy has six more days to get out of my house.

God ... please let him be gone.

Cersei and I stop for an iced coffee before heading west. We pass Wash Your Tail, a pet wash and bakery that opened a year ago. I've never been inside because I'm loyal to one of my patients who owns another dog wash and pet supply store here in Scottsdale. Today, I make one exception due to the sweltering heat. Pulling Cersei toward the store, I open the door and gulp breaths of cool air before looking around.

Pet lovers and wagging tails fill the aisles of the bustling store, so I tighten my grip on Cersei's leash as we weave our way around the displays.

"Good morning. Is there anything I can help you

find? Or are you just looking around and soaking up the cool air?"

Busted!

I smile at the blue-aproned man giving me a disarming grin. The ends of his floppy brown hair curl around his ears and tease his eyebrows. The mischievous twinkle of his hazel eyes holds my attention.

"First time in here. So I'm just checking you out. Thanks."

His smile swells and I feast on it until ... it hits me.

"Things!" I choke on what comes out as a half laugh and a hard cough. "I'm just checking *things* out. Not you. I meant to say thank you. But the 'you' got a little too anxious and devoured the word 'things.' So ..." I tuck my chin and scratch my forehead and mutter, "Just tell me to shut up."

Every inch of that exceptional smile and a slow nod await when I risk a glance up at him. "Take as much as you need. And can I say ... what a gorgeous creature?"

Heat gathers along my cheeks. "Oh gosh ... thank you. I'm Sophie."

On a chuckle, he shifts his gaze to Cersei. "Well, I meant your white floofer, but you're equally deserving of the compliment, *Sophie*."

For the record, I'm not this awkward. When I'm not taking in stray men or drooling over strangers, I'm entirely put together.

Smart.

Educated.

Confident.

Okay, somewhat confident.

And now that I think about it ... I'm questioning my intelligence.

I blame Jimmy. He has royally annihilated my psyche, rattled my confidence, and demolished my sense of trust and good will.

If this dude meant my dog, then he should have looked at her when he said it. Now I feel presumptuous and stupid.

It seems to be the new theme in my life.

"Kidding. I'm such a kidder. Of course I knew you were talking about my dog. Her name is Cersei. And now I'm going to exit the store and never return." I suck on the straw of my iced coffee and turn to slither toward the door like Hercules the garter snake.

"Nothing beats a classic standard poodle. Doodles have taken over the world. It's nice to see a purebred."

I turn. He's good. Too good. "Yeah." I nod. "Only ... I'm not sure if she's classic or a purebred. The vet thinks she might have something besides poodle in her. So she could be a doodle. But don't worry, I don't really see her taking over the world. She's scared of shadows, the trash truck, and her tail until she realizes it's attached to her body."

He laughs, pulling a treat out of a drawstring bag hanging from the waist of his pants, then he holds it up to me.

"What is it?" I ask.

"Dehydrated lamb lung."

I shake my head. "No thank you. Just coffee for me. But Cersei might like it."

The tiny bit of his smile that faded while showing me the treat quickly returns. He lets Cersei sniff his fisted hand before opening it and offering her the treat. "She really is gorgeous." He scratches behind her ears.

"Thank you." I smile.

Cersei's brown eyes track him, waiting to see if he's going to offer her another treat.

"I'm Shep. If you have any questions, let me know."

I slide my blue-framed glasses higher on my nose and blow my bangs away from my face as I nod several times and whisper, "Thanks," with the composure of a fifteen-year-old girl at a BTS concert.

Cersei sniffs butts and licks everything she can as I pull her around the store, sipping my coffee and letting my gaze navigate to Shep and his charming demeanor.

"Focus, Sophie," I murmur, reminding myself that I have a squatter at my house because I've habitually fallen for the sexy, nice guy façade. I've spread my legs in the name of charming and handed over my house key after hearing the words "I love you."

If there's rehab for total suckers, then I need to admit myself.

"Miss, your dog stole that treat from the bin back there," an older woman says to me with a disapproving scowl on her overly made-up face as she hugs a purse-sized gray fluff ball close to her and kisses its head.

"Oh ..." I frown at Cersei. "Drop it." I need another hand as I grapple with the leash, my coffee, and a stolen tendon treat. I shift my coffee to my hand that has her leash so I can grab the tendon. She doesn't release it. Instead, she hunches down, butt in the air, and growls at me. "Drop. It," I say in my own growly tone.

Launching into a game of tug, she inches her backside toward a tall swivel display of collars and leashes.

"Cersei!" I pull harder to keep her from making a bigger scene. I lose grip on the tendon. Thankfully, the leash catches, but the sudden jerk sends my iced coffee flying.

"Oh my god," I whisper. There's coffee everywhere, including my evil mutt and the treat police holding her perfectly groomed dog.

She's silent. Eyes wide, lips parted.

"I'm ... *so* sorry."

"Trade?" Shep bypasses me and holds out his hand with another treat in it.

Cersei releases the tendon and takes the treat.

"Good girl," Shep says, scratching her chest as she triumphantly chews the treat.

Good girl? Is he serious? There's coffee everywhere because she was being anything but good. I'm as speechless as the treat police.

"Let's get everyone cleaned up." Shep acts as if this happens every day.

"This is an eighty-dollar top," treat police lady squeaks.

"I'll compensate you for your shirt," Shep says.

"No! I did this. I'll pay." I snap out of my stupor and

19

fish some cash from my purse, handing it to the angry lady painted in coffee. "I'm incredibly sorry." Then I snatch the towel from Shep and crawl on my hands and knees, cleaning the mess while my dog ...

Actually, I don't know where Cersei is at the moment.

"I've got this." Shep squats next to me, pressing his hand onto mine to stop me from cleaning anymore of my mess. "Finish your shopping. It's no big deal."

"Um ... t-thanks ... I'm only getting the tendon. And I promise never to return."

He laughs, cleaning the coffee at a much faster rate. "That would be a shame. We'd hate to lose your business over a little spilled coffee."

"I uh ..." I'm so embarrassed I can't string together more than a few mumbled words.

"I'll meet you at the register in a sec. Boss needs me in back, but you have to promise to return for another visit."

Never. Ever.

I gulp and nod once.

He disappears to the back of the store for a few minutes before meeting us at the register. I'm third in line behind the treat police.

When he totals her products, I toss my credit card on the counter. "It's on me."

She glances over her shoulder, still hugging her fur ball. A tiny smile, that resembles the feeling of a truce, bends her lips. I'm sure it helps that I'm paying for nearly a hundred and fifty dollars in food and toys after having already paid for her shirt.

This is the most expensive trip to a pet store that I've ever made.

"How kind of you." Shep winks at me.

I glance away, biting my lips together, waiting for this misery to end.

After he takes care of the next customer, I set the tendon next to the register and risk a quick glance and apologetic smile.

"What's your last name, Sophie?" he asks.

"Ryan." I sweep my gaze around the store to keep from staring too long at him.

"Can I get your phone number?"

"Oh ..." I clear my throat and force myself to make eye contact again. "I'm flattered. Really. But I'm not dating right now."

That is code for: *I will be single for the rest of my life because I have lost all dating privileges for eternity. And I'm pregnant.*

Shep presses his lips together for a few seconds in an unreadable expression. Have I hurt his feelings?

"The phone number is for our system. With your name and phone number, you can start earning reward points with each purchase. You get a free dog wash just for giving me your name and number."

If an asteroid struck the earth right now and killed all of humankind, I wouldn't be mad. Not one bit. I wouldn't be alive either, but spiritually, I would feel grateful.

Stupid really is the worst feeling. It's worse than rejection and embarrassment. Everyone gets rejected at some point in their life. Everyone has something embarrassing happen to them—even celebrities and dignitaries wind up with toilet paper stuck to the soles of their shoes.

But stupid is preventable. It's the result of assumption. I'm the ass who assumed, and I couldn't feel more stupid.

"Four-eight-zero-seven-three ..." I give him my number as quickly as possible so I can get out of here and never return to use my store credit or free dog wash.

CHAPTER *Four*

"ANNE IS READY FOR YOU. How was your weekend?" Nora, my technician, asks as I stand from my desk chair and adjust the high waist of my pants.

I've been an optometrist in Scottsdale for three years. I'm the only doctor in my office with a small staff of four.

"Well..." I give her a gummy smile "...I had an argument with Jimmy. I think we might be breaking up."

I am a sinner, a repeat offender, with nowhere to repent. Jimmy was my last chance to save face with ... well, everyone I know. And he failed, which means I failed. It's humiliating, and I can't tell anyone the whole truth.

"On Saturday," I prattle on so she doesn't focus on the Jimmy disclosure, "I had an embarrassing encounter at Wash Your Tail with a moderate to severely sexy employee there. And yesterday my mom called to let me know Prince Harry died, and she'd really like me to fly home this weekend for the burial. How was your weekend?"

"Oh my god! Prince Harry died?" Nora's head jerks back, mouth agape. "How ... what the ... your mom knows him? *You* know him? I thought you said you're from Michigan."

"Prince Harry is ... *was* ... my mom's orange Tabby cat."

Nora covers her mouth and snorts. "You had me. I honestly thought you had connections to royalty."

"I do." I check my teeth in the oval mirror on the wall. "My mom is a royal pain in my ass. She honestly thinks her cat dying warrants me spending hundreds of dollars to fly home for a backyard burial."

Nora steps aside as I squeeze past her to head to the exam room, her smile falling into a somber expression. "Sorry to hear about you and Jimmy."

"Thanks, it's uh ... pretty heartbreaking."

Embarrassing. Shameful. Degrading. Disconcerting.

"Are you going to talk about your encounter with the 'sexy' pet store guy?"

I toss her a grin over my shoulder just before opening the door to the exam room. "You mean when I verbally vomited on the floor in front of him and rolled around in it before spilling my coffee everywhere and making the most cringe-worthy assumption that he was trying to ask me out on a date when he was only trying to enroll me in a rewards program?"

Nora grimaces.

"No. I don't think we need to talk about it. But thanks."

✳✳✳✳✳

THAT NEXT AFTERNOON, I arrive home to the pungent smell of sardines in my house. "Jimmy! What did I tell you about eating sardines? Not. In. The. House."

Cersei greets me with her whole backside wagging as I slip off my heels.

He shuts off the TV and shoves the last bite of saltine cracker and sardine into his mouth. "I'll have you know, I talked with my mom today," he mumbles with cracker crumbs flying out of his mouth onto my floor. "She's doing well. Thanks for asking."

I frown at his flippant attitude, as if I'm the bad guy.

"She said we need to take the things that are most irritating about each other and work past them. Conditioning of sorts until it no longer feels so irritating. So I'm going to eat sardines in the house until you get used to it, and I'll try to ignore the way you baby talk to Cersei. Like ... she fucking knows *who's the good girl*. But if you need to keep asking her, then I'll learn to ignore it." He rolls his eyes before standing (more crumbs falling from his lap to my floor) and takes his plate to the kitchen.

"Jimmy..." I rub my temples "...did something happen to you? Have you had a stroke? Did you hit your head?"

He narrows his eyes. "Uh ... no. Why?"

"Because you have *four* days left here. Four. Days. Then you're out. We don't need to fix what can't be fixed. We don't need to become more tolerant of each other. We need to get the hell away from each other."

"My mom also said couple's therapy is a good idea."

"No! Gah! No! No! No! You aren't listening to me. I don't want to be with you. I don't love you anymore. And it's not because there is anything wrong with me."

Cringe.

I might have an addiction to falling in love, and that part *is* on me.

"Oh ..." He crosses his arms over his chest. "So you're saying it's me? Something is wrong with me?"

"Yes! Something is wrong with you. But I have no time nor the desire to figure it out. If you want to see a therapist, by all means ... go for it. In fact, I encourage it. But I'm done. We are over. Get that through your thick head."

Jimmy scoffs. "I don't have insurance or a job. How exactly do you expect me to pay for therapy?"

"Holy shit! So this couple's therapy ... you want *me* to pay for it? You want me to pay to save a relationship I want nothing to do with? Are you out of your mind? This is what I'm talking about. Who are you? The Jimmy I met online was not stupid. He was smart and *charming*. He was funny. He used to crack jokes at other people's ignorance. You are officially the butt of your own jokes."

He bites his lips together and closes his eyes while sighing. "I looked in the trash ... in the bathroom." He shakes his head. "You're late. You haven't started your period. No tampons or wrappers. Are you pregnant? Are we having a baby?" Jimmy sounds pathetically hopeful, like the answer to all relationship issues is a baby.

I keep waiting for someone to jump out of the corner and yell, "Gotcha!" This is a joke. A prank. Any minute he's going to grin and put an end to it. He's going to laugh at me while packing his bags. He wants the last laugh. I broke up with him, so he's making me pay by putting on this act and driving me insane.

Fine.

I'll accept his win. *Bravo, Jimmy. You did it. You drove me to complete insanity. Made me look like a fool, AGAIN. Now get the hell out.*

"That's messed up, Jimmy. Who riffles through the trash looking for tampons? That's not even something that a married man should do. There are lines in relationships. Lines of decency and personal privacy that should never be crossed."

"Just answer me. Are you pregnant?"

"Sorry to disappoint you, Jimmy. No. I'm not having your baby."

He nods slowly, his expression wilting into something pathetic and sad—but mostly just pathetic. "Sophie, they repossessed my car today. Did you even notice that? Did you take two goddamn seconds to think about someone besides yourself? You're preaching about human decency. Well, where's yours? What kind of monster kicks someone while they're down? Haven't you heard the saying that you should never look down on someone unless you're offering them a helping hand?"

I let him live with me because he needed help. I didn't break up with him when I wanted to break up

29

because he was in a low spot—he'd lost his job—but Jimmy is living in a chronic state of need. If I wait for him to be in a better place, he will never leave my house.

"Four days, Jimmy. Or I'm calling the police." I snap my fingers and Cersei follows me to my bedroom, where I change into shorts, a white tank top, and sandals before taking my dog and leaving the house again.

It's my house, yet I'm the one who's always leaving to avoid spending any more time than necessary with the biggest mistake of my life—okay, one of three.

CHAPTER *Five*

IT'S PACK DAY. After I leave the shop, my six best friends and I head to an old park that's rarely occupied by more than birds and occasionally a homeless person or two. Today, however, we have company. A white poodle and a dark-haired woman in really *short* shorts, a tank, and chunky, clear-framed glasses. I can barely hide my grin, anticipating the level of awkwardness she'll display when I catch her attention.

On a weathered wood bench, Sophie You-Can't-Have-My-Phone-Number Ryan has her nose buried in her phone screen while Cersei runs free until she notices us and freezes with a little growl.

"Cersei, come," Sophie calls her just before glancing over her shoulder at me and my pack.

Her eyes bulge behind her glasses. "Cersei, come!" Jolting to her feet, she shoves her phone in her back pocket. "You," she says a little out of breath while attaching a leash to Cersei.

"Me." I grin. "I know ... I know. I took your number, but I never called. Such a dick move on my part."

She presses her lips together, but it doesn't hide her smile. "That's a ... lot of dogs."

"They're not all mine." I release their leashes. Sophie tightens her grip on Cersei and curls her shoulders inward as my pack runs past her toward a mucky pond. "The two greyhounds are mine: Julia Roberts and George Clooney."

She snorts. "Seriously?" Her delicate fingers curl her sun-bleached brown hair behind her ears. It's a blunt cut that juts below her chin with bangs that like to tease her eyelashes behind her glasses. No long wavy locks to toss over her shoulder. It's basic.

I think I'm a new fan of basic.

"Seriously." I shrug.

"And you stole the others?" Cersei lies down when she realizes her mom isn't leaving quite yet.

"I walk dogs from the no-kill shelter. It's where we got George and Julia."

She glances back at the dogs and releases a nervous laugh. "You uh ... let shelter dogs just run freely?"

"Sure. Why not? They need a chance to just be dogs. Play. Run. Dig. Sniff. Hump. I mean ... don't we all deserve to have those basic needs met?"

Again, she tries to suppress her grin. "Well, uh ... we were just leaving. Enjoy your evening." She tugs on the leash.

"Is Cersei a Lannister?"

She crinkles her nose, and it pushes her glasses up a fraction as she nods.

"Game of Thrones. Nice. But why Cersei? I'm partial to Arya."

"She wasn't my dog originally. I sort of ... inherited her." A sullen expression dissolves her smile.

"Well, better you than her ending up in a shelter. You're a generous woman, Sophie Ryan."

Her eyebrows form two sharp peaks as she bites her lips together and offers several easy nods.

I'd love to know what she's not saying.

God she's adorable. It's the glasses. I can't say that glasses have ever done it for me before, but they're doing it right now. And I'll never forget the image of her face filled with embarrassment while she gnawed her lower lip after the coffee incident. Is it messed up that I found her irresistible during the most disarming moment? There's a certain element of sex appeal to her vulnerability.

"About the other day ..." she says.

"Shit happens. No big deal. Don't give it another thought."

She nods slowly. "Easier said than done. But ... thanks. Anyway, I'd better ..." She jabs a thumb over her shoulder.

"So what is your story, Sophie Ryan?"

"Um ..." She's fidgety, like she's itching to leave. "I'm an optometrist."

"Ah ... that explains the glasses. Blue frames the other day. Clear frames today. I bet you don't wear the same pair twice in one week."

With a guilty grin, she gives a little shrug.

JEWEL E. ANN

"So you're a doctor?"

"Yes. A doctor of optometry." She won't even look at me.

"At the store you said you're not dating. Are you married? In a relationship? Tired of me being so nosey?"

She chuckles, eyeing my pack of dogs. "Not married. Not in a relationship. Life's a little complicated now. That's why I'm not dating."

"Maybe you just haven't found the right guy."

Again she laughs, shaking her head. "There could be a lot of truth to that statement, but ..."

"What's your idea of the right guy?"

She gives me a quick side glance. "I'm still figuring that out."

"Tall?" I ask, pushing my shoulders back, chin up.

Sophie presses her lips together to hide her grin as she shrugs. "Tall is good."

"Thick, dark hair?"

I don't think she has enough muscles in her face to hold her reaction much longer. "It's definitely preferred to no hair."

"Good with dogs?"

"Wouldn't hurt." Her amusement begins to break through her cool façade.

"Great personality?"

"As long as it's not overcompensating for said guy lacking in other departments."

On another sideways glance, she gets a full dose of

36

my confident (maybe a little cocky) smile. "I should get going. It was nice running into you again, Shep."

Cersei jumps to attention, and Sophie leads her toward the sidewalk.

"Listen, I feel bad for taking your number and not calling. So ... I'll definitely call you this week." A sense of pride warms my chest for cleverly twisting her presumption at the store to my advantage.

"I'm sure you're a great guy, but I can't go out with you." She doesn't even look back at me.

"Whoa ... there you go again ... assuming. I'm not wanting to go out with you. I just said I'd call you. To ... you know. Converse."

Her confident strides come to a halt. "To converse?" She glances over her shoulder.

"It means—"

"I know what converse means, Shep." She rolls her curious eyes.

"Great. We'll converse soon then."

See, Millie? There are ways to meet people that don't involve filtered pictures, exaggerated descriptions, and swiping right.

"That's..." her lips twist for a few seconds before she slowly shakes her head and grins "...not a good idea. Bye, Shep."

CHAPTER *Six*

SOPHIE

"HEY, JULES." I hug my best friend before taking a seat across from her on the patio of our favorite Mexican restaurant.

She slides a margarita toward me.

I smile, but I don't take it even though it makes me salivate. Instead, I grab my water and take several long gulps before diving into the basket of warm tortilla chips and fresh salsa verde.

"So ... what did I miss?" she asks. "You said you had so much to share with me, and you didn't want to explain via text. I was gone for only a week. Did I miss something big? Did you and Jimmy get back together?"

I cover my mouth to keep from spewing corn chips all over her. "Um ... no." I cough a few times.

"New guy?"

"Not exactly."

I've never felt so backed into a corner. I'm seriously hating life right now.

Jules curls her thick blond hair behind her ear on one side, exposing her gold loop earring. "Soph, what is it? You look like you're in pain."

39

"You love me no matter what, right?" I swipe some of the salt from the rim of my margarita glass with my finger.

"Yes ..." She draws out her answer while squinting at me.

"I'm in a bit of a pickle." My nose crinkles. I do not want to tell her this, but I have to tell someone, and I'd rather eat my own hand than tell my family.

"A pickle?"

"So ... you know how I said that Jimmy was going back to school after he sold his mom's house and that we were going to take a break as soon as he found his own place so he could focus on school and spend as much time as possible with his mom?"

Jules offers a slow nod.

Pinching my lower lip, I draw in a brave breath of air. "I sort of lied about that."

"About which part?"

Covering my face with my hands, I mumble, "All of it."

"What are you talking about? What does that mean? You're still with him? Or he's not going to school?"

"Jules ..." I clear the whininess from my throat and choke on my pride. "After I let Jimmy move in, after *everyone* warned me that it was a bad idea, and I swore that I knew what I was doing, that I was right and everyone else was wrong ..."

"Sophie, don't say it." She winces.

"After Jimmy moved in, I realized I didn't love 'at

home' Jimmy. He didn't help around the house. Dirty clothes everywhere. He never put dishes in the dishwasher. Toilet seat left up with piss everywhere. Shoes on my coffee table. Just ... *everything!* It all eviscerated my attraction to him. And every time I mentioned anything, he just rolled his eyes and said, 'It's a house, Sophie. You're supposed to live in it, not treat it like a goddamn museum.' The romance died. He became this charity case that I started resenting. He stopped trying to be romantic. Sex became this foregone conclusion that since we shared a bed, sex was a given."

"So ..."

I frown. "So I made up the story about him going to college because I didn't want everyone thinking that I, *yet again*, fell for the wrong guy and let him take advantage of me. I was so adamant that I knew what I was doing, that Jimmy was different."

"Okay. I see that. And you're right, instinctually I want to say, 'I told you so.' Just like your family would say the same thing. But it is what it is. You have terrible taste in men. You make terrible decisions when it comes to men. I think that's been well established. That's on you. Your life. Your choices. It only affects you. And Jimmy's gone. Who cares what the details were surrounding it? You have to let it go. What your family doesn't know about the past won't hurt them."

I feel an inch tall, not even. "Jimmy's not exactly gone."

"Not *exactly* gone?"

41

"Um …" I fiddle with my napkin. "I had it all planned out. But on the very day I was going to break up with him, he lost his job."

Jules pinches the bridge of her nose. "And let me guess, you didn't break up with him."

"He was really distraught. He had this mini breakdown. All upset about his mom having to go into assisted living. He went on and on about his terrible father who left them years ago. Then he started getting down on himself for never finishing college. And I couldn't. I thought it might be best to let him get into a better mental state. Find a new job. Find a place of his own. After all, like I told everyone, I didn't offer to let him live with me because we were dating; it was because he had to sell his house … well, his mom's house. And he needed a *temporary* place to stay."

"He's *still* living with you, and you haven't broken up with him? How did I not know this?"

Maintaining a permanent cringe, I shake my head. "It's … I've just … I don't talk about it because it's disgraceful. So I finally got the nerve to break up with him, stand my ground, and he rejected my 'proposal' to break up. *His* ridiculous word, of course. He blamed my upcoming period, which isn't upcoming at all. Then he went on and on about some thirty-day shit. And now his mom has him believing that we just need to work it out. He won't leave. He's in denial. I gave him a week. I told him I'm calling the cops if he's not out. Then he made me feel like I'm kicking him out onto the street."

"Has he found a job?"

I shake my head. "He says he's looking. He's said that for the past two months. Come to find out, it's not that he can't find a job; he just can't find one that pays better than unemployment."

"Oh my fucking freeloader. How, Sophie? How did you let this happen again?"

"I don't know!" I brush nonexistent crumbs off the table. "Why does being nice have to make me such a doormat? Why can't I find a good guy? One of the things I loved about Jimmy was his devotion to taking care of his mom. And I thought, *That's the guy I need.* Someday when I'm old and frail, I want to have a devoted husband. In sickness and in health."

"Sophie ..." Her head eases side to side.

This is what I've been trying to avoid: that look of disappointment. I stare at my margarita, so desperately wanting a sip, a buzz, anything to wash away the Jimmy fiasco.

"Maybe you should consult an attorney."

"We're not married. That's ridiculous. It's my house."

"Jacob, my neighbor, owns rental properties, and he's constantly complaining about it. Evicting someone isn't always easy. It would seem that someone who does not have their name on a piece of property or any sort of lease should not have any claim to staying there, but I bet Jimmy would find someone to make a case for him."

"No." I shake my head over and over. "Jimmy can't

afford an attorney. No one will be making a case for him."

"What if his mom pays for an attorney?"

"Pfft ... that's ridiculous. She has no money either."

Jules brings her drink close to her lips and pauses. "What about his aunt?"

"She lives in Tennessee. And I feel like getting him shipped off to Tennessee is a long shot. It's just ... ridiculous and sad. And his aunt probably wouldn't let him live with her anyway. And what does that say about Jimmy?"

"Or you? For dating him?"

I completely deflate. "I know! I've been trying to figure out what drew me to him in the first place. This is really embarrassing. And to add more misery to my already tumultuous situation, there's a sexy pet shop guy that's been flirting with me. And I'm pretty sure he's interested—"

"NO!" Jules nearly silences the restaurant.

My cheeks turn red as Mother Jules scolds me with one word.

She lowers her voice again. "You need to get your life figured out before you so much as smile at another man. Do you understand me?"

I nod, hiding behind my glass of water.

Jules holds up her glass. "To better choices."

Our glasses clink.

"What's wrong with your margarita?" Jules asks, eyeing the half-empty water glass in my hand.

"Oh ... uh ... nothing."

"Bullshit."

"Not bullshit." I can't look her in the eye.

"Oh my god! You're pregnant!"

I shake my head. "Shh ... no. I mean. Gah! It's not what you think."

"If you're pregnant, then it's what I think, Sophie."

Rubbing my eyes behind my glasses, I grumble. "I'm not supposed to tell you or anyone for that matter. So if I tell you, you can't say a word."

I feel like I *need* to tell her. It will give the urgency of my Jimmy situation much better perspective.

"Oh my god ... you *are* pregnant."

"Yes, but—"

"Does Jimmy know? This changes things, Sophie. You're evicting your child's father. Sophie!"

I frown. "Are you done? Can I speak?"

"Yes. Speak. Explain how you let this happen."

"It's not Jimmy's baby—"

"Sophie Elizabeth Ryan!"

"*And* ... it's not my baby."

Her head jerks backward, face wrinkled. "What does that mean?"

"It's my sister's. Chloe and Mason have been trying to have a baby. She's miscarried four times. I only knew about the first time. They stopped telling family because it's been too painful."

"Oh, Sophie ..."

I nod. "Yeah, it sucks. She has endometriosis. Of course, they could keep trying, but emotionally it's taken its toll. Chloe can't imagine going through yet

45

another miscarriage. And when she told me they had frozen embryos and were looking into a surrogate, I volunteered. I knew by then that things with Jimmy weren't going to work out. And ... I knew I needed to take a break from dating. This felt right. One hundred percent right. But we're not telling anyone until they're ready. So three months? Four months? I'm letting them decide."

"That's ..." Jules shakes her head. "I don't even know what to say. That's really generous of you. I mean, you haven't had a child of your own yet. And the first one you have you're giving away. You're a better person than I am."

I shrug. "It's not mine. Her egg. His sperm. I'm just a vessel."

"So pet store guy ... you know better, right? It's all about the baby now."

I laugh. "Yes. I have a baby to grow and a squatter to evict. My plate is absolutely full. Pet store guy is not in any equation of mine."

She eyes me with distrust. "I don't care how sexy he is. I don't care how much you dream of finding your prince. He's not the one. Now is not the time."

With a tight smile, I nod. "Yep. I know."

CHAPTER *Seven*

"WHERE HAVE YOU BEEN? I made dinner, and now it's cold." Jimmy grills me from *my* sofa the second I open the front door.

"I had dinner with Jules."

"And you didn't have the decency to call?"

It takes a minute for my fisted hand to uncurl, releasing my keys onto the narrow entry table. They scrape along the wood like Jimmy's words along my last nerve.

"We broke up. You are not welcome here, yet there you are ... adding another layer of dried sweat and body oil to my sofa, eating my food, and watching my TV. I asked you to leave, but you're too selfish and childish to do it without being physically removed from the premises. So that's what I'm going to do. In the meantime, my whereabouts is none of your business."

"*We* didn't break up, Sophie."

"You are—" Just as I start to unleash on him again, my phone vibrates. I stare at the unknown number for a few seconds before answering it. I don't care who it is. At this point, I'll talk to a telemarketer for the next hour. Anything that doesn't involve Jimmy.

"Hello?"

"Hi. It's Shep."

Nope. This is not good. He shouldn't be calling me. I'm off men, off drugs, off alcohol, excess caffeine ...

Jimmy fades away. I snap my fingers, and Cersei jumps off the sofa and follows me to my bedroom. "Shep. Shep. Shep. Why does that name sound familiar?"

"Cute. But I can actually *hear* the smile on your face. Nice try."

He's not wrong, but I wish he were. I have no business smiling because of any man. "What are you wearing—doing?!! I mean doing. What are you doing?" I pinch my eyes shut. I can't believe I asked what he's wearing. Maybe he didn't hear me.

"Fishnet stockings. A black lace thong. And a Spanx bodysuit," he says in a deep, rich voice.

I snort, cupping a hand over my mouth "Pretty fancy for a Wednesday, don't ya think?"

"Pretty nosey for a first conversing date, don't *you* think?"

"It's not a date." I roll onto my side and pet Cersei. "I'm not sure why you're calling me. Do you think using my phone number for personal reasons violates ... something?"

I have no clue.

"Good question. I'm not a lawyer. What's your take on it? Should I hang up? Do you think asking about my current clothing situation violated me? I'm on the fence. I mean, it was rather forward, but I'm a sucker for curiosity so there's that."

As I fight my grin, I'm relieved that he can't see me.

"Well, I don't know. But if this is your way of pursuing me, then I'm not interested."

"Interested in what? I'm not selling anything. We're just conversing like two normal humans. But if you're not a converser, then I'll hang up."

Who is this guy? My teeth pin my lower lip to keep from giggling.

"What do you want to converse about?" I surrender, a little, because his utter *strangeness* has piqued my curiosity. We are going nowhere, but now I'm wondering how we get to nowhere.

"Tell me what you were doing when I called you."

"I'd rather discuss hemorrhoids, tax audits ..."

"That bad, huh?"

I laugh. "That bad."

"Vibrator battery go dead on you?"

I snort. "Funny, but no. I have a backup."

"Fascinating. Tell me more."

"Should I be worried that a guy I met days ago at the pet store is calling me to talk about vibrators? Feels a little stalker-ish."

"Again, you asked what I was wearing. I'm just following your lead."

I can't help but laugh. For a guy who has zero chance with me, he's persistent. Sadly, I find his persistence a needed distraction from my problems.

"What do *you* want to talk about?"

I'm tempted to say "nothing" since I'm not the one who called him. "Is Shep short for Shepherd?"

"Yes."

"What time do you walk your dogs in the morning when it's over a hundred degrees by nine?"

"Four."

"Shut up! You do not walk your dogs at four in the morning."

He laughs. "I do. I walk them at four. Exercise at five. Shower at six on the weeks that I have them."

"The weeks that you have them?"

"I have shared custody with my ex-wife."

"Shared custody of dogs? Is that a thing?"

"It's very much a thing."

"Well, that explains why your marriage failed."

"What does?"

"You walk your dogs at four in the morning. I could never marry someone who routinely woke up at four in the morning."

"Why?"

I shake my head even though he can't see me. "Because he'd wake me up. I have a terrible time getting back to sleep if I wake up early in the morning. I'd be chronically sleep deprived and incredibly cranky all the time."

"I see. I guess that means we'll never get married."

With a nervous laugh, I bite my tongue. We'll never get married for a lot of reasons, but his four a.m. routine is low on the list. "How long were you married?"

"Five years."

"How long have you been divorced?"

"A year."

"Do you miss her?"

"I see her way too often to miss her."

"Do you miss being married?"

"I miss some things about it."

"Like?"

"I miss going out with friends, our couples' friends. I miss barbecues. Golfing with her on Friday afternoons. I miss quick trips to vineyards and long walks with the dogs. I sometimes miss the woman I married, but I never miss the woman I divorced." He sounds normal.

They all sound normal at first.

"What do you *not* miss about her?"

"Sorry, Sophie. I think it's my turn again."

"Fine, but nothing personal."

"You just grilled me on the history of my marriage. That's personal."

"You brought it up. I was just *following your lead.*"

"I see what you did there. Cute. Okay. Why did you choose to be an optometrist?"

I hesitate because I don't want to tell him. It's the most ridiculous and uninspiring reason. "Good pay. Good hours."

"Liar."

I laugh. "You don't know if I'm lying. We've known each other for less than a week."

"You just gave me the most generic answer ever,

which means you don't want to tell me the real reason. Why is that?"

"A guy. God ... I've never told anyone, I mean *anyone*, this before. I don't know why I'm telling you."

"Because I'm safe."

I grunt. "I don't know if I'd call you safe, but ..." I sigh. "I decided my junior year of high school that I would go to optometry school. My best friend, Jules, had a brother who was four years older than us. After his second year of undergrad, he declared he was going to be an optometrist. I had such a huge crush on him. Jules never knew. She still has no idea. I thought he'd help me through school. I thought it was the perfect chance to get close to him."

"But?" Shep draws out that one word.

But. Yeah, he has no clue. There's a big "but" to this story.

"But he died in a car accident two weeks after I started the optometry program."

"Jeez, Sophie ... that's ... well ... that's a terrible story."

"What? You asked me!"

"I did. But you make something up if the truth is ... a terrible story."

"Wow. I'm sorry I don't have something as heartfelt as missing my ex because we used to golf and go to vineyards together."

"That's not what I miss most about her. It's what sounds most engaging. Most romantic."

"Did you ... did you lie to me?" I sit up and hold out

my phone to stare at it for a few seconds. Who is this guy?

"Six-thirty."

"Six-thirty what?" I ask.

"Walk the dogs at four. Exercise at five. Shower at six. Have sex with my wife at six-thirty. That's what I miss most. But I thought we'd ease into our tele-dating."

"Tele-dating?"

"Yes. We're dating via phone."

"We're conversing, not dating."

"No, Sophie. We *were* conversing. At least, that was the plan until you just had to know what I was wearing. You can't uncross that line."

"Uh ... I can and I did."

"Nope. I thought we'd discuss the weather, then move on to hobbies, favorite vacation spots, and maybe share our bucket lists. You're the one who initiated phone sex right off the bat."

I open my mouth then shut it. I do this several times without anything coming out. He remains silent.

"I'm wearing white fitted capris, a floral blouse, and no shoes. My toenails are painted hot pink. My hair is its usual stringy mess, even more so now because I'm on my bed and it's been a long day." I tug at my lower lip, waiting for him to make some well-calculated comment.

He says nothing.

I'm not sure we're still connected.

"Shep?"

"I'm sorry about your friend's brother. I'm sure he'd be proud of you for finishing what he never got the chance to do."

"Thanks," I whisper. "Now who's keeping my terrible story alive?"

"How tall are you? I was trying to estimate it. Five-three? Not even? You're very petite."

"Five-four."

"Just barely."

I laugh. "Just barely still counts. How tall are you? You're freakishly tall."

"I'm not. Six-two. Six-three if I'm trying to show off."

"Show off? Like a bird puffing out its chest and lifting his head?"

"Exactly."

I'm not going to marry him or even go out on a date that's beyond a phone call, but I can't remember the last time a guy made me grin so much. Jimmy has sucked the life out of me so incrementally, I didn't realize until this moment just how much I've missed this kind of *conversing*.

"I should go. Cersei needs her dinner, and so do I."

"It's been fun."

I bite my thumbnail. There's no way I'm agreeing no matter how much I'm thinking it.

"You have my number now."

"I do," I say as if it's no big deal.

"Goodnight, Sophie."

"Night, Shep."

CHAPTER *Eight*

SHEP

"WHAT? For the love of god, out with it." I say to Howie, my best friend, as I tee off. "You've had a constipated expression on your face all morning. Who died? Did one of your testicles fall off in the middle of the night? Is Caroline cheating on you with her boss?" I return my driver to my bag.

"It is about Caroline, but ... wait ... why would you think she's cheating on me with her boss?" He removes his ball cap and scratches his closely shaven head before repositioning it.

"I don't *think* she is. I'm sure she's not, but sometimes you have to do the math." I release the brake on the golf cart and speed down the path.

"And what's the math?"

"One: You've said your sex life is in a rut. Two: Millie said Caroline's boss used to manage a fitness center, and she blew out a disturbingly deep sigh when she said it. Three: Millie and Caroline are in a book club that predominately reads romance novels. One plus two plus three equals six."

"And what is six?" Howie asks.

"The answer. I'm just trying to be a little more original than two plus two equals four."

"Shep, dude, good thing we're friends, or I'd really be worried about your one plus two plus three state of mind. You need to get on a dat—"

"Don't say it." I skid to a stop and hop out, grabbing a five iron. "If you turn into Millie and start talking about dating apps, I will divorce you too, but it will be my idea not yours."

"How else are you going to meet someone? Get laid? Get an occasional hand job ... if you're working at a pet store every day next to a woman in her fifties?"

"Maybe a customer comes in." I line up my club and smack the ball. It's a shit shot. Howie's in my head. "Maybe she's a single woman with olive skin, dark hair just below her chin, wispy bangs, and sexy glasses that instantly demand attention. And you know about her. A feeling because she gives you a look."

"That's uh ... *really* specific, man. Does said woman exist?" Howie struts to his ball a good fifteen yards away from mine. After he drives it straight toward the hole because no one's in *his* head, he makes his way back to the cart.

"Her name's Sophie. She's an optometrist. She has a poodle or maybe a doodle named Cersei Lannister. Granted, she's single but unavailable. It's a new status, I guess. Anyway, I'm looking into it."

"Well, from the sounds of things, twelve plus forty plus seventeen equals sixty-nine. That's your lucky number, Shep."

I grin. "Shut the fuck up. What were you needing to tell me? Something about Caroline?"

"Oh, yeah, that. I already mentioned it. Slipped it right in there without you noticing. Sometimes I do that to Caroline too."

I smirk. We're friends because neither of us are capable of taking life too seriously. "Condolences to Caroline, *Pencil Dick*."

Howie laughs. He's able to laugh at himself better than any human I know. "I really deserve some sort of award. With my familial Puny Pecker Syndrome, I have to use my dick, three fingers, and a toe to get the job done properly."

With a fist at my mouth, my entire body vibrates with silent laughter. I have actual tears in my eyes. I just ... can't with him.

"Anyway, Millie asked Caroline to ask me to convince you to get onto some dating apps, preferably at least one that Millie's on as well. But now that you're on the verge of nailing a doctor with sexy glasses, I can't make the dating app case anymore."

"I'm not nailing her." I hit the gas toward the green. "We're having some intense phone sex, but that's it." I give him a grin that says I'm joking. "And when I go all Morgan Freeman on her, I can practically hear her panties dissolving. But I digress ... Millie just wants me on the same dating apps so she can check out her competition. *As if* my idea of fun is hanging out with my ex and letting her scroll through my phone."

"Fair enough." He hops out of the cart. "At least I

can tell Caroline that I asked, and you said no. That should earn me some decent head or at least a lick or two while she fondles my one testicle that didn't fall off in my sleep."

I bark a laugh and shake my head.

"But seriously, Shep. I'm glad to hear that you're not moping around, still beating yourself up over your failed marriage. Way to get back in the saddle."

I dig into my pocket for some cash to get a beverage. "I wouldn't call this 'back in the saddle.' I'd call it a concerted effort to prove Millie wrong. I think her favorite pastime is imagining me still pining for her and reveling in the fact that it was she who ended our marriage with her horrid lying and desperate need for control, as if I was a warden in her life and not her husband."

"Shit ..." Howie rests his club on the ground like a kickstand. "Caroline's getting ready to leave me, isn't she?"

I shrug. "One plus two plus three, man. You know women like to do everything together."

As Howie's face settles into a deflated frown, my phone vibrates.

I grin. "It's her."

"Millie?" he asks.

"Sophie." I accept the call.

"Dr. 69?" Howie says way too loudly.

I roll my eyes and walk toward the cart. "Hello?"

"Hey, whatcha up to?"

"Who is this?"

"Oh, um ... it's ..."

I grin. "Kidding. So ... what are you wearing?"

"High waisted cream pants, sleeveless blouse, and a lab coat."

"Boring ... try again."

She giggles. "*Just* a lab coat, black heels, cat-eye tortoise shell glasses, and pale pink lip gloss."

"Damn ..." I might have to adjust things down below if she keeps this up. "Cat-eye tortoise shell glasses, huh?"

"They're very vintage."

"What's the address? I'm overdue for a good eye exam."

Sophie's laughter is the best sound I've heard in so long. "What are you doing?"

"Golfing."

"Must be nice. Some of us have to work."

"I'll do that later. Priorities."

She grunts. I think it's a jealous grunt.

Howie hops into the cart and pinches his nipples, licking his lips, and rolling his eyes back in his head. He's making it difficult to prove all the women wrong who say men never grow up.

"It's hard for me to feel bad for you having to work, when you're clearly not working at all right now," I say.

"I had a patient reschedule, so I thought I'd recip-rocate the kind gesture and call you to converse."

"Oh, you called me for phone sex."

"No." She coughs. "No phone sex. Just conversa-tion. So ... it's sunny out today."

63

I laugh. "Such a rare occasion in Arizona."

"Who ya golfing with?"

"My friend."

"A four-legged friend?"

My grin doubles. "Two-legged. A thirty-six-year-old toddler."

Howie gives me a look.

Yes, buddy. I'm talking about you.

"Then I'll let you go so you can talk about me. Make sure he knows we're *just* friends and I'm fully clothed, getting ready to give some lucky human twenty-twenty vision."

As entertaining as Howie can be, and as much as I love golfing, I'm bummed that I'm not someplace else so I can keep talking with said new friend "Okay, *Jesus.*"

Laughter bubbles out of Sophie. "Bye, Shep."

CHAPTER *Nine*

SOPHIE

"CAN YOU KEEP IT DOWN?" Jimmy grumbles from my sofa while pulling the blanket over his head.

I wonder if prisons cater to the nutritional needs of pregnant inmates because there's a good chance I'll end up killing Jimmy before he moves out. Legit, I Googled "how to kill someone without leaving a trace" before I went to sleep last night. Now that search is out there ... in cyberspace, even though I erased my search history. So Jimmy gets to live because I made a misstep in my murder planning. That's unfortunate.

"I'm meeting with an attorney today." I bob my herbal tea bag in lukewarm water. I already had my one cup of coffee. It wasn't enough.

"I cleaned both bathrooms yesterday, in case you missed that," he says from under the blanket. "Don't forget to tell your attorney *that*."

"My name's on the mortgage ... in case you missed *that*."

"You know ..." He throws the blanket aside and sits up straight.

I jerk my head to the side when I see him—all of

67

him. "The hell, Jimmy! You're sleeping naked on my sofa? Gross!"

"You never had a problem with me naked on your sofa when you were naked on the sofa with me. Cancel your stupid attorney appointment, play hooky from work, and get naked with me, Sophie. My mom thinks our lack of physical intimacy has contributed to the wedge between us."

"That's great, Jimmy." I remove the tea bag and drop it into the trash bin. Then I get Cersei her breakfast. "I'd love to hear how these conversations with your mom go. Does she know you haven't made any effort to get a new job? A place of your own? Does she know you've let yourself go? Does she know how much you smell? Has she seen your greasy hair and pale skin? I honestly didn't know one could live in Arizona and be so pale."

"Sorry, Queen Sophie. I wasn't genetically blessed with your pigmentation. Is that why you're having second thoughts about me? I'm too white?"

"Yes. If it weren't for your pasty white skin, I'd marry you tomorrow. It's all about that and nothing at all to do with your lack of employment or the divot your ass is making in my sofa. The piss on my bathroom floor. The scratches on my coffee table from your shoes. The *big* hint I gave you just a week after you moved in here ... when I suggested you sleep in the guest room."

"I thought you wanted privacy to use your vibrator."

What?

Why do men assume all women use a vibrator? I don't even own one.

"What would that say about you as a lover?"

He shrugs. "Nothing. Just because I jerk off in the shower doesn't mean you're a bad lover."

He has a point, but it's a moot point because it's a distraction from the real issue.

"If I get a job, will we be good?" Jimmy asks.

I grab the piece of toast from the toaster and spread peanut butter on it. "Would it make a difference in your train of thought if I told you I was planning on breaking up with you before you got fired? I let you live with me *temporarily*."

"I'm not sure what you mean by making a difference in my train of thought." He scratches the back of his head and yawns. "But it would explain why we've had so little sex. Did you ..." He has the audacity to look confused or maybe a little offended. "Did you have sex with me on my birthday because you felt sorry for me?"

"Yes." That feels good. I can't believe how quickly and easily that came out of my mouth. The reminder of just how low I stooped on his birthday doesn't feel as good.

"Jesus ... don't sugarcoat it. That's pretty fucking terrible of you."

"Terrible of me? Terrible of me to let you live here while you've looked for a new job and a place to live, even though you have *not* looked for a job *or* a place to live? Terrible of me to buy your food? Terrible of me to have sex with you? Are you really going to pretend that our sex life was such a deep emotional bond that the thought of me having it with you just because it was your birthday was some sort of betrayal and insult to your sensitive heart? You have tried to have sex with me while I'm sleeping."

Jimmy frowns and turns on the TV. "Once. And I thought you'd wake up and participate. Instead, you kneed me in the fucking groin."

"You startled me!"

Jimmy shakes his head but remains silent.

I finish eating and brush my teeth for work.

As I open the door and sling my handbag over my shoulder, Jimmy clears his throat. "I still haven't seen any tampons in your trash. If you're pregnant, I'm never moving out. No way am I letting our kid grow up in a split family. I did that, and it's not what I want for my kid."

Oh, Jimmy ...

✳✳✳✳✳

HERE'S the nice thing about working with four other women ... one of us is always having her period. If someone would have asked me if I could ever imagine myself stealing dirty tampons from the trash in the employee bathroom to plant in my trash bin at home, I would have laughed and cringed at the same time. Who ... who would ever do such a crazy thing?

Me.

Desperate me.

"Whoa ... what are you doing?" Nora's gaze focuses on the clear plastic bag in my hand as I come out of the bathroom.

I should have grabbed a paper bag. It was a last-minute decision.

"Is the trash full?" she asks.

"Um ..." I swallow hard and slide the bag behind me, so she stops staring at it. What if it's hers? "I've been having heavy periods. So very heavy. And my doctor wants to see what I consider a really heavy period. So I'm taking this to her so she can see how heavy it is."

Oh my god ... was that really my best excuse?

Nora's face sours. "Did she ask you to do that? It's kinda weird."

"I thought the same thing. But ... I'm not the gyne-cologist."

"Are you going to put it in the fridge? Surely, you can't just keep it in your purse. It will start to smell. Then again, how sanitary is it for you to put it in the fridge where everyone keeps their lunches?"

"True. Maybe I'll just grab some ice and put it in the car. I'm done early anyway because I have a meeting with my attorney."

Nora nods slowly. "Ice. Good idea. Hope you're not meeting with your attorney for anything major."

"Nothing major." Aside from Jules, I haven't told anyone that Jimmy is still living with me despite our breakup. Stupid squatter. I slide past Nora then turn back toward her. "Nora?"

"Yeah?"

"Keep this between us. I don't want anyone needlessly worrying about me until I know something for sure."

"Absolutely. I do hope it's nothing. The pill might help lighten your flow. It did for me."

"Yeah. I'll keep that in mind."

After my last patient, I run home to plant the dirty tampon in my trash. I've reached a new low in my life. Never saw this day coming. I'm sure my sister and her husband would be really proud of their surrogate carrying around someone's dirty tampon.

I put the cart before the horse. Implantation of the embryo should have happened after the boyfriend (exboyfriend) eviction. But things went quicker than I imagined. And when a date was offered to ... get me pregnant ... I agreed because Chloe thought Jimmy and I had broken up. It was the only way she would have agreed to let me be her surrogate. And we had, in my mind. It all seemed like an afterthought. After all, how long does it take to break up with someone?

"I want to break up."

"Why?"

"It's not working for me. I'm sorry."

Cue a few tears and maybe a fleeting plea or two.

"If that's what you want. I'll pack my stuff now."

A few more tears.

Load up the shit.

Done.

If only …

"Home for a nooner?" Jimmy asks while making a mess in my kitchen. The house smells like burnt butter and bacon.

"Go to hell, Jimmy." I rush to the bathroom, plant the tampon in the trash, flush the toilet, and wash my hands. "No time to play, Cersei." I pause just long enough to give her a quick kiss on the head as I scurry to the front door so I'm not late for my appointment.

"You look beautiful today."

I stop, one foot out the door and my back to Jimmy who followed me.

"You look beautiful every day. And maybe I should have told you that more. Maybe I should have tried harder to make you feel loved and appreciated. Because I do … I appreciate you. And I'm going to do better. I'm going to find a job. I started looking today."

I inch my head back to see him, chin pressed to my shoulder.

He slides his hands in the pockets of his shorts. He's dressed. In real clothes. I hadn't noticed when I walked in the door.

"If I'm honest, you intimidate me. I still can't believe you ever gave me the time of day. You … a beautiful, smart doctor. Totally put together. And kinder than anyone I have ever met."

He shaved too.

The longer I stare at him, I realize he's also showered. I can see a tiny glimpse of the guy I met online.

"You have no idea how taking care of my mom has impacted my life. It's the reason I haven't finished college. It's the reason I wasn't a great employee and got fired. I've needed this break, emotionally and physically. I've been falling into a depression, but I'm going to do better. I'm out of it now. I'm sorry. I don't want to lose you."

My Jimmy had tattoos down one arm. And it was sexy. I've been blind to them for months.

My Jimmy had abs for days. My Jimmy was king of the smolder. All it took was one look and I lost my clothes and all inhibitions. I haven't seen that Jimmy for months.

Now, I see a tiny glimpse of that Jimmy. But it doesn't erase the image of the unkempt freeloader on my sofa. I recall his pathetic attempts at seducing me when he hadn't even brushed his teeth.

No smolder.

No game whatsoever.

Some things can't be disguised by tattoos and abs. And I know ... I just know that if I have another weak moment (like *so* many before now), I will regret it. And it's not just me now. I'm pregnant.

"I have to go," I whisper.

CHAPTER *Ten*

"WHAT DID YOU FIND OUT?" Jules asks as I answer the phone in my car after leaving my attorney's office.

"He's going to check on a few things and get back with me. But apparently, I might have to formally evict Jimmy. I first need to give him written notice that he has five days to leave. If he doesn't leave, I can file an eviction lawsuit against him. If I win, which I will, and he still doesn't leave, I file a Writ of Restitution to have the sheriff remove him. God ... how did this happen? *And* ... Jules ... he showered and shaved. He said he's looking for a job. And he said all the things I needed him to say months ago."

"Too late. You can't. Sophie, hear me clearly. I will not let you take him back."

"I'm not taking him back. I just wasn't expecting him to say the things he said. For a second, not even a full second, I felt sorry for him. He said I intimidate him and expressed how he was slipping into a depression, but he's going to do better and he loves me. It was ... sweet. I mean it was half-empty boxes of stale donuts and a slew of wadded up fast food bags all over my coffee table too late, but still ..."

"No! Hell to the no." Jules's voice escalates. "We are

not going there. Nothing about Jimmy is sweet any longer. If he brings home a dozen puppies, it's not sweet. If he makes you dinner, lights candles, and offers to go down on you all night ... it's not sweet. Got it?"

"I'm *not* taking him back." I laugh. "Just calm down, Jules. I'm one hundred percent sure of that. I think it's nothing more than a glimpse of hope that we can end this amicably as adults. No lawsuit. No attorneys. No gossip. Nothing but two people who go our separate ways. I hate conflict."

Jules hums. "I don't feel your level of optimism. But I hope for your sake that Jimmy surprises us and does the right thing."

"Me too. Hey, someone else is calling me. Gotta go. I'll call you tomorrow."

"Bye, babe."

I switch over to Shep. I didn't expect him to call again so soon, but I'm giddy that it's him, and that makes me cringe. I shouldn't have called him the other day. It was a really weak moment, an escape from Jimmy. Now I've encouraged this ... whatever *this* is. "Just be honest ... am I your only friend?" I ask him without a "hello."

"That's harsh. And no, though I have a sneaking suspicion *I* am your only friend. Just checking in on you. Making sure you're not home alone knitting your dog a hat, watching horrible reality TV, and dreaming of dating someone in the dark or marrying a guy the same day you meet him because a small room full of TV execs thinks you're a perfect match."

"I liked the show where they dated naked. I bet you're a little too self-conscious to do that, huh?" I've known this guy two seconds, maybe three, yet it feels natural and easy to talk to him like we've been bantering for years. Maybe it's easy because it's going nowhere. There's no risk for either one of us.

"Where are you?"

I catch myself grinning and immediately force a frown. "Driving home. Where are you?"

"Driving range. You should meet me."

"We're conversing. Meeting would be next level. I can't do next level."

You can't do any level!

"It's not a date. My stroke is way off. I need you to take a video of my swing so I can analyze it later."

Laughing, I shake my head. "I'm sure someone else can take a video for you. Didn't you have a toddler friend who golfed with you? Or a stranger is fine. Just flash them that perfect smile of yours."

"You like my smile, huh?" He's such a flirt.

It does *things* to me. Or maybe that's the tiny human growing in my uterus. "It's not awful."

"Topgolf. Bay 208. See you soon." He disconnects the call.

I shake my head again. I didn't agree to meet him. I'm not his personal videographer.

"Nope," I murmur to myself, cruising toward home. *Turning around …*

Heading to Topgolf.

It's a video. No big deal, right?

❋ ❋ ❋ ❋ ❋

TELLING myself I'm just doing this to avoid Jimmy, I make my way to Topgolf. The host escorts me to Bay 208. And the sexiest guy I've ever seen shoots me his killer grin while standing with one foot crossed over the other, hand resting on his golf club. I nearly do a one-eighty and take my foolish self right back to my car.

"Heels for golf?"

I glance down at my black wedges. They look great with my yellow floral romper. "Neither my wedges nor I were planning on golfing today. And I'm not golfing. I'm taking a video of you. Then I'm leaving because I'm hungry. I skipped lunch."

His gaze leaves my wedges via my legs. It's a slow inching of his gaze that I can feel in places I've banned myself from feeling a man's gaze.

You're pregnant.

You're going to get cankles.

Stretch marks.

Hemorrhoids.

Shep's eyes find mine, and his ruddy lips pull into a sly grin as his tongue slides along his lower lip. He nods. "You can take them off, but not yet. I'm not done looking at you in them. Best view I've seen in a long time."

Jesus ...

The late afternoon sun feels like ice compared to Shep's words. I start to say something smart, witty, but my voice won't work.

"Don't look so shocked, Sophie. Surely you've looked in a mirror." He hands me his phone. "Take it from several angles."

I nod repeatedly, rubbing my nervous lips together. Shep hits one ball after the next as I take the video.

"You don't have a ninety-degree angle when you hinge your wrists at the top of your swing. See?" I show him the video and pause it.

He stares at the screen for several seconds before shifting his attention to me. "Dr. Ryan ... do you golf?"

"Probably better than you, Shep."

His entire face blooms with something resembling utter happiness. Christmas morning. Fourth of July fireworks. "Take off your shoes."

"I'm hungry."

"I'll feed you in a minute. Take off your shoes."

"You're not feeding me. That's the definition of a date." I cross my arms over my chest.

"Sex defines a real date. Take off your shoes."

Shep has a Master's degree in making me blush. Fight or flight. I really need to flee the scene.

"Well..." I slip off my wedges "...I'm not sure *sex* defines a real date." I take the club when he hands it to me. "I've been on many dates where I haven't had sex."

"Really?" Shep bends down to place a ball on the tee. "Huh ... well, it's been a while since I've dated, so

81

maybe I'm not the best judge." He stands straight, peering down at me with an innocent grin, but I can't stop thinking about his statement.

Sex defines a real date.

"Let's see it, Sophie."

I don't even think. No practice swing. No nerves.

Whack!

Shep whistles, tracking the ball in flight. "Damn, Sophie. I'm really turned on right now."

"Again." I tap the club next to the tee.

Shep eyes me, but he can't hide his shock or maybe his pleasure. He tees me up again.

Again, I drive it perfectly.

And again, he whistles. "Looks like you have some explaining to do."

"When I was five, my dad qualified for the PGA. Dalton Ryan. A car accident ended those dreams. He broke both arms. He's golfing again, but he never made it back to that level. So I've been golfing about as long as I've been walking." I slip my feet back into my wedges while holding out the club to him. "Now, I'm going home to grab a late lunch."

"I think you owe *me* lunch. Since you've bruised my ego a bit."

"Can one bruise the ego of a stalker?" I twist my lips and scratch my chin.

"Come on." He nods toward the exit. "Lunch is on me. We'll discuss my low-level stalking skills later."

I shake my head, despite my smile, as I follow him to the exit. "I said I was going home for lunch."

As soon as we step outside, he turns. I nearly walk straight into him.

"You've been on my mind. It's distracting." He eyes my mouth, and I take a step back for safety and sanity reasons.

"So calling me to meet you here and eating lunch with me will get me off your mind?"

He grins. "Yes. I'm just waiting for you to do something annoying. Golfing better than me is annoying, but not in the right way. Let's eat. Maybe you'll get some lettuce between your teeth, and it will distract me from the rest of you."

"What makes you think I'm getting a salad?"

"Sushi?"

I know the right answer is no. I *know* the right thing to do is go home. But when I'm in Shep World, Jimmy doesn't exist. I don't think about the baby and how disappointed, and probably angry, Chloe will be if she finds out I lied about Jimmy. Shep doesn't know I have the worst luck in men. And he never has to know that because we will never be more than friends.

I don't have to say a word. Shep knows my answer is yes.

"Hiro?"

I nod again. Wait ... should I have sushi if I'm pregnant? "On second thought ... let's do True Foods Kitchen. It's in—"

"I know where it's at. Meet you there."

"Okay."

He gestures. "After you."

I eye him for a few seconds before heading toward my car. After about ten steps, I turn around. His gaze is still stuck to me, and that grin ... it's a little obnoxious.

"I'm in trouble, Sophie. So much trouble." He shakes his head slowly.

No.

No one is in trouble.

It's not a date.

It's food.

I'm pregnant. My ex is at my house. Shep can admire my golfing skills or even gawk at my legs as I walk away, but that's where it ends.

✳✳✳✳✳

"Happy hour. Good call," Shep says as I approach the entrance.

"Hi. Do you have reservations?" the hostess asks.

I cringe. "No."

"I can seat you at the bar?"

"Perfect," Shep says, resting his hand on my lower back as the hostess offers us two open stools and hands us the happy hour menu.

"Cozy." I opt for a nervous laugh, tamping down my nerves as we climb onto the stools at the crowded bar.

He angles his body ever so slightly, and his bare knee touches mine.

"Can I start you off with something to drink?" the bartender asks.

Shep nods for me to order.

"Uh ... I'll have the strawberry lemonade."

Shep orders a beer and returns his attention to me. I wait for him to question my drink order. Do I not drink? If not, then why?

He doesn't.

"So when are we going golfing?"

I smile. "I'm not dating you, Shep."

"Who said anything about dating? Just friends golfing."

"I have friends who golf with me." My dad. He's the only one who golfs with me.

"Maybe ..." He narrows his eyes.

The bartender serves our drinks.

Shep takes a sip of beer. "But do you have friends who look at you the way I look at you?"

My lips wrap around the straw, and they don't let go until I figure out how to reply to his comment. "How do you look at me?"

"Like my dogs look at me."

I laugh. "You think I have treats in my pocket for you?"

"No. Well, *do* you have treats in your pocket? Now that I think about it, I can't imagine a better trait in a woman than carrying treats in her pocket."

I giggle, shaking my head.

He winks at me. "No. What I meant was ... when I see you, I get really excited. And I can't stop staring at you and waiting to see what you'll say to me. Hoping it's something that lets me know you're excited to see me too."

Whoa … I need to get out of here.

"Well…" I play it cool and mess with the corner of the cocktail napkin "…I'm not sure if my friends wag their tails when they see me, but we usually hug and say 'hi' in a high-pitched squeal."

"That's good." He hides behind his glass bottle, pausing before taking a long swig. "So tell me why you're not dating. Not that I'm interested in dating you. I'm asking for the rest of the single, straight male population."

"Oh? Is there a weekly 'Single, Straight Male' newsletter that goes out? Are you like Editor in Chief?"

He takes a long pull of his beer and rubs his lips together. "Something like that."

I drum my fingers on the side of the glass, smearing the condensation. "Can I be honest without *not* being honest with you?" I glance over his shoulder for a second, organizing the thoughts that get jumbled before they make it to my tongue. "Maybe it's not dishonesty. Maybe it's lack of transparency." My gaze returns to him. "If you're not wanting to date me, which you're clearly not, and you have a friend, albeit a man toddler friend, and I have another friend who I share my darkest secrets with, then can we be friends who share the good stuff? Just the good stuff? Can we be each other's escape from the bad stuff? I *need* an escape right now. So we don't have to *lie* to each other. We simply aren't transparent about everything."

Most ridiculous idea *ever!*

Shep studies me through a series of slow blinks and another swig of his beer while I maintain a low level of feigned confidence, my fingers drumming a little faster on my glass.

"But seriously, are you married?"

I shake my head.

"Engaged?"

Headshake.

"Betrothed to another? Are you a princess running away from her royal duties? Has your future husband been offered a dowery?"

I snort and bite my lips for a few beats before nodding. "You caught me. That's the one."

Shep smirks. "If I had a dime for every time I've met a betrothed woman with a dowery ..."

I playfully nudge his knee. "You'd have exactly ten cents."

"Give or take." He shrugs. "So being your friend means I get the watered-down version of you?"

After sucking on my straw, I gulp while shaking my head. "Absolutely not. You get the *best* version of me. You get what my patients get. When I arrive in the exam room, I'm happy. We *converse*." I wink. "We chitchat about the good stuff in life. Nobody unloads a dump truck of unsolvable problems. And life is good. It's like customers showing up at Wag Your Tail. It's all about the friendly interaction. As crazy as it sounds, but it's no less true, we often give the best of ourselves to complete strangers or acquaintances."

Shep nods slowly, the cogs and gears at work in his handsome head.

I shrug, my smile falling into a more somber expression. "It's all I have to offer right now. I'm sorry."

"You're really not going to tell me why you're not dating?"

Concealing my smile with twisted lips, I shrug. "I like being mysterious."

"Are you questioning your sexuality?"

"Not yet." I chuckle.

"Can I get you something off the menu?" the bartender asks.

I study the happy hour menu of five items. "We'll take one of everything."

"You got it." The bartender snags our menus.

"Hungry?" Shep's eyebrows slide up his forehead. He has the most perfect features. Handsome and well-groomed (like a dog), yet intentionally rugged with his shadow of dark facial hair (also like a dog). And those brown curls around his ears ... I want to slide my fingers through them.

"Starving." I grin.

"Where do you put it?" He sneaks another quick scan of my body.

"I have a thing for over ordering. Leftovers are my jam."

"I'm here. There won't be any leftovers."

I squint at him. He ignores my glare.

"Do you have family around here?" I ask.

"Is that an approved topic?"

I shrug. "Only if your family brings you joy."

His face lights up, which makes me feel good too. He likes his family. I can tell from the look in his eyes. "My parents manage several properties they rent for vacation homes. They spend most of their time in Sedona, but my childhood home, which they still own, is in Phoenix. They play golf and sip cold drinks with friends every day. I plan on following in their footsteps when I retire."

My laughter bubbles to the surface so naturally. Everything about Shep is easy. Everything else feels complicated. For once, I just need easy. Shep World isn't my reality; it's an escape. I *need* this escape, just for a little bit. No one has to know. They wouldn't understand.

"Good plan." I smile. "My sister questioned my profession when I decided to be an optometrist. She called it a boring profession. It's not boring to me. I like it. And when I retire, I think golf and cold drinks with friends sounds perfect. I don't think people take enough time to be present. To appreciate life without fast-forwarding to the future. We waste so much of *now* in preparation for tomorrow or the next day ... or the next decade. Is it really a race? Can we not slow down before we die, or even before we retire?"

"A golfer who lives in the moment ... you're really killing me, Sophie. We stay friends, right? When you marry this other guy and take over the throne, you won't forget about me, right?" He holds up his bottle of beer.

I won't have a baby belly for months, so what will it hurt to just ... live in the moment?

I clink my lemonade glass to his beer bottle. "No promises. Let's take it one day at a time."

"One day at a time." He bobs his head a few times like he's mulling it over.

Our food arrives and we eat every bite. I find out that Shep has a sister who is five years older than him. She's married with two kids. They live in Seattle. She's a stay-at-home mom, and her husband TJ is a welder for a shipping company.

"I have a sister too." I toss my napkin aside. I'm so full. "She lives in Tempe. Her husband is an analyst, and she teaches English at a private school. She's three years older than me."

"And your parents?"

"They're divorced now. My dad lives in Santa Monica, and he's remarried. My mom lives in Detroit, where I grew up. Her cat died recently, and she wanted me to fly home for the burial. I did not, so now I'm on her shit list."

Shep smirks and slides his plate away from him as the bartender clears our dishes from the counter. "Tragic. That's pretty awful of you."

I chuckle and nod.

"How did both you and your sister end up here?" he asks.

"I moved here first after my best friend moved here. My sister's husband had the chance to relocate to offices in Tempe, so they took the transfer here to be closer to me."

"Wow. You abandoned your mom."

"We did not abandon her." I shake my head several times. "My grandma is still alive and in Michigan. Mom plans on moving here when Grandma dies. She wants to be close to her grandchildren."

"Oh, does your sister have kids?"

Biting my lips together, eyes slightly flared, I shake my head. "Not yet. They're trying, so hopefully soon. She's had several miscarriages. It's been rough on them."

"Sorry to hear that. Have they considered adoption?"

"Not yet. They still haven't given up hope of having a child of their own. There's a lot of options now."

"And you? Are you planning on a family some day?"

"Of course. The future of the throne depends on it."

Shep barks a laugh, and it's warm and inviting. I find myself leaning into him a bit more like people do after a few drinks, tipsy because Shep World (I'm trademarking that) is a beautiful place.

He brings his finger to the bridge of my yellow-framed glasses and slides them up my nose a fraction of an inch as he grins. "What do you think your husband will be like? Amazing, probably. I bet he cures cancer or solves the climate change crisis. Some awesome shit like that. And he no doubt rides an actual white horse."

I gobble up his words, his proximity, everything about him. And I think about his guesses regarding my fake husband and his hypothetical awesomeness. Who needs to cure cancer or solve climate change? Small, good deeds should be enough. Like … having a baby for two people who cannot do it on their own. If we can infinitely change the course of one person's life for the better, then that's enough to feel fulfilled.

"Can I get you anything else?" the bartender asks.

"We're good," I whisper without taking my gaze away from Shep's. I like our little world. It's such a different life than my reality right now. A magical alternate universe. It's like immersing myself into a book where I can't wait to turn the next page. And sometimes I have to put the book down and return to reality, but I anxiously anticipate the next time I get to dive back into Shep World.

"Who leaves you?" I ask without a delay of thoughts from my brain to my lips. I've thought it. Who leaves someone like Shep?

The joy that's been on his face for the past hour starts to fade, and he blinks, glancing away at nothing in particular. He starts to speak.

"Stop!" I hold up my hand. "Don't answer that. I'm new at this. It's my first time having a strictly … *positive* friendship. It's going to take some getting used to. So when I screw up, just kick my shin or something, and I'll do the same to you."

"So..." he scrapes his teeth along his lower lip "... this friendship will require shin guards. That's what I'm hearing from you."

I roll my eyes. "Pinch my arm. Whatever."

He tosses a wad of money onto the counter.

I dig through my handbag and slide a fifty onto the counter, pushing some of his cash back toward him. "We split it."

He shakes his head, but he doesn't argue. I'm not sure if I should be flattered that he tried to pay for it all himself or insulted that he didn't put up a bigger fight and insist on paying. Then I think of our conversation.

Mind games.

Friends shouldn't have to play mind games like lovers do.

As we make our way out of the restaurant, his hand finds my back again. "This you?" He nods to my blue Volvo.

"Yes." I unlock the doors, and he opens the driver's side for me. "Thank you."

Before I climb inside, he gently wraps his hand around my wrist.

Oh god ...

It's nothing. It's his hand holding my wrist. So why does it feel like everything? Why does it feel so hard to breathe? Why do I feel exposed like his touch just opened up my emotions and he can see right through me?

My gaze doesn't go to his; it slides to his hand on my wrist. "Wh-what are you doing?" I whisper.

"I'm touching you."

After a hard swallow, I manage another clipped question. "Why?"

"Because it's too hard to *not* touch you."

"W-we're just ... friends. Friends don't touch like this." I can't find an ounce of strength, a true shred of resistance, so everything comes out as a breathy whisper.

He releases my wrist and traces the pad of his thumb to the palm of my hand, circling it with a wispy touch that sends chills along my skin despite the ninety-degree temperature around us.

"What if friends *do* touch like this? What if we make our own rules? Isn't that what you suggested during lunch? Or what if we choose not to have any rules? Why complicate things with rules?"

Complicate? Is he suggesting no rules is ... *easier*?

"Rules..." I clear my throat, unable to tear my gaze away from his hand touching mine "...prevent lines from being crossed."

If he can't hear my heart beating wildly against my ribcage, then he's deaf. I can barely hear my own words past the *whooshing* in my ears.

One. Single. Touch.

Shep has proven that less is more—infinitely more.

"What lines? I don't draw lines," he says.

I choke on a nervous laugh. "Lines on the street keep cars from crashing into each other. Lines are good."

"Sophie ... are you afraid of crashing into me?"

Yes. I'm terrified of crashing into him. I'm terrified that I'll misplace my self-control whenever I'm with him. Being with Shep feels like a chronic state of intoxication. It's dizzying and reckless. It's a preamble to regret.

I pull my wrist away from him and lift my gaze.

"I've never had a friend like you before," he says with a smirk stealing his lips.

Another nervous laugh escapes me. "Well ... that uh ... makes two of us." I slide into the driver's seat and fasten my seat belt. "I need easy. I have no room for anything but easy."

"I'm easy, Sophie."

Lifting an eyebrow, I glance up at him.

Shep shrugs. "Am I proud of it? Of course not. Should I haphazardly share my joie de vivre with just anyone? Doubtful. Yet, here I am. So ... when can I see you again? That free dog wash expires soon."

Joie de vivre?

Who is this guy? I squint at him. "It does?"

Shep's whole face lights up. "No. I'm not so subtly suggesting you and Cersei come into the store soon. In case I have to spell it out for you."

"When are you there?"

"All the time ... except when I'm not." He shrugs.

I roll my eyes.

"You have my number. Call me when you're ready to get wet," he says.

With heat accumulating in my cheeks, my filthy mind leaves the station into dangerous territory.

Shep rests his hand on the top of my door. "Dogs shake and water from the nozzle splashes everywhere." His lips curl into a smirk. "But ... I like where your mind went when I said it."

My head swings from one side to the other as I check my seat belt as if I'm not sure it's secure. "My mind didn't go anywhere."

"It did." He shuts the door and struts down the sidewalk, glancing back at the last second as if to make sure I'm self-combusting in my seat.

I am.

When I get home, domestic Jimmy's in the kitchen, cleaning the sink. "I fed Cersei. And I'll take her for a walk in a bit."

I slip off my wedges and carry them to my bedroom. I don't know what to do with new Jimmy or maybe he's back to original Jimmy. "I'll walk her."

"Sophie, just put your feet up and relax. I'll make popcorn, and I saved you some of the chocolate ice cream."

"Why should I put my feet up?" I pause, my back to him. Did my sister come by? Did she tell him? God, does she know he's still living here? Did Jules say something?

"Because you started your period."

The trash.

Jimmy might be searching for a job, cleaning the house, and saving me ice cream, but he's also still digging through my bathroom trash for tampons, and that is the neon light that blinks the brightest.

Jimmy is not the one.

But ... he's here until I can get him legally removed from the premises, so he might as well make himself useful.

"Sure," I say. "Take her for a walk. Thanks." I opt for a long bath and inappropriate thoughts of my new friend.

CHAPTER *Eleven*

FOR THE NEXT FEW DAYS, Jimmy attempts to earn his keep: he feeds Cersei, takes her for walks, cooks, cleans, and even vacs out my car. It's more than I expected when he moved in with me. That should count for something, but it doesn't. I can't be with Jimmy when I know there's a Shep in my world. And I can't be with Shep while my sister's baby is in my uterus.

And even if I weren't with child, Shep could be a Jimmy, like Jimmy is a Tanner (the car and purse thief) and Tanner was a Benjamin (who slept on my sofa for a month with a fake cast while he dodged the police). These are my freeloaders—men who swept me off my feet before stealing my wallet, my time, my sofa, or my goodwill. Mostly, they stole my innocence in a non-virginal way.

And now, I'm susceptible to baby brain. Even more reason not to put myself in vulnerable situations such as a new relationship. Yet, here I am ... proverbially telling Shep, "Okay, but just the tip."

One day at a time. Shep is my friend. Period. If Shep World ends tomorrow, so be it.

Then why am I so excited about meeting him at the

store to wash Cersei? Oh ... that's right. I'm going to get wet.

"Good afternoon. If you need help with anything, just let me know." The salt-and-pepper-haired woman behind the register smiles at me as she refills a countertop display with biscuits.

"Is Shep around?"

"He's in the back unloading a shipment. Do you want me to get him?"

"Can you tell him Sophie's here?"

"You bet." She pushes open the door to the back of the store. "Shep? There's a Sophie here to see you."

"Thanks, Boss." His voice echoes.

"Listen, if he needs to finish what he's doing, don't let me stop him." The last thing I need is Shep getting fired like Jimmy because he's catering to my dog's needs while on the clock. It's a self-serve wash.

"It's fine," she says. "I'm sure he'll finish later. And if he doesn't, I'll have to do it. He's always slacking."

I cringe. "You know ... tell him I had something come up. I'll be back another day."

"What's come up?" Shep asks as he pushes through the backroom door, untying his apron and slipping it over his head.

Taking a second or ten to admire his fitted tee and toned arms, I clear my throat. "Finish what you're doing. I don't want you to get fired because of me." I shoot his boss a nervous smile.

She laughs. "Finally! Someone who knows who's boss."

He wads up his apron and throws it at her, hitting the side of her head. *Oh my god!* I can't believe he did that.

"I know you're the boss, Marta, but you don't actually have to be so bossy."

My eyes widen. I can't read her. Does she find him funny? God, I hope so.

"Come on, dirty bitch ... let's get you wet," he says.

Kill me now.

"Watch your mouth, young man. Or I'll wash it out with soap like my grandma used to do to me." Marta gives Shep the hairy eyeball.

"I was talking to Cersei, who is a bitch and she's dirty. I wasn't talking to Sophie." Shep nods toward the basin. "I would never call you a dirty bitch."

Without blinking, my gaze ping-pongs between Shep and Marta as I inch my way toward him.

"Nice glasses." He eyes my leopard print frames.

"Thanks." I try to smile despite the tension I feel between them.

"That shirt is nice too ... and an interesting choice."

I glance down at my white tank top and short denim shorts with a frayed hem.

"Hope *my friend* is wearing a thick padded bra," he says so only I can hear him.

Shit ...

"Or maybe I don't." Shep smirks while putting Cersei in the basin.

"I'll wash her." I reach for the hose in his hand.

"No. I've got it." He pulls just out of my reach.

I don't trust the look on his face. As he washes her, I maintain a good three feet from the basin, and he glances up occasionally and gives me a look. He's enjoying this. He's enjoying my discomfort, my distrust.

"Anyone ever tell you that you look a lot like that girl from High School Musical? My granddaughter loves that series."

I turn toward Marta as she says that. "Vanessa Hudgens?" I chuckle. "Thanks. That's quite the compliment."

"Your smile. Your eyes. I've always thought she was stunning. You're definitely Vanessa's twin in the most stylish glasses I've ever seen. Well, your hair is shorter and lighter, but the face is identical."

"You are stunning," Shep says, bringing my attention back to him along with a second round of blushing.

"She said Vanessa is stunning."

"She said you look like her. And *I* said *you* are stunning."

"Well ..." My palpable nerves make my voice shake. "You're my friend, so you have to say nice things to me."

"I'm your friend..." he lathers Cersei "...so I'm honest with you."

"You've known me two weeks. We're still in the polite stage of our friendship." I narrow my eyes at him, but I can't entirely hide my grin.

He turns on the water again and begins to rinse

Cersei. "I'm not *that* polite." With a flick of his wrist, he sprays water all over the front of my shirt.

My white shirt.

My *thin* white bra.

I might as well not have a shirt or bra on. He can see *everything*.

"Shep!" I jump back, jaw unhinged. At first, I pull the material away from my breasts, but it's not helping. I'm too wet. My shirt is too wet. So I cover my arms over my chest.

"Oops. My bad." He redirects his gaze to Cersei, but his grin doesn't budge.

I glance around and find a restroom just past the coolers, scurrying to it and locking the door behind me. "You shit, Shep," I mumble, inspecting the two dark circles in the mirror, nipples popped out like cherries atop cupcakes. Grabbing a wad of paper towels, I scrub the wet cotton with frantic circular motions, cursing Shep under my breath. It does nothing but break down the paper towels and smear pieces of it along my shirt. Why don't they have an eco-friendly air dryer?

"Sophie?" Shep knocks on the door.

"We are no longer friends!"

"Bullshit. Open the door. I have a dry shirt for you."

I crack open the door.

"Let me in."

I shake my head. "Give me the shirt."

"I will, after you let me in."

"I'm not letting you in. Where's Cersei?"

"Marta is drying her, and she's going to clip her nails for you too. No extra charge."

I blink a few times. *No extra charge*. Does he think he's winning? Does he think a free nail clipping makes up for this?

"Jesus ... you're going to get fired. And honestly, you deserve it at this point. I'd fire your ass for spraying down a customer. I hope the nail clipping comes out of your paycheck."

"It will come out of my paycheck. Now let me in." He pushes the door open despite my resistance. As he shuts it behind him, I snag two more handfuls of paper towels and cover my breasts.

"Give me the shirt."

He hands it to me.

I hold the paper towels against my chest with one arm and snatch the shirt from him with my other hand. "Now get out."

"My buddy, who was supposed to golf with me Friday afternoon, had to cancel. You should come with me."

"I have to work."

"That's a lame excuse."

"Says the guy with a job he doesn't take seriously."

"Reschedule your patients." He slips his hands in his back pockets.

"Sorry, *Mom*, I can't reschedule patients on a whim because your cat died." I go with a ridiculous clown grin.

"I'm playing at a course in Sedona. My parents'

place is empty because they're in Colorado visiting my aunt and uncle. Take the whole day off on Friday. We'll come back Sunday evening."

I chuckle. "No. We're friends." Glancing down at my drenched shirt, I frown. "Just barely friends. But friends who don't have weekend getaways. And again, I have patients Friday who have been on my schedule for months. Also, we met two weeks ago. This is not only *not* happening; it's ridiculous that you'd even suggest it."

"What are you waiting for? You're a grownup. You have the means. You're your own boss. Don't wait for your hair to turn gray and your joints to stiffen before playing golf and sipping cold drinks with friends."

I shake my head slowly.

He takes a step closer. I retreat a step, my butt hitting the pedestal sink.

"There are four bedrooms and a sofa sleeper. We don't even have to sleep on the same level. All the doors have locks, so I won't have to worry about you sneaking into my bedroom at night."

It's impossible to keep from giving him an eye roll.

"Say yes, Sophie. Be old as fuck with me without actually being old as fuck."

On an unavoidable laugh, I nod. As cautious as I need to be because my impulsive decisions have led to my current situation at home, at my core, I like spontaneity.

I also like Shep's outlook on life, even if he's on the

verge of losing his job. "Fine. Now get out of here so I can change my shirt."

Shep's smile makes everything inside of me melt. I don't know why I'm so hesitant to be his friend. I've never been friends with a guy like this. My guy friends are either from school or they're boyfriends or husbands of my friends. Why can't we be friends?

Oh that's right ... we're friends who touch. Friends without rules. Friends without lines. What could possibly go wrong?

CHAPTER *Twelve*

THURSDAY NIGHT I eat dinner with Jimmy. He has news. I like news, especially since I know he's been looking for a job. I don't want to have to give him written notice or start the formal eviction process.

It's my house.

We've broken up.

He just needs to get back on his feet to realize he can stand just fine without me.

"I got a job."

I grin. I knew it. This is the best news of the week. "That's awesome. What's the job?"

"It's in sales. I'm selling timeshares. And the good news is I do it from home, so I don't have to invest in fancy suits or wear a stupid uniform. The hours are flexible, and there are lots of opportunities to earn bonuses."

"Well, sounds like a good fit. I know you hate wearing uniforms, and you have never been a fan of suits. When do you start?"

"I started today."

"Oh ... wow. That's good. How did it go?" What is that saying about catching more flies ... more flies with honey than vinegar? That's the goal. Be nice. Be sweet.

Jimmy leaves. Mission accomplished. Neither the baby nor I need to hold a grudge. I stab my fork into the broccoli and cut it in half. We did it. Jimmy has come to his senses. Found a job. And no one in my family will be the wiser.

"Good. Really good." He nods. "I've ordered a desk. I had to use your credit card, but I'll totally pay you back. And you can use the desk, too, in the evenings when I'm not working. And I'm not asking you to pay half. I'm totally cool with covering the full cost. It's a business write-off for me."

Honey, not vinegar.

My fork drops out of my hand and clinks on the plate. Slowly bringing my napkin to my face, I clear my throat. "First, where did you get my credit card? Second, why are you ordering a desk for my house? Third, why haven't you found a place to live?" With a shaky voice, my composure teeters on the edge. The honey is gone.

"Um ..." He rolls his eyes from one side to the other, confusion lining his forehead. "I got your credit card out of your purse this morning before you left for work. I didn't want to bother you while you were in the shower, but I also needed to get Cersei out for her walk before it got too warm. And I need a desk for my computer, which I will also be paying you back for as soon as I get my first paycheck. I actually have one more unemployment check coming, and it might cover part of the computer. And for the record ... I didn't use your credit card for the taxi to the Apple Store. I had a new customer credit for downloading the app. And I'm not moving until we have a chance to make this work. Like ... really work. Now that I have a new job and I've been doing basically everything around the house, I'm more than earning my keep. And you should be happy."

This isn't happening. Any minute I'm going to wake from this nightmare, and Jules and I will laugh as I tell her about my disturbing nightmare because this isn't real. No. There's no way this is real.

Scooting my chair back with a slow screech along the tile, I unfold my body and make cautious, calculated steps to my bedroom. Any sudden movement will end with a steak knife shoved into Jimmy's carotid artery. And I need to keep calm. Calm for the baby. Calm to stay out of prison.

I retrieve the five-day written notice for him to move out. Returning to the kitchen, I grab a pen and sign and date it. "Here." I smile while gritting my teeth. "You have five days to move out or I will have you legally evicted. Keep your desk and computer, just get out of my house." I gently set the notice on the table beside his plate, forcing control with each measured movement, but my hand shakes as I rest the pen on the paper.

See ... I'm being calm. So calm. Smooth and sweet like honey. No need to commit murder.

My fork rattles on my plate as I carry it to the sink, scraping most of my dinner into the garbage disposal. The problem with non-confrontational people like myself is we don't let off enough occasional spurts of steam to prevent an acute nuclear meltdown.

"Baby ... what the heck?"

"I'm not..." *breathe, breathe* "...your baby." After placing my plate and fork in the dishwasher, I ease the door shut and turn toward him. "Jimmy, you have to wake up. I'm not your girlfriend. *We* are not together. I broke up with you. I've been extremely generous letting you stay here until you found a job and a place of your own. I asked you to leave. Your denial of reality should be embarrassing for you. I know ... I really know you're not this dense, this stupid. You have a job. Please get out. Go your own way before this gets any further out of hand. Don't be the person who's made to look like a complete fool. You are not my boyfriend. You are officially a squatter."

I am a complete fool for letting a man use me for the millionth time.

He studies the notice, eyes in tiny slits while his head inches side to side. "You've ... what? Has this just been lying around, waiting for the right moment to spring it on me?"

"Jimmy, for god's sake. I gave you a week to get out and that was nearly three weeks ago."

"But I got a job. We were good. I've been doing my part around here. I've been doing *more* than my part. I've been raising your dog. You could say I've been raising your child."

"Cersei is not a child. She is, in fact, a dog. It's not

even close to the same thing. And I never asked you to do it."

"Yet, I did do it. And I've never complained."

I rest my hands on my hips and gaze at the ceiling. "Where is your dignity? You are a good-looking guy. And when you're driven to work hard and do things for other people, you can even be charming. Someone else will see that, and they'll want to be with you. But that's not me. Not anymore."

He rips the notice up. "I don't accept this. You owe me now. I've been doing *everything* around here, and I'll move out when I'm good and ready and not a day earlier. If I have to get an attorney to prove that I've earned my keep, then that's exactly what I'm going to do." He storms out of the kitchen toward the guest room. I want him out, but him no longer sleeping naked on my sofa, after watching movies until the wee hours of the morning, has been a tiny win.

"And Sophie?" He turns just before closing the bedroom door. "Squatter is not a politically correct term."

I rub my temples. I'm too pregnant. Too tired. And too pissed off to care about hurting Jimmy's politically correct feelings.

"Informal settler is the correct term." He shuts the door.

THE NEXT MORNING, I finish packing a few things for my weekend in Sedona, including Cersei's bag since there's no way I'm leaving her here with Jimmy. I'm not letting him gain any more ammunition to fight me over this eviction.

He's ruined relationships for me. Maybe not forever, but close. He's robbed all trust I've ever had in men. He's definitely destroyed any possibility that I will ever let someone move in with me again.

"Where are you going?" Jimmy eyes my suitcase as I wheel it out of my bedroom.

I see he's regressed, returning to his spot on the sofa, back in his boxers and an old tee. I'm guessing a shower and house cleaning are not on his agenda. "I'm going out of town for the weekend. Cersei is coming with me, so you don't have to worry about anything except packing your shit and moving out."

"Who are you going with? Jules?" He ignores my moving out comment.

"No. A different friend."

"Who?"

If Jimmy can selectively choose to acknowledge my words, then I can play the same game. "Come, Cersei." I sling her toy and treat-filled bag over my shoulder.

We cruise through the light morning traffic to my office where I told Shep to pick me up, after giving him a tiny lie about needing to check on a few things before leaving town. I can't risk Jimmy seeing me leave for the weekend with another guy. He can't be trusted not to do something to retaliate. More than that, I don't want

Shep to see that my miserable asshole ex-boyfriend is still living with me. Jimmy can't reside in Shep World. And Shep can't reside in my real world. It's … complicated.

Even if it's not my fault (of which I haven't decided), it's embarrassing. Really, it's humiliating at this point. The people we date are tiny glimpses into the people we are. And right now, Jimmy is the worst version of himself and clearly representative of something that must be wrong with me.

"So this is where you do your doctor thing."

I turn toward Shep's voice, messing with a few things on the desk to look busy at my important task which apparently involves untangling paperclips and organizing pens by color. "Yes. This is where I do my doctor thing. Are you ready?"

He bends down and scratches Cersei behind her ears. "Had I known you were bringing her, I would have requested Julia and George for the weekend. Not that Millie would have agreed, but it would have been worth a try."

"Millie? Your ex-wife's name is Millie?" I usher him and Cersei toward the door and set the alarm behind us.

"Yes."

"Interesting. I had it different in my head. I imagined an Emma or Scarlet. Maybe a Gwen or Abigail."

"Sorry to disappoint." He laughs as we make our way toward a red Shelby Mustang.

"I love your car."

"It's my dad's car, but thanks."

After we load my stuff, Shep slides into the driver's seat, and suddenly I feel suffocated by his nearness— all the things money can't buy like his wayward hair. The sharp angles of his face. That ornery smile. I swear he always looks as if he's winning at something or hiding a secret. So maybe he works at a pet shop and drives his dad's car, and maybe that should be a concern since I'm a magnet for men in financial "situations," but it's not. We're friends. That's it.

Is he hiding something from me? I hope so. I hope he's hiding a secret. Or ten. As of recently, I've decided I'm in the camp that doesn't believe lack of transparency is the same as a lie. Self-preservation has its place in the world. It's a pillar of individuality.

I'm so full of shit.

Nonetheless, I lean my head back and take a deep breath; it's a Shep World weekend.

Speaking of ... Shep smells clean, not like a body that's been stuck to a leather sofa for weeks, emitting a toxic mix of sweat, oil, and farts. Inhaling Shep takes me on an evening drive from the redwoods of California to the coastal highway. He's crisp and refreshing. Alluring and a little reckless. I'm afraid if my dad nicked him with a weed eater, I'd rush him into the house, screaming and crying fat tears. I'd make him a bed of newspapers, give him a water dish, and stock up on worms and guppies.

Snorting a laugh, I press my lips together and glance out the window.

"Everything okay?" he asks.

Is everything okay? My thoughts somehow jumble together, making a weird comparison between the sexy guy next to me and an injured garter snake from my childhood. That's probably not normal or *okay.*

"Everything is just fine."

"I'm glad you said yes to this weekend." He gives me a quick glance and that winning grin before slipping on his sunglasses and starting the car.

"You like having your ass handed to you on the golf course, huh?"

"Sophie, if you're the one doling out the ass-kicking, I'm in. Anything to be with you."

What?

No. No way. He's not allowed to say those words. Those are illegal words. Shep clearly doesn't have that many friends. His friendship skills suck. I'm trying to banter with him, but he's hell-bent on reminding me that we have no lines and no rules. We're free falling, and I can't find the damn cord to deploy the chute, while he's grinning as if he doesn't care how we land or if we live to tell about it.

"You're a good distraction," I say. "You're not dramatic like my girlfriends. And I could use an opportunity to regain my faith in men at this point in my life."

"Well crap. That puts a lot of pressure on me ... representing the entire male species. If I screw up, you'll die alone."

I laugh. "Exactly. So don't screw up."

Taking an exaggerated inhale, he blows it out just as slowly. "Doing my best." He leans forward. "Music? Or do you want to entertain me with your deepest, darkest secrets?"

"Music. Definitely music."

He hooks his phone up to a cassette adapter. It's funny, but the car is old. What did I expect?

"Summer Days" by Martin Garrix plays and it brings an instant smile to my face. Shep has good taste in music. Shep has sexy taste in music. It's the perfect song for a sunny day in a Mustang.

CHAPTER

THiRTeeN

"YOU CAN HAVE the master bedroom here on the main level." Shep leads me to the bedroom with wood floors and a huge area rug under the king bed. On one side, a private balcony overlooks the pool. The other side opens to a spacious en suite bathroom with a soaker tub and walk-in shower. His parents' house is breathtaking.

All I can think is … this is so weird. What am I doing here with the guy from the pet store?

The gated entry. The panoramic view of the glowing red rocks.

The infinity pool and hot tub.

I'm in awe.

"It's your family's house. You take this room. I'll stay in another room. A *guest* room."

"Too late." He sets my suitcase at the end of the bed. "I've already laid claim to the bedroom downstairs."

"But…" I nod toward the door "…there's another bedroom here on the main floor."

"Yes. But I want to make you feel as comfortable as possible. Give you as much space and privacy as you need. So I'll be downstairs. Cersei can have the other bedroom up here."

"Shep ..."

"Get settled. We have a tee time in an hour." He disappears down the stairs with his bag.

I stare ... and stare at the view. Then I plop back on the bed and gaze at the ceiling fan. I can't believe I'm here. With him.

A few minutes later, Shep emerges from the basement in black shorts and a white golf polo. I've changed into a black skort and a white sleeveless polo.

"Wow ... we match," I say, trying to hide my amusement while eyeing him. "I can change. I packed another option."

"You don't want to match with me?" He fiddles with the buttons to his polo and adjusts the collar.

"No. I mean ... it's fine with me if it's fine with you. My shirt's wrinkled, so ... whatever." That's my comeback. *Brilliant.* "Got any food in the fridge?"

"Yeah. You hungry? I guess I should have planned for lunch before golf."

I shake my head. "It's fine. I'm a snacker. That's all." I'm *not* a snacker. I can skip a meal and not feel hungry. But I've read I need to eat small meals and frequent snacks to keep any possible nausea at bay. So far, I haven't felt anything except some slight tenderness in my breasts.

"Fruit? Meat? Cheese?"

"Sure."

He chuckles. "A buffet it is." I take the food from him as he pulls out several trays from the fridge.

"Looks like someone planned for a party. All this food on trays."

"No. My mom knew I was bringing Howie, so she made sure to leave food. If it were just me, I think she'd let me starve."

"Howie? The toddler?"

He grins and nods. "Does he know about me? Did you talk about me the day I called you?"

"I may have given him some details about you," he mumbles.

"What details?" I dig into the food.

"He knows we're friends. He's happy that I have a ... *friend.*"

I narrow my eyes.

"He and his wife were friends with me and Millie. I don't get to see him as often because we no longer do things as couples."

"Maybe I should hang out with you and Howie." A whole different, Jimmy-less life, I think in my delusional head. Sounds magical. "You know ... since this is all a friend thing. I could go golfing with you two. A threesome."

Shep coughs, spewing out some cracker crumbs. "N-no. Don't say it like that."

"That's what it's called. Do you think Howie would be opposed to a threesome?"

"St-stop." He fists his hand at his mouth and laughs.

"Well..." I shrug, keeping my smile well hidden behind a handful of grapes "...it's just an idea. You two can discuss it later. Oh, and tell your mom thanks for me. This is all really good."

He nods several times while his throat bobs. "I will. Maybe." He brushes the crumbs off his hands into the sink. Then he leans his hip against the counter and crosses his arms over his chest. They're tan and defined.

I give my eyes a few extra seconds to admire them before refocusing on the food. "Maybe?" I say, covering my mouth as I chew.

"My parents don't know you're here."

"Me? Your *friend*? I'm *your* secret?"

His head bounces a few times. "Perhaps."

This makes my day. He has at least one secret. Me.

"Are you not allowed to have girls at the house when your parents aren't here? No parties? No loud music?"

"I'm avoiding a million questions. You're my first female anything since my divorce."

I chew slowly for a bit before nodding. "Men and women can be *just* friends."

"I'm sure it's a hard sell for some people. But not us. We know otherwise. Right?" His question is weird, or maybe it's the way he's posing it to me like I actually need to answer him, instead of a foregone conclusion or anything rhetorical.

"Yes. We're just friends." I pop a piece of pineapple

into my mouth. "Despite your juvenile attempts to see my nipples."

His face comes to life. "It was a successful attempt. Not juvenile. Well planned with a solid payout."

I roll my eyes. "You didn't see anything."

"Oh, I saw everything. I could sketch your nipples if they robbed a bank."

"Stop." I laugh, returning the food trays to the fridge. "Stop talking about my nipples."

"You brought them up. Don't get me wrong, I was hoping you would. Like ... really hoping. I've been meaning to compliment you on them. That day at the store, I wanted to give them a slow clap or something special like that. Maybe a ribbon like at the state fair."

I can't stop giggling as I fist my hand over my mouth to keep from spitting residual bits of food from my mouth. "Let's go. This conversation is over." I fill a bowl with water for Cersei and set it on the tile floor.

"It's not over. It's just shelved until later." Shep follows me to the door. "I still have some things to say about your nipples."

"Stop!" I cover my face for a brief second as we make our way to the Mustang in the circle driveway. "Friends don't talk about each other's body parts like this."

He opens the car door for me. "Really? Huh. That's too bad. Good thing we don't have to be like other friends. And I've critiqued a few things about Howie. Poor guy is seriously pecker challenged." He shuts my door after I secure my seat belt.

✳︎ ✳︎ ✳︎ ✳︎

"I'M PAYING," I say when we arrive at the golf course. The woman at the counter smiles at Shep and then at me.

"Sophie ..." Shep starts his protest.

"No. You drove. I'm staying at your parents' house. And I've eaten their food. I wouldn't feel right if I didn't at least pay for our golf." I sign for the eighteen holes of golf and turn toward Shep. "Ready?"

"Ready. Thanks for paying. It's quite kind of you."

Yes. They all say this. The men I manage to attract into my life find me quite generous. I'm not sure taking advantage of me is their initial intention or a byproduct of a hidden flaw they possess. Or maybe it's my flaw. Maybe I'm an easy target. Who am I kidding? I'm the Mother Teresa of garter snakes.

Shep is different, not that I know this for certain. I just know that he will never move into my house. It's Shep World. Separation of church and state.

As the afternoon progresses, Shep whistles every time I make a perfect putt or land a chip shot just inches from the hole. It doesn't get old. I'm tempted to suggest we play another eighteen holes. As far as friends go, Shep's a pretty good one. Jules might have to up her game.

"Welp." As we walk toward the cart after the last hole, Shep stops and waits for me to turn. "I'm not worthy." He drops to his knees and holds his putter in front of him as he bows.

126

"Stop." I giggle before continuing to the cart, so he'll stand up and not embarrass me.

"Let's grab a cold drink." He lumbers to his feet and joins me in the golf cart, gunning it toward the club house.

"You're a good golfer, Shep. Kept me on my toes the whole time."

"You on your toes. Me on my knees. Sounds fair." He tries to sound defeated, but I don't miss the enjoyment pulling at his lips.

We order drinks at the clubhouse and find a table with a great view. There isn't a bad view in Sedona. Again, Shep orders a beer and I ask for a lemonade. While I wait for him to carry our drinks (which he bought) from the bar, a guy with short blond hair slows his pace and stops at my table, taking off his golf glove.

"You took my table."

I lift my eyebrows. "Oh? I'm sorry. I can move." I start to scoot my chair backward.

"Don't. I may have exaggerated a bit." He grins. "I sat here yesterday, but I was by myself. I wouldn't mind sitting here today with you if you don't mind."

"I mind, Trace." Shep sets our drinks on the table and sits across from me.

Trace eyes Shep with something that resembles contempt. "Well, doesn't that just fucking figure."

Shep sips his beer. "What's that?"

"Good luck, miss." Trace shoots me a tight smile before sauntering in the opposite direction.

"Are you cock-blocking me, Shep?"

He pauses his beer mug at his lips. "Cock-blocking implies I blocked you from having sex with that asshole. Is that what you're implying?"

"I'm implying that if you were a girlfriend of mine, I would still be talking to him, and maybe my *girlfriend* and I would have invited him to join us for drinks."

He lifts a brow, beer still paused at his lips. "And then you would have had sex with him?"

I shake my head. "Not my point."

"What's your point?" he asks then takes a pull of his beer.

"My point is there are some drawbacks to us being friends, specifically you being a male. People assume we are a couple."

"Do you routinely ditch your friends for random guys?"

"No. Not my point."

Setting his beer on the table, he shrugs. "You don't have a point, Sophie. Unless ..." His dark eyes lift to mine.

"Unless?" I stir my lemonade with the straw.

"Unless your point is that you're in need of cock."

"What? No! That's not it at all."

"You're the one who accused me of cock-blocking you from a guy who jumps anything that moves. What else am I to deduce from that?"

"I'm joking. Geesh ..." I glance out the window with a slight headshake.

"I'm just saying..." he continues "...we're friends. And you should be looking at the upside to my gender.

If … and I'm only saying *if* … you need a cock, I just so happen to have one you can borrow." He grins like he *borrowed* that smile from the devil himself. "That's what friends are for."

"No." I choke on my lemonade and clear my throat several times. "That's not what friends are for."

Shep rubs his chin, scratching his scruffy jaw while inspecting me. Amusement clings to his full lips. In equal parts, I want to strangle him and kiss him. This new acquaintance—friend—of mine is unlike anyone I've ever met. I think in a good way, but honestly, I'm not sure.

"You could murder me, and no one would know where to look," I say.

His eyes narrow for a few seconds. "Interesting. Tell me more."

"I told the people I work with that I needed the weekend off for personal reasons. I'm the boss, so no one questioned me. I think they suspected issues with my ex. My best friend is in Vegas this weekend for a wedding, so I didn't bother to tell her where I was going. My mom is still upset about me not attending her cat's funeral, so she doesn't know. And I only talk with my dad every month or two, so he doesn't know either. My sister … well, she'd totally lose it. I irresponsibly, recklessly left town with complete abandonment to stay with a guy I've known for less than a month."

"Why would your sister lose it?"

Averting my gaze to a couple walking into the club-

129

house, I shrug while thinking about the embryo inside of me. "She's just a lot more cautious than I am."

Shep leans back and rests his hand on the table, softly drumming his fingers. "I'll think about it. The murder. I wasn't planning on it, and I've never done it before. But now that you've offered it as an option, I feel obligated to at least consider it. And I'm always game to try new things."

My grin remains restrained for a moment. "Sure. Take your time. Just let me know what you decide. Or ... don't. I suppose a good homicide requires a certain element of surprise."

He smirks. "I'd imagine so. But again, I've never done it, so I can't speak from firsthand experience. I would have researched this a bit had I known ahead of time. I guess my head is spinning right now because we somehow jumped from me offering you my cock to you offering to let me murder you. I think..." he rubs the back of his neck "...a lot has changed since the last time I dated—I mean—made a new friend."

Shep glances over my shoulder and sits up straight. "Shit. Be cool. There's a couple headed our way. They're going to try to engage us in conversation. Don't do it. Don't say a word. Just let me handle it. Okay?" Shep sounds so serious.

I stiffen, anticipating their approach.

"Hey, how are you?" a man's voice booms behind me.

Shep plasters on a fake smile. "Hey. Good. Thanks."

The middle-aged gentleman and his wife stop at our table.

"Great day," she says.

I smile. Shep nods.

"I'm Tony and this is my wife, Deb." He holds out his hand to me.

"Hi. I'm Sophie. It's nice to meet you."

Shep kicks my foot under the table. I shoot him a quick scowl. Really, what was I supposed to do? Ignore them?

"Tony was just saying it's been a long time since we've seen Shep." Deb rests her hand on Tony's arm.

"Yeah. We saw your parents last month, and I honestly couldn't remember the last time I saw you. It's been a while. How the heck have you been?" Tony asks.

"Been good. Thanks. Hope you enjoy the rest of the day. It was good to see you."

I pull my lips tight, amused by Shep's attempt to dismiss them as quickly as possible.

"Yeah ... we just finished our round for the day. We'll be back early in the morning." Tony widens his stance and crosses his arms over his chest like he's settling in for more conversation. Nothing about his posture says he's leaving any time soon. "Gonna throw some steaks on the grill tonight. Deb's making some salsa. She's been growing upside-down tomatoes like it's nobody's business. Got 'em coming out our ears. We should drop some off for you. You like tomatoes, Sophie?"

"Yes. I love—" I grunt and scowl at Shep when he kicks me *again*.

"We're only here until Sunday, and the fridge is stocked with more food than we'll be able to eat. But thanks anyway. Enjoy your steaks. It's been good talking to you." A stiff smile remains cemented to Shep's face.

"I love your glasses." Deb nods to my glasses.

They're basic red frames today.

As I open my mouth to thank her, Shep scoots back in his chair. "Speaking of twenty-twenty vision ... would you look at the time? We need to let Cersei out."

"Cersei? As in ... Game of Thrones?" Deb asks.

I nod, biting back my urge to also say Cersei is my dog.

"Oh lord ... Deb and I have watched that series three times. Can you believe it? It's almost embarrassing, like we don't have a life or something."

Shep's brows slowly lift as his lips curl inward. This time I kick him under the table. He's being a bit too obvious.

"You know what's another good show to binge watch?" Deb asks.

Then she tells us about every show we need to watch—covering Hulu, Netflix, HBO, Showtime, and other streaming services I've never heard of before now. One of the shows has a main character who is transgender, which leads into Deb and Tony expressing their concern for their granddaughter who recently revealed that she's transgender. We learn the names of all of her transgender friends and their new transgender names and how confusing that is for family and friends to keep track of new names and proper pronouns. On the heels of that admission, they go into great detail about their upbringing and how woke they are now—totally supportive of the LGBTQ community (although they miss a few letters)—Tony says, "The LB whatever etcetera etcetera people," and I cringe wondering if anyone else hears him.

It's not that he's meaning to be disrespectful; he'd just be better off not saying anything at all than saying it all wrong, even if it's an accident. My "squatter" comment doesn't seem as bad now. While I notice my own smile feeling stiff and beginning to crack, I glance at Shep and he's wearing the same cringe-worthy expression.

They just won't shut up.

"Oh. Excuse me." I interrupt and bring my phone to my ear.

Deb stops talking for a few seconds.

"Oh no! I'm so sorry. Let me get where I can talk in private," I say to my phone and the imaginary person who I'm talking to. "Shep. We have to go. It's an emergency." I don't know why, but I jump to my feet and grab his hand, pulling him to stand. "So sorry," I mouth to Deb and Tony.

"Take care," Shep says as I lead him to the door and straight toward the Mustang, keeping ahold of his hand the whole time.

"Before I sound like an insensitive ass by thanking

you for getting us out of that torturous situation, can you confirm that you just took a fake call and there is no real emergency?"

I laugh. It's all I can do as I start to release his hand when we get to the car.

His grip tightens as he stops, turning me toward him. Nothing ... he says *nothing* which feels intimate because he's holding my hand and we're really close.

That sly grin of his makes an appearance two seconds before he speaks. "This was a good idea."

In lieu of speaking, I return several lightning quick nods that don't require breathing. When he appears satisfied with my level of discomfort, he releases my hand and opens the car door for me.

CHAPTER
Fourteen

It's a fifteen-minute drive to his parents' house, and I can't find anything to say, but neither can he until we walk in the front door.

"I'll grab a quick shower and put something on the grill."

"I'll be in the pool," I say, hustling to the bathroom to put some distance between us while my thoughts untangle from his … *Gah!* His everything. It's not okay for friends to have inappropriate thoughts about each other, yet here I am, my mind in the gutter.

As I finish slipping on my bikini, my cell phone rings. "Hey, Jules. How's the wedding?"

"It's rehearsal dinner later. I'm getting a pedicure at the moment. Just seeing how you're feeling."

"I'm fine. Why?" I adjust my top and inspect myself in the full-length mirror.

"Just seeing if morning sickness has hit."

"Oh. That. No. Not yet. Maybe I won't get it. Not everyone does."

"I hope not for your sake. I think it should be a rule that if you're carrying a child for someone else, you shouldn't get sick."

"You haven't told anyone, have you? Chloe would kill me if it got out."

"Of course not. I can keep a secret, ya know. So what are you up to this weekend? Jimmy still trying to woo you with his lazy ass?"

"No. I golfed this morning."

Not a lie.

"Is your dad visiting?"

"No."

Not a lie.

"Who did you golf with?"

"Myself."

Half lie.

"Can you do that? Can you play golf by yourself?"

I chuckle. "Yes. You can play golf by yourself."

Still, not a lie.

"Sophie, the switch to open the cover to the pool is in the box next to the heat lamp," Shep yells upstairs.

I press my hand against my phone's speaker, but I'm not sure it's fast enough.

"Who's that?"

"Who's who?"

"Sophie. I heard a guy. Something about a pool cover?"

"It was Jimmy."

Here come the lies ...

"It didn't sound like Jimmy. And you don't have a pool. Where are you?"

"Nowhere—"

"Sophie, you're in Sedona."

138

I cringe. Jules and I follow each other's location. Stupid, stupid me for forgetting to shut that off.

"I am." I bite my lips together and wait for her to ask the questions so I can determine how many lies I can believably feed to her—how deep can I dig this hole I'm in.

"Why?" she asks.

"Golfing."

"With whom? And don't you dare say you're in Sedona golfing by yourself."

"Listen, there are a lot of nice resorts in Sedona. I absolutely could treat myself to a getaway. Massages. Peace and quiet. Golf. Good food. And with Jimmy the squatter at my house, I think I deserve a getaway."

"You invited Jimmy the squatter to live with you. I'm not buying the 'poor me' act. Sorry."

I roll my eyes. She's not wrong. But friends don't punch each other in the gut like that.

"And while I'm not denying that you can't get away to Sedona by yourself, it doesn't explain the man's voice I just heard. And your location doesn't show you at a resort. It shows you at a house."

"What if I rented a VRBO?"

I need to bail. The water's getting too high.

"Did the guy come with the VRBO?"

"Fine! I'm here with Shep. But it's not what you think."

"Shep?"

"The guy from the pet store."

"Dear god, how did you completely fail to heed my

warning? I told you to stay away from him and *all* men. You have a serious problem, Sophie. You're in Sedona with another guy while you still haven't evicted the last guy from your house? AND you're pregnant. What. Are. You. Doing?"

Jules hasn't met Shep, so she can't possibly understand Shep World. She doesn't know that it's not real.

"Calm down. You're getting worked up about nothing. We're golfing. That's it. Think of him as you or any of my other friends. Female friends. Nothing is going on. Nothing will be going on."

"Sophie, I love you," Jules says in the same tone one might use to talk someone down from a ledge, "but you are delusional. I don't want to tell your family, but you're being very reckless and irresponsible. Do you see this?"

"Jules, I'm good. It's golf. That's it. I have to go, but I promise we'll talk when I get home."

"Sophie—"

"Muah! Bye, bae, love you." I disconnect the call and toss my phone onto my towel before easing my way into the pool and swimming to the edge, resting my arms on it while soaking up the view. This is heaven.

Since nobody knows if heaven is real, I'm inclined to let this fantasy play out. Golfing, friends only, platonic fantasy of course.

"How do you like your fish?"

I turn toward Shep's voice and his shirtless body

with low-riding swim trunks. He has much better abs than my friend, Jules, but I won't tell her that.

"Cooked. But actually, I'm not a fan of fish." I am. But it's on Chloe's Please Don't Eat List for me—for her baby.

"Steak?"

I nod. "Well done, please. And can I help you with anything?"

"Nope." He starts the grill.

I focus on the new view—him—instead of the one behind me. It's hard to say which is better. One makes me feel at peace. The other makes my head dizzy with inappropriate thoughts.

"No glasses." He gives me a quick glance. "Can you even see me?"

I grin. "Yes. I have okay vision without them. Twenty-fifty."

"So I look a little fuzzy, but still sexy, right?"

"I wouldn't know. We're friends. I don't think about you that way. I suppose some women might find you moderately attractive."

Hot as fuck, if I'm being honest only with myself. Where's my morning sickness? I didn't think horny pregnancy hormones started until the second trimester.

"Well ..." He deposits a filet of fish on the grill and disappears inside the house for a few seconds before returning with a piece of red meat for me. "Moderately is good, right? I mean ... you're a moderately good golfer, and I'm moderately attractive."

I don't take the bait. "Tony and Deb ... they were a chatty couple."

"Midwesterners." Shep closes the lid to the grill and sits on the edge of the pool, submerging his legs. "Illinois or Indiana. I can't remember. I just know that they can talk for days. One random topic bleeds into another with no escape. They think 'nice talking to you' means 'please keep talking.' It's a train wreck."

"You do realize ... I'm from the Midwest." I kick off the side of the pool and swim toward him, giving him a fake scowl.

Amusement twitches his lips. "That's probably why you were good at getting us out of that situation. You knew the only thing that would work was an actual fire in the building or a made-up 9-1-1 emergency."

I swipe my hand along the surface of the water, sending a spray in his direction. He flinches, turning to the side for a few seconds as if he can dodge the inevitable. This friendship thing is interesting. On the inside, I'm dying to find some friendly excuse to be near him again, for him to touch me again. On the outside, I have to play it cool because cool is what's called for when you're in my situation.

"Watch it, Sophie."

"Watch what, Shep?" I swim a little closer until there's maybe three feet between us. "Are you feeling defeated? Are you going to tell your mom that your new friend outplayed you and splashed water in your face? Will she call my mom and ask my mom to tell me to be nice to you?"

"Are you bullying me?" He tilts his head and narrows his eyes. "I didn't take you for a bully, but I'm feeling a little bullied."

I stick out my lower lip. "Sorry. Am I too much for you to handle?"

Something crosses his face, and it's chilling—thrilling. A drug I don't need, but I think I might like it a little too much if I take even the tiniest hit.

"You have no idea how much I can handle." He stands, sauntering to the grill. "The question is ... are you ready to be handled?"

"I'm ready for dinner." I cave because I'm only fifty percent confident that I'm not in over my head with Shep. Those aren't good odds for a woman with my history.

As he flips the meat, I climb out of the pool and wrap up in a towel.

"Dinner's not quite ready." He closes the lid and turns. His gait in my direction turns into a slow prowl, or at least that's how it feels to me. "Can I get you something to drink? Wine? Beer? My parents keep the bar well stocked. I can make you anything you want?"

I take a step back before he steals all the oxygen. "Water is fine."

He eyes me for a few breaths. "Are you okay with me drinking?"

I nod. "I'm not an alcoholic. I'm just taking a break from alcohol for a while."

"A cleanse?"

With a tight smile, I shrug a shoulder. "Sure. A cleanse."

"But you're still eating red meat?" His lips twist as he studies me.

I shiver, even though it's still nearly one hundred degrees. "Baby steps."

Baby, minus the steps.

"Water it is." He heads into the house to get our drinks.

I drape my towel over the back of a chair and pull on a coverup that doesn't cover up all that much.

"Here you go." Shep sets a glass of ice water on the table under the pergola and nods for me to take a seat. Then he disappears inside again, only to return a minute later with that charcuterie tray from earlier and two boxes of crackers pinned between his arm and torso.

"I love that you speak my language." I pluck an olive from the tray.

"Appetizers are your language?" He glances at me with a playful grin claiming those sexy lips.

"Yes. And this ..." I lean back, closing my eyes for a few seconds. "Sunshine. Time away from home. Golf. Dinner poolside with..." I smirk to let him know I'm about to feed his ego and I know it "...with my new friend whom I find to be really good company."

He takes a pull of beer, smiling the whole time. Cersei plops down in the shade under the table, and I rub her belly with my foot.

"I couldn't agree more," he says.

Sometimes you meet someone, and everything just clicks. I clicked with Jules from a very early age. It's as if you're recognizing something from another life—a familiarity you can't see or remember—but you feel it. People say it all the time to make sense of feeling such an instant connection with another human. My problem? The feelings I have for Shep are a little jumbled. I need to sort through them and ditch the highly inappropriate ones.

"When did you start playing golf?" I ask.

"High school. I dated a girl whose dad was a caddy."

"No joke?"

Shep shrugs. "No joke."

"And your love of dogs?"

"Man's best friend. It's in my DNA."

I laugh. "That's fair." This is hard. I want to dive into his past, his marriage, his divorce, but that will open the door for him to quiz me. If Jimmy doesn't exist in Shep World, then maybe Millie doesn't belong here either. "So, did you go to college?"

Shep sips his beer. "Nope. You?" He smirks.

I chuckle. "Nah. I just did the online optometry degree. You know, the one you can get with a weekend course for four hundred and ninety-nine dollars?"

"Is that so?" Shep tries to suppress his grin, playing along with me. "They let anyone be a doctor these days."

"They really do. So ... what did you do right after high school if you didn't go to college?"

He shrugs a shoulder, looking so cool it's having a very heated effect on me. "This and that."

Do I want him to be serious? Do we have to be serious if this isn't our real life?

With feigned deep concentration, I nod. "I've done a lot of that but not much this."

"Finally..." Shep stands and heads to the grill "...a woman who just ... gets me."

I close my eyes and absorb the sun. "This is a good life. Think of all the hours people work for so few moments of true bliss."

"The good life is Dr. Ryan in a swimsuit calling her time with me 'pure bliss.'"

Without opening my eyes, I grin. "I was referring to the pool and the sunshine."

"Were you, though?"

I peek open one eye as he drops the fish and steak onto our plates. "You're awfully confident."

"Hopeful." He smirks, setting the plates on the table.

"Hopeful? What exactly are you hoping for?"

He heads back into the house and returns a minute later with a bowl of mixed greens, a bottle of salad dressing, and a loaf of French bread.

"I'm hoping Sophie Ryan agrees to be my friend again tomorrow."

Twisting my lips, I bob my head side to side. "One day at a time."

We eat in comfortable silence for a few minutes, sharing an occasional flirty grin as if we're acknowledging all the tip-toeing we're doing around conversations that normal friends would have on a weekend trip to Sedona.

"You know ... you're right," I say.

He glances up, squinting.

"Midwesterners. We're an interesting breed."

One corner of his mouth quirks into a half smile. A reluctant smile.

Cutting my steak, I blow out a slow breath. "My dad used to over-greet people all the time. I don't think he does it anymore. I suppose Californians aren't into as much small talk. Every time my dad would pass someone on a walk or even just in a store, he'd greet them. I used to say, 'Who was that?' and he'd shake his head and say, 'I don't know.' But you thought he knew them because it wasn't just a quick, friendly 'hi.' It was more. 'Hello, there. How are you doing today?' As if a complete stranger is going to unload how they're truly doing. They're not. Not even Midwesterners.

"And usually, we'd be walking in opposite directions. Did he really expect people to stop and go into detail? 'Hello. Since you asked, my wife is cheating on me, and I just found out I have prostate cancer. Thanks for asking.' Hi. Just say hi. Right? Hi and a friendly smile is enough. It's actually more genuine than the excess. Don't force people to lie and say they're fine. And don't even get me started on how this sets you up for sounding like a fool when you leave the Midwest and everyone you pass does *not* say more than hi. I can't tell you how many times someone has just said 'hi' to me and I've replied with 'fine, thank you.'"

When I return my gaze to Shep, I realize he's stopped eating. With the biggest smile, he seems to be hanging on my every word, completely enamored with me or my Midwesterner confessions. It's an amazing feeling to have someone look at you like this. We click. That's all there is to it.

"Hi," he says after a long pause.

My grin matches his as I say, "Fine. Thank you."

"It's nice being with a happy person." He rolls the bottom of his beer bottle in a circle on the table.

"What makes you think I'm happy?"

I'm not happy. My ex-boyfriend won't get out of my house.

"It's an aura thing. A definite vibe."

I roll my eyes. "I get mad. Trust me. I get moody and angry."

"Everyone does. But the sun never ceases to exist, not even on cloudy days."

"So Millie was still shining when you divorced her; it was just a cloudy day." It slips.

Dammit!

Why did I say that? We were doing so good.

Shep's smile falters a bit. "Millie wasn't and isn't the sun."

I scoff. "And I am?"

"Unequivocally."

Silence.

More silence.

It takes me several moments to find a breath let alone find actual words.

"You're a nice friend." It's all I can manage, and as the words slide past my lips, they feel cheesy and generic. *Unequivocally* inadequate.

"I really am." That smile ... he's so self-assured, and I'd say arrogant, but it's not really arrogance at all. Shep's playful. I adore that about him. This friendship might ruin me for all other men. Does he know this? Is it secretly his intention?

"Why are you not married?" he asks.

That came out of the blue. He's poking holes into my perfect little bubble.

"Uh ..." I stab my fork into my salad.

"What's wrong with you?"

I snort and wipe my mouth. "Why does something have to be wrong with me?"

I'm a gullible, overly sympathetic, fool for love.

Shep doesn't ever need to know that.

"My expectations are apparently too high."

"Sexual expectations?" He's a relentless tease.

Favoring self-preservation, I ignore his question. "I think I just prefer to be with someone who has a purpose in life. Who has initiative. Who does his part in life."

"Maybe the men you've been with have decided you're their purpose in life. You should feel flattered."

"In that case, I fear there's a fine line between feeling flattered and feeling suffocated."

He hums. "Maybe. Tell me your idea of the perfect guy."

"Perfection doesn't exist."

"Tell my ex-wife that." He frowns.

"I will." I grin. "My idea of a *good* guy. Let me see ..."

"Dark, wavy hair? Mesmerizing eyes? Lover of animals? Tall and moderately sexy?"

I laugh as Shep drones on with his self-description, yet again. We've played this game before. "A guy who makes me laugh."

"Done." He winks.

I shake my head despite my grin. "Someone who has a job he loves but isn't married to it. Someone who feels like I bring out the best in him, but deep down he knows it's not me. It's him. He doesn't need me, but he wants me. Someone who values our time away from each other because it only makes our time together that much better. I don't want to be the air in his lungs. Just ..." I try to find the right word.

"Just his hidden sunshine on a cloudy day. You're good with being felt, but not always seen," Shep says.

I nod.

He closes his eyes. "I feel you."

My heart scrambles to understand this new rhythm it's found in the presence of Shep. When I realize it's struggling too much, I stand, carrying my half-eaten dinner to the kitchen. Cersei follows me, plunking onto the cold tile floor in the hallway.

There's a shift happening. And I'm trying so hard

to stop it, but it's like fighting gravity. His nearness at my back is an invisible touch on my skin.

I place my plate of half-eaten food in the fridge, not wanting to waste it. Maybe later, after he goes to bed, I'll get the munchies. Shep slides the charcuterie tray in the fridge before I can move. His bare chest presses to my back. The sheer material of my coverup does nothing to block the heat from his skin so close to mine.

I slowly turn.

Baby in your womb. Squatter at your house. Focus!

Shep doesn't move. He just ... gives me this look. He's good. Too good. "Do you think friends sometimes kiss?" he whispers as his fingers ghost along my palms.

To save myself, I try to imagine how he might look and smell if he didn't shower for a week. Would his ass be as sexy if it were imprinted in my leather sofa, stenciled in sweat and grime?

I draw in a shaky breath, keeping the rest of my body unmoving. "Uh ... my friend Jules has kissed me on the cheek. But it uh ..." I start to lose my breath under my fading voice. The rapid thumping of my heart tramples my confidence.

Shep ducks his head, bringing his lips unbearably close to my cheek before pausing. "Here?" he whispers.

"Yeah ... that's my ... cheek ..." If I could stop panting, I wouldn't feel so parched.

My eyes close when his warm lips touch my cheek. The kiss is slow and silent. Maybe an illusion. It's okay to indulge in an illusion, right?

"What about here?" he asks, dragging his lips from my cheek to my jaw. Jules doesn't kiss me quite like this. It's the lip dragging that seems a little excessive for friends.

"K ..." I can't even manage the O part of granting him permission to kiss my jaw. Jules has *never* kissed my jaw. I should tell him that. It's not fair ... to Jules, of course.

"Here?" he whispers in my ear as his lips feather along my earlobe. "Sophie?" His mouth slides down my neck.

I swallow hard. "Yeah?"

"Do you want to be *best* friends?" His fingers interlace with mine, and he guides me toward him while he backs us out of the fridge, letting the door close behind me.

He works his mouth back up my neck as I ready myself for the moment I know I won't be able to stop.

Ruff! Ruff!

Cersei not only barks, but she also jumps up on me, forcing me to step back.

Forcing Shep to release my hands.

Damn you, dog!

Cersei's trying to save me from myself. So why am I so pissed off at her right now?

Ruff! Ruff!

"Do you need out, Cersei?" Shep asks because he's nice. A real dog guy.

I want to put her leash on and tie it to a post. She wasn't supposed to be my dog. Car and purse thief bad decision left her with me. Without her and her bad timing, I might be ...

Having sex!

"Let's take her for a walk. The sun's getting ready to set. We'll get some views from the trail just down the way."

I was anticipating naked Shep being the stunning view tonight. "Sure." I scrounge a smile and pin it to my face, even if it is a little crooked and painful.

"Let me grab a shirt and shoes."

I nod several times. "Yeah. I'll get dressed."

By the time I slip on my shorts and midriff tee, Shep and Cersei are already waiting at the door. I feel fifteen, taking tentative steps toward the door while my first date waits for me.

Shep? He's cool. Cool as if he didn't just kiss me intimately.

"Ready?"

I nod.

Cersei will be sleeping on the floor tonight. No way in hell am I letting that little bitch sleep with me after what she just did.

CHAPTER
Fifteen

IT's like it never happened.

We take Cersei for a walk. Shep tells me all about his favorite trails and water holes around Sedona. My hand dangles at my side, begging to be taken by his hand, but he never does.

My house has a Jimmy infestation. I have no business dreaming about Shep holding my hand. Yet ... I wet my lips repeatedly, hoping he'll wet them for me, hoping he'll feel the sudden urge to pick up where we left off before evil Cersei Fucking Lannister decided to be so rude.

He never does.

Evening snacks. Small talk. Fetch and a final pee outing for Cersei.

Then Shep stands from the sofa. "We have an early tee time in the morning. I'll let you get some sleep." Shep locks the doors and shuts off all the lights except for the accent lights under the kitchen cabinets and the one in the hallway leading to the master bedroom.

"Okay." I glance at my watch. It's ten o'clock. What are we? Seventy?

"If you want to watch TV, it won't bother me. I can't hear much downstairs."

"Okay." I press my lips together.

We're going to bed at ten on a Friday night. After he kissed me. What did I do wrong? Why am I being punished? Is this karma for not being kinder to Jimmy?

"Night."

I nod once. "Night."

Shep disappears down the stairs.

"Go to bed. On the floor." I point to the bedroom.

Cersei runs into the bedroom and jumps up on the bed.

"Off." I point to the floor.

She whines before jumping down and settling along the wall by the air vent. I shower and climb into bed, resting my hand on my abdomen. It doesn't feel real. I'm not disappointed that I haven't had morning sickness, but at least it would make this pregnancy feel real.

As I lean over to shut off the light, my phone chimes. I gaze at the screen a few seconds. "Really?" I mumble to myself before answering it.

"What are you doing?" I answer.

"What are you wearing?" Shep says.

"You're *downstairs*."

"I am. That's why I can't see what you're wearing."

I laugh. It seems to be a reoccurring theme with him. "A nightshirt."

"Whatcha up to this weekend?"

Curling onto my side, I play along. "Hanging out with a friend in Sedona."

"Guy friend or girlfriend."

My face aches because I can't seem to wipe this grin from it. "Guy."

"Just friends?"

"Just friends."

"Is golfing your favorite pastime?"

"No. I like to crochet."

"So you're sixty?"

"Says the guy who goes to bed at ten on the weekend."

"Sorry. I was in a hurry to call you."

More giggles, the kind that linger in my belly long after the giggling stops.

"What do you crochet?"

"My grandma taught me to crochet hats and scarves, but they don't come in as handy here in Arizona as they did in Michigan. My current project is a baby blanket for my sister."

"Oh, is she pregnant now?"

"No ... uh ... she's not. But it will take me awhile to finish it, so ..."

"You're a nice aunt. Or future aunt."

"You have no idea. So is golfing *your* favorite pastime?"

"It's up there, but I have to say I enjoy brewing even more than golfing."

"Brewing? As in beer?"

"Anything."

"Anything?" I laugh.

"Beer. Ginger beer. Kombucha. Vinegar. Sake ..."

"That's a little unexpected, Shep. I didn't see that coming."

"So you're surprised?"

"I am."

"Perfect. I like it when I can be a little unpredictable."

"Oh, Shep ... you are anything but predictable."

We converse for the next two hours. It's absurd. We're in the same house. Yet, it's fun in the way that building a fort and sleeping on a pile of blankets and sofa cushions is fun even if there are perfectly good beds available.

Waking at four in the morning, I can't get back to sleep, so I slip out back, open the cover to the pool, and turn on the pool's lights. It glows in the early morning darkness. I shrug off my nightshirt and step into the cool water, wading my way to the infinity edge and resting my arms on it.

"And you led me to believe you weren't an early riser."

"Shit!" I glance over my shoulder. "I'm not wearing anything!"

Shep sits on the edge of the pool in his swim trunks, no shirt, like he did last night. "I see that."

"Yet, you're staring at me." I keep one hand on the edge so I don't sink, and use my other hand to cover my breasts while drawing my knees up to hide my other area.

"I am. How are you this morning?"

"I'm naked."

"How did you sleep? Naked as well?"

"Would you mind turning around so I can get to my towel and shirt?"

"Our tee time is at six. Want me to take Cersei for a walk while you get ready? Then we can grab breakfast. Sorry. Nothing is open this early, so I hope you're good with cereal or toaster waffles." He's enjoying this too much.

Shep can't beat me at golf, so he's trying to clench a poolside victory.

I will not shrivel into a ball of embarrassment, pleading for him to be a gentleman and turn away. I am done. Done. DONE letting men take advantage of me.

"Who doesn't love toaster waffles?" I don my most confident smile as I swim toward him.

His grin incrementally swells until I start up the corner stairs and he realizes I'm getting out of the pool. Naked. Giving no fucks that he's watching me. That grin of his falters a bit like it did yesterday when I handed him his ass on the golf course.

I towel off, shaking a bit from the chilly air, but more than that, I'm way out of my element here—a first-time stripper on the stage. Only I'm not trying to look sexy. I'm shooting for unaffected. Indifferent, yet confident.

Tossing my towel aside, I slip on my nightshirt and then step into my panties. Shep doesn't blink. Not once.

"Hope it's real maple syrup. And I'll walk Cersei.

She's my dog." I saunter into the house, resisting every urge to run and scream, *"Oh my god! I just let him see me naked!"*

By the time I emerge from the room, Cersei is ready for her walk. Shep's waiting by the door, looking his usual hot self—wavy, wet hair, a fitted tee, jogging shorts, and a lidded cup of coffee in each hand.

"Hi." He grins.

I return the sentiment. "Fine. Thank you."

He breaks into a spontaneous laugh—one that makes my tummy do those weird flips again.

"I added soy milk and sugar to yours." He bends down, causing me to freeze in place and have a mini heart attack. The second his lips press to my cheek, I feel it like a zing of electricity all the way to my toes. I need an "anti" pill.

Antibiotics to combat bacteria.

Antihistamines for pesky allergies.

Antidepressants for dealing with the Jimmies of the world.

Anti-shepherds to prevent my legs from spreading because the pet store guy has a great smile and knows how I like my coffee.

"Wh..." my voice trembles "...what makes you think I'm a soy milk and sugar girl?" I take the coffee with a shaky hand, and he opens the door.

"It's what you ordered yesterday when we stopped for coffee on our way out of Scottsdale. I'm observant."

We step outside.

"Like I observed that birthmark on your inner thigh." He adds this unnecessary detail.

Don't react ...

I have a birthmark on my inner right thigh. It's really high up my leg. Shep didn't miss anything last night while I was in my bikini or this morning when I was in ... nothing.

After taking a sip of coffee, I clear my throat. "Today, you need to focus on not letting your wrists break too soon on your swing."

He laughs. "We're talking golf now, huh? I like talking about all the things I've observed about you more than I like talking golf."

"I'm just sharing what I observed about *you*."

We cut through a rocky area that leads to the trail.

"Are you hurt?" I interrupt the crunch of our footsteps over the terrain with my question. I'm feeling brave again. I want to figure out this man, but not cross a line. Maybe just nudge it.

"Hurt?" He gives me a sidelong glance after sipping his coffee as Cersei treks ahead of us.

"Did Millie hurt you? Did losing her leave a scar?"

What am I doing? I'm breaking my own unspoken rules. I'm digging on land that's not mine. Am I hoping to discover something about Shep that makes it easy to walk away unscathed? I continue, "I can't imagine loving someone then losing them and it not leaving a mark. Even if losing them also leaves a bad taste in your mouth or resentment. I've thought that about every man I've loved or thought I loved. I couldn't stop

161

thinking about the things that made me love them in the first place. And I grieved those. And I think that grief leaves a mark."

"Is this your idea of happy talk?" He shoots me a quick glance, eyes squinted.

Busted. My nose crinkles as I adjust my glasses. "Forget I asked. I'm still learning how to navigate this new kind of friendship."

After a minute or so, he exhales a long breath. "I'm not hurt. Maybe men don't experience relationships the same as women do. I think we treat it like a snake shedding its skin. I don't think it has to hurt unless you don't want to let go. Unless you feel like something is being ripped away from you. Maybe men don't give anything away. Maybe we loan a piece of ourselves, but when it's over, we take it back."

"Well ..." I don't know how to respond to him. "Yay for you." It's impossible to keep all the sarcasm out of my voice.

"Maybe I just haven't met anyone worthy of truly owning a piece of me."

"Your heart is a rental?"

Shep chuckles. "Perhaps."

We make our way up a hill, and he grabs my hand. I glance down at his hand around mine.

"Look." He guides me to the right just as the sun slides up the horizon and outlines the red rocks. "The sun ... she's amazing. Don't you think?"

She ...

✳✳✳✳✳

SHEP toasts waffles and drizzles them with real maple syrup while I change into my golf attire.

"Anything else, my queen?" he asks in a dramatic tone while setting my plate on the table next to a fresh cup of coffee and a red juice.

"What's in the juice glass?"

"Beet juice. It helps your golf game. I figure you need all the help you can get." He sits next to me instead of across from me so our knees touch.

I could move mine, but I don't.

"Is that so?" I sip the juice. It's quite tasty.

"I was courteous yesterday. You're my guest, so I let you win. Today, all bets are off."

"Bets?" While cutting my waffle, my gaze narrows at him. "When did we make a bet?"

"Now. Right now. Let's make this interesting."

"I'm listening. Don't bet so much that you have to get a loan from your parents to pay me. Be smart."

He blinks several times, a neutral expression, before clearing his throat. "No money. Something else."

"Such as?"

"Sex."

I choke on my waffle and reach for the beet juice. "W-what?"

"If I win, we have sex tonight. Friend sex, of course."

I don't ask what "friend sex" means. It doesn't matter. He's not winning.

"And *when* I win?"

He shrugs. "Name it."

"What if I want to reserve it? Reveal it after I win."

"God. You're full of yourself, Dr. Ryan."

"Just being factual instead of delusional. And you didn't let me win. I'm not stupid. I heard you cussing under your breath yesterday every time you shanked your ball and I hit the hole."

"Deal. You can reserve your demand for tomorrow morning ... when you're naked in bed with me, telling me what you would have requested from me had you won."

"Friends don't have sex. This much I know."

He brushes me off with a headshake as he focuses on cutting his waffle. "You know nothing. Sex can be sex. Like wine can be a buzz without getting drunk."

"I'm not drinking wine."

"All the more reason to have sex. Good god, Woman, what do you do for enjoyment? Friends don't let friends go dry in *every* way."

I stop feeding him any more information about me. Instead, I finish breakfast with a knowing grin on my face. I *know* I'm going to be victorious today.

✳✳✳✳✳

THIRTY MINUTES LATER ... we're on the first tee.

"Remind me to stop and get condoms on the way back to the house," Shep says behind me.

I swing and it's *perfect.*

For the first nine holes, I keep a steady lead, but not an unreachable one. The last nine holes get more interesting. I intentionally give him the lead for a few holes because I enjoy seeing the extra bounce in his step. I enjoy watching him twirl his putter like a majorette. By the fifteenth hole, I stop making intentional errors, slowly creeping up on him. By the eighteenth hole, we are tied.

Shep plays it cool, but that's all it is. An act. He's sweating.

"This one's for all the chips. You feeling lucky, Sophie?"

I've noticed Shep gets extra chatty—dare I say like a Midwesterner—when he's feigning confidence.

"I'm feeling what I'm feeling, Shep." I drive one straight down the fairway.

Shep's ball lands in a sand trap, which means I'm going to have to make a shitty shot just to keep him close.

We make it on the green, tied again.

"Do you like to be on top or bottom?" he asks, again revealing his nerves.

"I think you know the answer to that."

Shep putts and misses it by a fraction of an inch, taking three steps to tap it in and out of my way. He's good. His only tell he's giving is the slight muscle twitch in his jaw.

My shot is a lot farther back and downhill. It's easily two if not three shots for a good golfer. Just to keep him sweating, I mosey to the cart and grab my towel to polish my putter, sip my water, and remove my glove. Eventually, I line up with my ball, and without much thought, much planning, or even that much focus on the hill in its path, I tap it.

It rolls.

A little left.

A little right.

Gaining speed.

Maybe too much speed.

But ... probably not.

Clink.

In the hole.

"I like being on top, Shep. Get used to it, *friend*."

SHEP DOESN'T SAY much on the way back to the house, and by much, I mean anything. I don't either. I take my victory lap in silence. It's much better this way. I'm silently gloating that I'm not gloating.

After feeding Cersei, I change into my swimsuit and head to the pool. Perched on an inflatable chair with a drink in the drink holder, sunglasses on, I smile at Shep when he emerges from the house with his bruised ego. I'd say it's not an attractive sight, but I'd be lying. Shirtless Shep is always an attractive sight.

"I think we should finish off that charcuterie board for lunch. Shower. Go shopping. And grab dinner at a nice restaurant. My treat." I flash him a huge grin.

"Is that your prize? Making the plans for the rest of the day?" He dives into the pool.

I flinch as water showers on me.

He breaks through the surface just inches from me, shaking his head like a dog.

I turn away even though my glasses are already a mess. "No." I take a sip of my drink. "It's not my prize. It's a suggestion. You can make a counteroffer."

"No. I accept your offer. Minus the shopping. I'm not much of a shopper."

"My *friends* shop with me."

He frowns. "What are you looking for?"

I shrug. "Nothing. Just browsing."

His face sours. "Gah ... you were the perfect friend. You have a dog with a cool name. You're sexy as fuck. You wear the most stylish clothes and always wear a different pair of glasses. You golf. And you swim naked in my pool early in the morning. You were perfection, Sophie. Until ... you suggested a shopping trip and used the word *browse*." He rests his arms on the side of my floating chair, head bowed on them in defeat. "Why'd you have to ruin it?"

I lift a hand to his head and thread my fingers through his hair, something I've been dying to do since the day we met. "Fine. Shopping will be my prize for winning today."

He grumbles and lifts his head. "*Fine.*"

※ ※ ※ ※ ※

Following lunch and showers, we go shopping. Shep drags his ass behind me like a dog learning to walk nicely on a leash. After an hour of *browsing* without making a single purchase (which drives him insane), we find a nice restaurant. We're seated at a table outside with string lights above us and the perfect view of the sunset.

"Thank you for going shopping with me today," I say, resting the cloth napkin on my lap.

He glances up from his menu, unable to fully conceal his scowl. "You earned it."

"I did. Didn't I?" I let my grin outshine the shadow of his scowl.

It only takes a few seconds for his lips to fight their own smile.

We order appetizers, drinks, and main dishes to share. Shep continues to wordlessly grapple with his loss today—forced smiles, limited eye contact. A bruised male ego might be more incurable than cancer. I won't apologize for being the better golfer. Nor will I apologize for the hour I dragged him in and out of stores.

Friends know that being together is all that matters. Sometimes I go to my least favorite Italian restaurant with Jules because it happens to be her favorite. Sometimes she goes to foreign films with me even though she hates subtitles. That's what friends do.

"Do you have a hard time drinking beer at restaurants since you brew your own?"

He shrugs, chewing his food for a few moments. "Not really. I said I brew things. I didn't say I was good at it."

I giggle. I'm not good at crocheting either. "It's been a good weekend. Thank you for inviting me. Even if you never invite me again."

"You're welcome." Shep pauses his fork at his lips and smiles.

"And?"

He swallows. "And what?"

"You're supposed to say how much you've enjoyed our weekend together. And then you're supposed to say you'll definitely invite me again."

"You want me to tell you how much I've enjoyed getting my ass handed to me on the golf course? You want me to tell you how much fun I've had shopping? Then you want me to tell you that I want to do it again?"

"Well, when you put it that way ..."

The waiter leaves the check. I reach for it, but Shep beats me to it.

"I said my treat."

"I know what you said." He retrieves cash, a lot of cash, from his pocket.

It's probably an entire week's pay.

"Shep, I wouldn't have picked this restaurant if I had known you were going to insist on paying. Now I feel bad."

"You should. I've been taken to the cleaners by you today. You should definitely feel bad."

I recoil as he hands the waiter the cash and tells him to keep the change. Shep grabs the bag with our leftovers in it, and we make our way through the restaurant to the car.

He opens my door, but I don't know why at this point. After I fasten my seat belt, he hands me the bag to set on my lap.

"Any other stops before we head back to the house?" he asks when he gets in the car.

I shake my head, keeping my gaze out my window.

"Good. I'm sure Cersei is ready for her dinner," he mumbles.

When we return to the house, I don't wait for Mr. Chivalrous to open my door. I head straight toward the house to feed my dog.

"Are you mad?" Shep calls.

"No." I take three more steps to the door and stop. "Yes." I whip around. "I'm so fucking sorry you feel *taken to the cleaners*." I reach into my purse and pull at least two hundred dollars from my wallet. It should cover dinner and his time wasted shopping with me. Then I throw it at him, but it scatters all around us instead. "You're a shitty friend, Shep. And a sore loser."

His lips part, eyes wide and unblinking like the rest of his body remains unmoving. "Sophie ... I ... it ... it was a joke. I was joking. I didn't mean it. I didn't mean to make you feel bad." He bends down and picks up the money.

Well, shit.

Now I feel stupid. And hurt. And ... I don't know. Just really frustrated because I like this imaginary world, but it's starting to feel real. And it's not real. Real is the baby inside me. Real is Jimmy. Real is having to face Jules when I get home.

After he gathers all the money, he steps closer and shoves it into my purse. I keep my jaw set, eyes on his chest, refusing to look up at him.

"I'm a terrible loser. The worst. Yet..." He takes my chin and tips my head up, forcing me to look at him "...

if someone's going to hand it to me in golf, I want it to be you. If someone's going to drag my ass in and out of stores, I want it to be you. I said it before and I'll say it again ... *anything* to be with you." His fingers drift from my chin to my jaw, gently cupping it.

I reach for his hand, covering it with mine because I don't want him to stop touching me. If it isn't real, then I don't have to say no. "Shep?" I whisper.

His gaze affixes to mine. "Yes?"

I take one step closer until there are no more steps to take. "Want to be *best* friends?"

He grins and I feel it like it's a physical touch. "Yeah, Sophie," he whispers, lifting his other hand to my face too. "I really do."

We kiss.

I drop the sack of leftovers to the ground.

Shep holds my face, angling me where he wants me so his tongue can reach deep into my mouth, mingling with mine, overwhelming me with a friendship like no other. He backs me into the house, never letting his lips leave mine.

Cersei jumps on him.

He keeps guiding me backward toward the bedroom, shaking off my spastic dog before closing the door and leaving her on the other side. I unbutton his jeans. He pushes the straps of my dress down my shoulders. "Fuck ... Sophie." He rests his forehead on mine and stops my hands from breaching the waistband of his underwear. "We didn't stop for condoms."

"I'm ..." I'm out of breath at just the thought of

what we're going to do, feeling like my whole chest might explode if we don't keep going. He didn't bring them. Does that mean he's stupid for not planning ahead? Or does it mean he's truly my friend? "I'm ... well ... it's fine. You can't get me pregnant. I promise."

He sucks in a harsh breath when I tug down the front of his underwear. His hands go straight to my face again, our kiss growing eager and impatient like the rest of our bodies. It's been so long since I've felt this out of control.

We're just friends. Temporary friends.

Friends without boundaries. His hands leave my face, limitless without those boundaries as he fights with my dress, eagerly dragging it up my legs in one direction while shoving it down past my breasts in the other direction. We manage to back up enough for the bed to catch us when we fall. I search for anything to grab, finding real estate with his shirt, tugging it up his body and over his head while he inches down my body.

Every move we make is a little frantic and clumsy, our clothes half on, half off. He tugs on my panties, getting them only to my knees before he plants his mouth between my legs. I claw at the mattress with one hand, and my other hand clutches his hair while my back arches off the bed.

"Sh-shep ... god ..." My body twists. "Just ... yes ... god ... yes ..." I tighten my grip on his hair, pleasure unfurling in every direction.

He hums in response to the fractured, barely

coherent words falling from my lips. Crawling back up my body, he laps his tongue over my nipples then up my neck to my mouth. The room fills with the sound of our moans and a slight creak of the bed as his hips rock, rubbing against my leg and the bed. He's having sex with me ten different ways without *actually* having sex with me yet.

His tongue in my mouth.

One hand in my hair.

His other on my breast.

My belly.

Finally sliding between my spread legs, filling me with his fingers. This is the most magical friendship in the history of friendships.

For as impatient as this started, he's found his rhythm, and it's so fucking slow I'm ready to scream. I turn my head to the side to catch a breath and make a plea. "Shep ..."

He captures my mouth again, showing no mercy. He heard me say I can't get pregnant, right? What's he waiting for?

Flipping me onto my stomach, he kisses my back, the curve of my butt, and down the back of my legs before he nudges my knees apart and grips my hips.

The pillow muffles my drawn-out groan as he plunges into me. My fingers curl into it, gripping it tighter and tighter each time he rocks his hips, his teeth claiming the skin on my shoulder, one hand next to mine and his other hand sliding beneath my pelvis, the pads of his fingers stroking me.

"I need you to *not* be good at this," he whispers in my ear.

"W-what?" I ask, a little distracted by our current activity, straining my neck to look back at him.

He kisses me before biting my lip as an evil grin bends his mouth for a split second before releasing it and flicking it with his tongue. "This. Sex. I need you to be a little bad at it." He slows his pace. My orgasm is happening in under ten seconds regardless of his pace. "I can be a proud man, Sophie." His hand next to mine slides along the mattress to my breast, squeezing it hard. "But I'm not too proud to admit I need a win today."

I close my eyes, jaw slack, as I tear through the tape at the finish line.

The creaking bed gets louder, the headboard tapping the wall a few times while Shep gets his well-deserved win. He is the master, of that there is no denial. He rolls over, taking me with him so my face hovers over his and our shallow breaths mingle.

I grin. "I did my worst."

I haven't seen Shep this tired. His heavy eyelids blink once as a tiny smile twitches his lips. "*Best* friends."

As much as I love Jules, she will never live up to this, no matter how many times she agrees to go to the movies with me.

"Well, you look pretty tired." I run my hand through his hair, letting the damp strands by his ears curl around my fingers.

His brow furrows. "Oh, little girl..." he kisses my neck down to my breast "...you are so very wrong."

What talent or stamina he lacked to get the job done on the golf course, he more than makes up for in the bedroom. After he proves he has what it takes to finish the back nine, I sit up and swing my legs over the side of the bed. "Friends," I say. "Only friends. You will never live with me. Understood?"

Shep chuckles. "Wow ... okay. What about that made you think I was that fucking needy?"

I peer at him over my shoulder, at every inch of his gloriously naked body. Cersei whines behind the door.

"Do your thing. I'll feed your pooch. And I'll do it without feeling like we should shack up together. Does that work for you?"

I roll my eyes before grabbing my dress and scurrying off to the bathroom to "do my thing." After my second shower of the day, I make my way to the pool where Shep's reclined in a lounge chair, staring at the stars, jeans back on but no shirt. He tucks his hand behind his head and glances over at me while I recline in the chair next to him.

"To reiterate ..." he says, "there won't be news of a baby in the coming months. Correct?"

With a nervous laugh, I shake my head. "Sorry. No babies for you, Shep."

"The pill isn't one hundred percent, even if you're taking it without fail."

"Thanks, Dr. Shep. I'm not ... well ..." I rub my lips together. *Where am I going with this?*

"You're not what?"

"You can't get me pregnant because I've sorta ... had a procedure." There. I'm not lying. I'm not sharing the secret I'm not supposed to share yet. That makes me feel better. A little. Rolling my head toward Shep, I give him a tight smile.

Worry lines his face, but he manages the hint of a smile. "I have a tee time for us again in the morning."

"Great. Then, I think I need to go to bed. And you need to sleep downstairs. Tomorrow morning we repeat the events of this morning, except I'll need a smidge more syrup on my waffles if you're going to over toast them."

He waits and waits, allowing my mind to go crazy wondering what's in that head of his. "This morning I watched you take off your clothes and swim in the pool."

I grin. "True."

"So ... if tomorrow morning will be a repeat of this morning, then ..."

I stand and smirk. "Night, Shep."

He says nothing for a beat, but as soon as I reach the door, he murmurs, "Night, Sophie."

I don't look back at him. He doesn't need to see the monstrosity that is my grin.

CHAPTER
Seventeen

SUNDAY MORNING, we do a repeat, minus the naked pool time. I sense his disappointment the rest of the morning. I'm certain he's going to use it as his excuse for losing a third time to me. Shockingly, he doesn't. Not aloud, anyway.

"Tell your parents 'thank you' for their generosity. The home. The pool. The food. I had a good time. Or don't tell them." I wink and open my door as he stops the Mustang in the parking lot of my office. "Since ... it didn't happen."

"Really? I have to give them all the credit for the weekend?"

I laugh. "You can take a little credit."

"Gee ... thanks." He climbs out to retrieve my golf clubs from the trunk while I grab my bags and let Cersei out of the backseat.

We load everything into my car and stop at the driver's door. Shep's hands find mine, our fingers lacing as he pulls me into his chest. I don't do this with Jules.

"So much for our conversing ... our exclusive tele-dating, although, it wouldn't be a bad idea to return to it," I say.

"Pfft. We can't tele-date now. We're friends. *Best* friends." He wears that mischievous expression like it was custom made for him.

"You should date," I blurt. It takes me a second to realize what I just said. I'm scared to death of this friendship. It would make things a lot easier if I knew Shep were actively dating. Not imagining anything more. Accepting what happened this weekend won't happen again. It was my pre-baby-belly last hurrah.

He narrows his eyes.

"As your friend, I'm telling you that you should date. I can give you dating advice as any good friend would do."

I can't. My dating life has been nothing short of a catastrophe. But saying it to Shep feels like the right thing to do. And for a second, it makes me feel normal. Just a woman—a friend—helping another friend. A woman with a good job. A woman living with her dog. A woman *not* housing a squatter.

Informal settler.

Shep kisses my cheek, pausing for a long moment before sliding his lips to mine and giving me a soft peck. "Don't worry, Sophie. I'm not going to sit around home drawing your name on notebooks and stalking you on social media. No trees will be defaced because I carved our names into them. I'm a grown-ass man capable of having sex without postcoital heavy spooning."

"Good. That would be pathetic." I release his hands and open my door.

"I have Julia and George this week. Let's meet at the park."

I smile, dropping into the driver's seat. "Sounds perfect."

And just like that ... we've figured it out.

No room for neediness or falling in love. Shep World can continue a little longer. It's innocent. And nobody has to know.

Just two grown adults exploring all the ways we can be friends. What could go wrong?

※※※※※

JIMMY.

That's what or *who* could go wrong. He manages to stay out of my sight for the remainder of Sunday, and I don't see him Monday until I arrive home from work.

"What the hell ..." I park on the street because my driveway is in the process of being torn up. Grabbing my bags and letting Cersei out of the car, I march through my yard, scowling at the men destroying my property and fueled by a special kind of rabid anger funneling into my veins.

"What the—" I start to unleash on Jimmy, but he holds up his hand, perched at his new desk, new computer in front of him, headset with a mic attached to his stubborn, dumb head.

I'm so angry I can't relax my hands to drop my bags. My legs root into the floor, and everything inside of me shakes as I wait for him to finish his sales call.

In *my* house.

With a desk he purchased with *my* money.

And *my* computer.

Fucker!

"Hey, babe. Missed you. Do you want the good news or the bad news first?" Jimmy slips off his headset and stands.

"I want you out of my house! What the hell is happening to my driveway?"

"Okay. Looks like we'll start with the bad news." He saunters toward me, slipping his hands into the pockets of his shorts. "Grammy died Friday. I was going to call you, but I didn't want to ruin your weekend. That's the bad news. The good news is that I will be getting some inheritance money. Mom floated me a loan so we could put in a new driveway like we've talked about for months. No more huge cracks and uneven parts. I think we'll have enough for a basketball hoop too."

Blink.

Blink.

Blink.

"Jimmy ..." I ease my head side to side. "You ... you need help. Serious help. You are delusional. Something is truly wrong with you. I gave you a five-day notice to vacate. You have one day left. Then I'm filing eviction papers. This ends with you being escorted from the premises by a sheriff. Is that what you want?"

"I'm paying for the driveway, Sophie. That's a big investment. It's equity in this house."

Oh my god. Oh my god. Oh. My. God!

He's digging his heels in. He's doubling down. He's going to drag this out. Court. Attorneys. I don't have time for this. I'm pregnant!

"I'm ..." I open my mouth to say just that but clamp it shut just as quickly. No. Jimmy Fucking Pain In My Ass doesn't get to hear about this baby before my parents. Before Mason's parents.

"Hey, Cersei." Jimmy bends down and rubs Cersei's chest. She likes him. I hate that. But he feeds her junk food and rubs her belly all damn day because he has no life. He's a parasite in my life. Is he going to attempt to take her too? Will we be like Shep and Millie? Sharing custody of a dog?

How can that happen if he NEVER MOVES OUT?

I'm fuming to the point I can't even speak. I need to go to my room and calm down for the baby.

Jimmy: One.

Sophie: Zero.

CHAPTER
Eighteen

"How was your weekend?" Nora asks, stopping at the door to my office. She was out on Monday.

"Good. Yours?" I scroll through today's schedule on my computer.

"Fine. Did you uh … hear back from your doctor? Is everything okay?"

I glance up, eyes narrowed.

"The bleeding," she says in a hushed voice.

"Oh. That. Yeah. Fibroid. No big deal. Thanks for your concern, though."

"That's good. Your first patient is here."

"Thanks." I close my eyes and exhale when she leaves my office. My life is an epic disaster at the moment. Ten balls in the air and I don't know how to juggle.

Midmorning, Nora catches me just before I go into the exam room. "Flowers at the front desk for you. They're stunning." She waggles her eyebrows.

I frown. Fucking Jimmy. I'm sure I paid for them. I didn't check my purse before leaving for work. Ten bucks says I'm missing a credit card. After the exam, I return to my office where Nora has set the bouquet on my desk. Snatching the card, I pull it from the envelope. What could he possibly say to justify this?

Hey, Sophie!

Hope you're having a great start to your week. So glad we're friends.

Jules xo

For some irrational reason, I get tears in my eyes. Jules has sent me flowers before, but only for special occasions like a birthday. Now I feel extra guilty for thinking that Shep could ever be my best friend no matter how well-honed his orgasm-giving skills happen to be. Maybe she feels bad about what happened on the phone. Maybe she feels that she did unfairly judge me and not trust me when I said that Shep is just a friend. And the fact that I had sex with him is making me feel a billion times more guilty in the presence of the wildflower bouquet dotted with the purple-pinkish echinacea. It's symbolic of strength and healing. It's definitely an apology.

Grinning, I call Jules and bend over to smell the flowers.

"Hey. Calling to spill all the details from your 'friendly' golf weekend?" she asks as soon as she answers my call.

"Funny. No. Wait ... is that what this is? Is this a bribe? Here I thought you were being crazy generous. *Overly* generous. Apologetic. A truce of sorts after our short conversation on the phone. But now I'm a little suspicious of your motive."

"What are you talking about? Bribe? My motive?"

"The flowers. I got them. They're beautiful. And way too much. Now I feel like a terrible friend. I should have been the one sending you flowers for lying to you or … misleading you."

"Is this pregnancy brain already? It's a little early for pregnancy brain."

"What do you mean?" I chuckle.

"Sophie, I didn't send you flowers."

"Um … yeah you did. Your name is on the card."

"Maybe Jimmy sent them."

"No. It says *Hope you're having a great start to your week. So glad we're fri—*"

Friends.

"Gotta go. I'll call you later."

"Okay. Let me know when you figure out who sent you flowers and gave me credit for them. Tell them thank you. And we need to talk—"

"Sure." I press *End*. I won't be thanking anyone. I call Shep, feeling all sorts of anger.

"Miss me already?"

"You cannot send me flowers."

"Flowers?"

"Don't. I know it was you. And they are too much. Friends don't send each other flowers for no reason. It's not my birthday. I didn't receive a job promotion. And nobody in my family died. *And* we don't exist."

"Your mom's cat died."

I scoff. "You sent me flowers because my mom's cat died?"

"No. I sent you flowers because I wanted you to feel as good as I do today."

"Shep, we are friends. You have no idea what it means to be friends. You cross all the lines and—"

"Were you pissed off at Jules? When you thought they were from her ... because I assume you called her first. Were you mad?"

"I ..." I clench my teeth and roll my eyes. "That's not the point."

"That's the only point. It can't be okay for Jules to send you flowers, but not okay for me to send you flowers."

I close the door to my office. "I'm not having sex with Jules. So don't lecture me on friendship etiquette."

"Well, Jules should address that if she feels it's unfair that I get to have sex with you and she doesn't."

Pinching the bridge of my nose, I bite my lips to keep from grinning. Not that he can see me. Still, I swear he'd detect the grin on my face from the sound of my voice. "Got. You *got* to have sex with me. Once. It was a one and done. And for the record, I wasn't thrilled about the idea of Jules sending me flowers for no particular reason. When I thought it was her, I called to tell her it was too much."

"And thanked her," he says.

"No."

"Yes. I'm not stupid, Sophie. Even if you thought it was too much, which I'm sure you would or did say to her, there's no way you would have been mad. There's no way you wouldn't have said *thank you*. So just tell me they're too much, then insert the big 'but' and finish your long speech with a 'Thank you, Shep. It's too much, but so sweet, and you've brightened my Tuesday.'"

I have this clawing urge to argue with him, to make some grand point about the level of inappropriateness. It's unsettling. *He's* unsettling.

He's also fun and spontaneous. Irresistibly sexy, yet effortlessly charming. I like the version of me with him. *That's* why the flowers are not okay. He can't be perfect. Perfect doesn't exist. And even if it did, I'm at the worst possible place in my life to receive it.

He wins. This time.

"Thank you, Shep. It's too much, but so sweet, and you've brightened my Tuesday."

"You're welcome. Millie is meeting me at the park with the dogs tomorrow at five. How does a five-thirty doggy playdate sound?"

"It sounds like you don't want me to meet Millie."

He chuckles. "You're not wrong. And uh … what did you mean when you said 'we don't exist?' Are we dead? Ghosts? What did I miss?"

Biting the inside of my cheek for a second, I lean my backside against the edge of the desk. "I've told you my real life is complicated now. You came into it at the worst possible time, in some ways. In other ways, you're a much needed distraction. An escape from reality. So when we're together, I pretend it's not real life. I wouldn't have had sex with you in real life."

"I see ... I uh ... is that a compliment? Or should I feel like you're embarrassed of me? And did we not use a condom because you had *a procedure* or because you didn't think you could get pregnant if you just pretended it wasn't real?"

I snort. "No. I'm not that stupid. Definitely the former. And yes, it's a compliment."

"So sending flowers to your work was breaking the barrier?"

"Exactly."

There's a pause. A long pause.

Is he questioning my mental state? I can't blame him if he is. On a scale of one to ten, my sanity, as of late, has teetered around the three to four mark.

"Okay," he says.

Again. I wait for him to elaborate, but he doesn't.

"Okay, we're good ... or okay you think I'm out of my mind?"

"A bit of both."

Biting back my grin, I nod several times. "So I'll meet you at the park?"

"Hypothetically, yes."

I laugh.

"See you at five-thirty. Gotta go, Sophie. Some of us have real work to do."

"I have real—"

He ends the call before I finish my protest.

I stare at the flowers. They're beautiful. For a few seconds, I allow myself to smile and feel good about his gesture.

CHAPTER
Nineteen

By the time I drive home the next day, I have a new driveway. Biting my tongue, I speed-walk past Jimmy to change my clothes, get Cersei and her gear, and practically run to the park.

It's five-forty.

"Hey ..." I say out of breath.

Shep's in shorts and a red tee with blue sneakers, one of them propped up against the tree at his back. His arms are crossed in a standoffish pose.

"Where's Julia and George?"

He frowns. "Millie is running late. We should just reschedule our playdate."

"Because now I'm going to meet her? Or because you're in a bad mood and won't be any fun?"

"Yes." He attempts a half smile. "All of the above."

I let Cersei off her leash to roam the park.

Shep's gaze roves over me in my pink jogging shorts, white midriff tee, and white sneakers. Pink-framed glasses, of course. "You look edible," he says with an odd blend of sex appeal and anger. It almost sounds like he's angry that I look edible, but I doubt that's the case.

"I do, don't I?" I give him the confident grin with

the matching response that he would give me if I complimented him.

This frees a bit more of his smile. I'm making it hard for him to stay grumpy. That's what friends are for.

"Come here." He doesn't move, a statue that's frozen in place, one that can only be admired.

I don't know why, because I know better, but I find myself taking those four steps to get to him.

Because he asked.

Because I want to.

Because I think a part of me needs this.

He drops his propped foot to the ground. Taking my hands, he pulls me into him until my cheek rests on his chest and his rests on the top of my head. Slowly ... so very slowly ... he exhales. It's food to my soul, feeling so needed, so appreciated.

"Hi," he whispers.

"Fine. Thank you." I grin.

In the next breath, he stiffens then releases me. "She's here."

I step back and turn.

Shep's feet pound the ground as he takes long strides toward the skinny blonde with fire engine red lips, tight denim capris, and really cute heels. I stay back, way back, just a stranger at the same park. No big deal.

"Sorry I'm so late." She hands the leashes to him. "I had to drop off some products and the lady was really chatty."

"Okay." Shep takes the leashes and greets Julia and George with kisses and pats their bellies before unleashing them to play with Cersei by the tiny pond.

Millie slides her sunglasses onto her head, craning her neck past Shep to me.

"Shit," I whisper, turning my back to them and calmly walking toward the pond.

"Hi. I'm Millie."

"Double shit." I cringe, slowly turning around and pinning a fake smile to my face. "Hi. Sophie."

She makes quick, confident strides toward me with Shep right behind her, a huge frown on his face. "Fun glasses."

I smile, stiff and awkward. "Thanks."

"How do you know Shep?" She slants her head to the side.

She saw me in his arms.

Shep sighs. "Sophie shops at Wash Your Tail. Her dog, Cersei, likes to run around with Julia and George."

Millie nods slowly. "So you're ... friends?"

"Yes," Shep and I say at the exact same time. It's too timed. Too obvious.

Friends who hold long embraces in the park.

Another slow nod from Millie. "Oh!" Her eyebrows jump up her forehead. "Are you the one?" She shifts her gaze to Shep. "Caroline said you were dating someone you met at the shop. You told Howie."

"We're not dating." I feel the urgent need to make that clear. "Just friends."

Shep eyes me while smirking. It's the I've-seen-you-naked smirk.

I return the you're-not-real-in-my-world scowl.

"Well..." Millie shrugs "...that's probably for the best. Shep's ... *a lot.*"

"I'm a lot?" Shep scratches his chin, jaw clenched.

Millie crinkles her nose into something akin to a half apology, more like a "sorry to be so brutally honest" smile.

"I'll drop them off at your place next Monday morning." Shep does a great job of dismissing her.

Millie lowers her sunglasses to her nose again. "It was nice meeting you, Sophie. Say ..." She digs into her purse and pulls out a business card, handing it to me.

"Jesus Christ ..." Shep mumbles.

She ignores him. "You have beautiful skin. I think you could keep it looking that way for many years. If you're interested in some skincare designed by some of the world's leading scientists, I'd love to give you some samples to try. I can also let you try some amazing products that are incredibly nutritious and so good for your body. I can speak from experience, they are life changing."

I stare at her card in my hand because I can't look at Shep. If I do, I won't be able to stop myself from giggling. He's fuming and it's hilarious.

"How generous of you. If I'm interested, I'll definitely contact you."

"Do. Really. I'd love for you to see what I've seen. I

can be reached anytime. Have a great rest of your week, Sophie."

"You're incorrigible," Shep mutters as she breezes past him to her car.

There's no way she doesn't hear him; he's not that discreet. Yet, she's clearly mastered the art of ignoring him.

After she gets into her car, I shift my gaze to him. I'm not sure why he looks embarrassed, but he does. Embarrassed and livid.

"It's funny, there have been several times that I've wanted to ask about Millie's profession, but I didn't because it didn't matter for our *friendship*." I hold up her business card. "Multi-level marketing. Interesting."

He shakes his head. "You have no fucking idea. Millie single-handedly ruined countless relationships with friends of ours and alienated so many family members because she is a walking sales machine."

"Some people do quite well. She's a natural."

"She's a disaster. And stupid. God, so incredibly stupid. She had a car, a perfectly good car, a nice car, an expensive car that was paid off. But her big corporate employer convinced her to take a new car. A bonus with all the strings attached. As long as she met her sales quota each month, she didn't have to pay anything for the car. But ... the months she didn't meet it, she had to pay over eight hundred dollars for that month's car payment. Which ... fine. I get it. For someone who doesn't have a car and who's really good at their job, then it appears to be a good deal. Sadly,

Millie is awesome at her job, except when she's not. And believe me, there's nothing worse than someone trying to meet a quota with only a few days left to do it. She became rabid. Relentless. No one was safe from her high-pressure sales, not even the person at the grocery store bagging our groceries. You know those 'no soliciting' signs? She thinks they don't apply to her."

Wow. Shep's had a lot on his chest. He's taking a hatchet to the barrier of Shep World, and I don't know how I feel about that. There are a million ways I could respond. I could play devil's advocate. I could pile on and wholeheartedly agree that Millie is, in fact, incorrigible. But I'd rather not talk about Millie. I like the version of Shep that doesn't involve him thinking about Millie because smoke shoots out of his nostrils, and it's not a pretty sight.

I'm stuck. Do I respond? Does he want me to respond? Do I change the subject? Then, will he think I'm being insensitive to his feelings?

"My new best friend sent me flowers today." Positive. I stick to the positive stuff.

It takes Shep a few seconds to adjust to my rapid change in subject. When his smile comes back to life, the tension melts from his shoulders and that deep line along the bridge of his nose disappears. "I bet you were really appreciative of it. Not irrationally mad or anything like that."

I spin one-eighty and take off toward the dogs and

the little pond, an extra bounce in each of my steps. "I would never act irrationally."

"I have a new friend too."

"Oh yeah?" I grin, but he can't see it because I stay several steps in front of him.

"Yeah. I'm thinking of inviting her to have dinner with me and my parents this Friday. What do you think she'll say?"

"She'll say no. Want to know why? Because your friend isn't real."

"She feels real. She's beautiful. She's smart. She's funny and *really* imaginative. She's quite possibly the best golfer I've ever met. And she indulges me in random conversation at odd hours of the day and night."

"She sounds amazing." I toss him a flirty glance over my shoulder.

"She's ... something. That's for sure."

I turn and he stops, eyeing me with curiosity. "You weren't sure you wanted your parents to know about our trip to Sedona, but now you want me to meet them?"

He shrugs. "Just testing the waters."

I laugh, shaking my head. "I can't meet your parents," I say with as much regret to my voice as I can possibly infuse. Right guy. Wrong time.

"Because I can't really be in your life?"

Scrunching my nose, I nod.

"Just give me this much honesty. Are you married

with kids? Is it a bad marriage? Am I an escape from a bad marriage?"

"No. I've told you that." I give him a sincere smile. "It's nothing like that."

"Have you escaped from prison?"

With my lips pressed together, I give him a slow nod. "Nailed it. You always nail the obvious. Am I that transparent?"

He shakes his head, fighting a grin. "What about this ... what if I want my parents to know that I'm not sulking after a bad divorce? What if I want them to see that I'm meeting people, even if the people I'm meeting are just new friends?"

My eyes narrow a fraction. "I'm listening."

"The story is that we are friends. That doesn't change. I go to dinner with my parents and you're there. Total happenstance."

"My date for the night stands me up, and you insist I eat with you and your parents?"

He nods. "Sure. Have you been stood up a lot?"

Shep earns a firm scowl from me. "No. I'm just putting together a scenario for why I would be at a restaurant by myself."

"And you're not worried that my parents' first impression of you will be you getting stood up?"

I tilt my head and narrow my eyes, trying to read him. "Are *you* worried about that being their first impression of me? Would that embarrass you?"

"I'm not the one getting stood up. Why would I be embarrassed?"

"I'm not actually going to get stood up, jackass. It's just an excuse."

"Why not just say that you're eating alone, and then I invite you to eat with us?"

"Because eating alone at a restaurant on a Friday night makes me look like a loser."

He laughs ... a little too much. "But being stood up doesn't?"

"Fine. My date had to cancel because he's a pediatric cardiologist who gets called into work because a heart just became available for one of his patients. A two-year-old. It's heartbreaking yet a miracle because her family has been waiting, slowly losing hope for months. He's a lifesaver. I'm so lucky to be his girlfriend. And although he has to cancel our date, he insists I go to his penthouse and make myself at home until he gets there to have mind-blowing sex with me. And it's going to be the best sex of my life because the whole time I'll be thinking ... he just saved a little girl by giving her a new heart with his talented hands and brilliant mind." I release a dreamy sigh.

The expression on Shep's face morphs into something sour. "You're right. Go with the scenario where you get stood up."

"Why? Because you don't want Dr. Amazing to overshadow you in your parents' eyes? In my eyes?"

"What? No. Christ. He's a fictional dude you just made up on a whim."

"I'll think it over." I bite my thumbnail as if the thinking has already begun. "And I'll make a split-second decision that night. Just go with my lead." I resume my trek toward the pond, retrieving a rope ball attached to my treat bag strap. "Cersei!" I throw the ball and all three dogs chase after it.

Shep clears his throat. "I once carried a girl three blocks to her house after she fell off her bike and cut her knee. And I was only twelve. But my hands felt talented, and I was a solid student in school, so you could say I had a brilliant mind."

I giggle. And giggle. He's jealous of my made-up boyfriend. The flowers are no longer the highlight of my week. This is it. This crazy conversation with Shep. "You should add that to your profile on your dating apps. I'd be all over that."

"I'm not on any dating apps. And you were all over *this*, but now you have an unhealthy fixation with a doctor who doesn't exist. And as your friend, I feel the need to bring you back to reality."

When Cersei returns with the ball, I throw it again, and again, three dogs chase it. "And what is my reality?"

He's going to fail at this because he has no real clue as to my reality. Our friendship and this past weekend have been nearly as "not real" as my doctor scenario.

"In reality, the date standing you up scenario or the dinner by yourself scenario is more likely because you can be a little persnickety."

I glance back, lifting an eyebrow. "Was that on your word of the day calendar? Have you been dying all day to call someone persnickety?"

"It's an app, not a calendar."

Damn him. Really. Damn him! Why does he have to be so entertaining, so funny, so sexy, so everything I can't have right now?

"Sometimes you really bumfuzzle me."

"Not a word." He rolls his eyes. "Nice try."

"It is." I tip my chin up, accentuating my confidence. "It means to confuse or fluster."

"Well ..." He smirks. "I believe I fluster you. You blush and bat your eyelashes as your gaze shifts to anywhere and anyone but me. My gaze goes straight to your nipples then because I know you're turned on."

"You know nothing, Jon Snow."

He grins, reaching out to snag the ball that George Clooney managed to fetch before Cersei. "I'm learning quickly. Observation is my strong suit."

"Conversing ... observing ... you have so many talents."

"Fucking ..." He winks at me. "Don't forget how talented I am at that."

"So Friday ..." I clear my throat and change the subject before I do that blushing and gaze shifting for which he has such a keen eye. "You'll have to text me the time and the restaurant."

"Is our playdate over?"

"It's not *our* playdate; it's for the dogs. And I really should head back home."

"Well, maybe we need to schedule a playdate for just the two of us. Do you want to play with me, Sophie?"

I don't want to laugh or give him any reaction what-soever. There's no need to feed his ego, to play his game. But it's really hard because he's good at this. Too good. "Golf? Do I want to play golf?"

He shakes his head. "Not the balls I had in mind."

"I'm not five. I don't do playdates anymore."

"Spoilsport," he says.

He's bringing out all my scowls today. "Spoiled brat."

"See ... you do know how to engage on a playdate. First, we call each other names, then you shove me. I shove you. Clothes come off. There's some inappro-priate language. Some begging. Likely grunting. You, of course, screaming. And then we go our separate ways and think about our actions."

"Cersei! We're leaving! Come, now!"

Those lips I want to kiss slide into a curved line of total satisfaction. "You shouldn't walk home alone. We'll walk you."

"No!" I cringe and hustle to recover with a nervous laugh. "I mean ... that's ridiculous and we both know it. You didn't walk me home last time."

"You don't have a home, do you?"

I shouldn't reward him with an eye roll, but I can't stop it. "You got me. I'm a homeless optometrist."

"Well, let's look at the facts. You don't want me to walk you home. You've never invited me to your place. And you had me meet you at your office last Friday morning instead of picking you up at your 'house.'" He air quotes *house.*

"I have not seen *your* house. Nor have you invited me," I say, tipping my chin up.

"Come to my house. Come inside. Come in my bed. Just ..." He smirks. "Come."

"Cersei!" Before I have a chance to yell at her anymore, I realize she's heeled right next to me. "There you are. Let's go." I attach her leash. "It was a one and done."

"What was?" he asks.

"Our activities over the weekend. Jules and I go to concerts, but we rarely see the same act twice."

"If you really like a band, and you just can't get enough of their greatest hits, then you'd go to more than one concert. You'd stalk them. You'd be a groupie. You'd go to all of their shows. And you'd throw your panties on the stage and pray they picked you for a private tour of their bus or jet."

Wrinkling my nose, I shake my head. "You need to know that a lot of my favorite bands or singers are female."

"Why are you being so difficult?"

"Why are you being so perverted?"

"You mean persistent."

"I mean perverted." I gaze at him over the frames of my glasses.

He presses his finger to the bridge of them and pushes them up my nose. "Kiss me."

I bat away his hand. "I'm not kissing you."

"Why? Afraid you won't be able to stop?"

"I can stop just fine. But I'm not kis—"

He kisses me. Asshole. Really. Worst friend ever.

I push at his chest to no avail. He slides a finger under my shorts *and* my panties like a pro with stealth precision. And ... *oh my god* ... my knees start to buckle. Then he pulls his lips away but leaves his fingers between my legs. Heat blooms along my cheeks and need makes its way to the very spot his fingers are stroking.

For fuck's sake. We're in public, even if I don't see anyone around us. There's Google satellites and shit like that.

Need wins.

I lunge for him, eager to have his mouth on mine again. But ... he denies me. And he does it with so much cockiness I could rip his throat out with my teeth.

One step.

Two steps.

Three steps.

He backs away from me, dragging his fingers (those fingers) along his bottom lip. Then he swipes his tongue along the same path. "Told ya. See you Friday. I'll text you the time and location."

There's not enough time to pull myself together or concoct the right comeback. In a flash, he and his dogs are twenty-five yards away without so much as a glance back at the remains of me and my scorched dignity.

CHAPTER *Twenty*

"I FILED a complaint with the court to begin the eviction process," I say to Jules as we watch her kids swim in the pool. Her husband is out of town for a few days, so I offered to buy pizza for her crew in exchange for pool time and BFF therapy, even if I do know it's going to lead to a major lecture.

"He's a dick. The world's biggest dick. I get why you're not supposed to tell him about the pregnancy, but still ... if he ever did love you or love himself for that matter, he'd move out and move on."

"Jimmy purchasing a new driveway complicates things a bit. It's ridiculous, just incomprehensible. It's *my* house. I didn't ask him to do that. So does that mean I can put a pool in my neighbors' backyard while they are out of town, and I'm magically entitled to live with them?"

"Exactly. This just blows my mind. You should be able to call the police and say you broke up with your boyfriend and he won't leave your house, and they should remove him from the premises. Period. I mean ... could you get a restraining order against him? Surely they can't let someone live in *your* house if they pose a danger to you."

"I can't go down that road. I have a reputation as a business owner in this town. I'm not going to let Jimmy drag it through the mud unless I can't avoid it. And sadly, I fear it's headed in that direction. But I want to do it honestly."

"You're a better woman than I am. Kylie, don't splash your sister!"

I lean my head back and soak up the remaining sunlight of the day.

"So ... how long are we going to beat around the bush? Do you think it's time we discuss your trip to Sedona?"

"There's nothing to tell. We golfed. Walked Cersei on the trails. Lounged by the pool. Ate good food. Chatted."

"Had sex?"

"No."

"Sophie."

"We didn't." I stare at the pool.

"Sophie."

"Jules," I mimic her like a child.

"Sophie."

"We just talked."

"Body language?"

I can't. She's too good. I snort. "It's ... not ..."

"You need help, Sophie. Your behavior is self-destructive. Have you thought about seeing a therapist?"

A therapist? God ... I can't imagine what a therapist

would do with the details of my life. The real ones and the "fake" ones.

"Okay, here's the thing ..." I sit up and swing my legs over the side of the lounge chair, giving her my full attention.

"Oh good. I've been waiting for *the thing*."

"He's not real—"

"Oh, Sophie ..." She facepalms her forehead.

"Just hear me out, Jules. I had no plans of pursuing Shep. None. But he called me, and I enjoyed talking with him. And taking the dogs to the park. Topgolf. Lunch. More talking on the phone. I don't tell him about my life and all its problems. He doesn't tell me about his."

That's a half lie.

"I can't expedite the removal of Jimmy from my house. And I can't change my mind about this pregnancy, not that I want to. I don't. This pregnancy is the one thing in my life that I feel most certain about. And because of this baby, I don't want to feel stressed all the time. It's not good for the baby. When I'm with Shep, it's like all the stress in my life disappears. It's easy with him. No stress. No expectations. Shep World is a fantasy. And sometimes, I need that fantasy. He's a good book. He's a break from life to meditate. A vacation. A long jog to clear my head. He's the best guy at the worst time, but we're making it work."

Jules lifts her sunglasses onto her head. "What does that mean, making it work?"

"I mean, it's mutually beneficial. I've been

completely upfront with him. We're living in the moment with no expectations."

"You've been upfront with him? So he knows about Jimmy? Knows about the baby?"

"No. That's the whole point. That's what makes Shep World such an amazing place. He doesn't see Sophie the doormat who has the worst luck with men. He doesn't see Sophie the woman who is pregnant with someone else's baby. Because here's something very important to remember ... Jimmy? The baby? They don't define me. They are not who I am. They are products of my choices, good and bad. Shep sees me. And even if this ends tomorrow, it's been really amazing to have had him see *me* and not my life's decisions."

Jules laughs, not with me, at me. "This Shep World sounds better than Disney."

"It is." I smirk.

"Being upfront with someone implies honesty. But you're not being honest with him."

"I'm being completely honest with him. What you mean is transparency. Am I being transparent with him? No. But I'm being *honest* with him because I'm upfront about not being transparent with him. He knows I'm not telling him about my "real" life. I've been vague about the reasons for it. He knows it's nonnegotiable. He can take me as is for as long as it mutually works for us, or we end it now. And so far, he's been good with our unconventional, potentially temporary, friendship. Maybe it's what he needs in his own life. Not everyone's needs are the same. Not everyone shares the same definition of honesty, transparency, and morality."

Jules sighs, inching her head side to side. "You should have been a politician."

"Because I'm a gifted orator?"

"Because you're full of shit."

Lying back in my chair, I blow out a long breath. "I don't know what you're talking about."

"Fine, let's do this."

"Do what?" I ask.

"Tell me all about Shep World. I know you're dying to share."

I'm *so* dying to share.

✳ ✳ ✳ ✳ ✳

FRIDAY MORNING I meet my sister and her husband at the doctor's office for the first ultrasound.

"How are you feeling, Sophie?" Dr. Munson asks when she enters the room.

"Good." I smile at Chloe and Mason standing in the corner of the room, holding hands and wearing huge grins. It affirms that I'm doing something completely selfless. If I have a legacy, I'm good with it being this—giving my sister and her husband a baby.

Even if I have kids of my own, this will always feel different. Not more special, just ... selfless.

"Nausea?" Dr. Munson asks.

"No."

"None?" She lifts an eyebrow.

"None." I shrug.

"Is that alarming?" Chloe asks. "I read that nausea is a sign of a healthy pregnancy."

"Twenty to thirty percent of women don't experience it. That doesn't mean they don't have healthy pregnancies. Is everyone staying for this?" She glances at Mason specifically, as she dons her gloves.

"We'll stay at Sophie's head." Chloe pulls Mason toward her as I recline back, my lower half covered.

Even though Mason can't see my naked body, it's a little weird watching him witness this: the internal ultrasound wand that will go inside of my vagina. Is it weird for him? If it is, he's not showing any sign of it.

"There's your baby." The doctor points to the screen. "And we have a heartbeat."

The room falls silent except for the rhythm of that tiny heart. Such a miracle. I'm not immune to the emotions in the air.

Mason kisses Chloe's head as her eyes fill with tears. She grabs my hand and says, "Thank you" with a frog in her throat.

I can't talk at all. I just nod.

My life is perfect.

My life is messy.

My life is a million miles from any destination I ever imagined.

I guess that's the purpose. Where's the fun in knowing where you're going and how you will get there?

"Do you need anything?" Chloe asks after the doctor and Mason exit the exam room to let me get dressed.

I need Jimmy out of my house. That's not a request I can make when she has no idea that he's still living with me. She only knows we broke up—way before we actually did. I swear I'm protecting her more than she's protecting me, and *I'm* the pregnant one.

"Vitamins? A spa day? Do all of your clothes still fit?"

I laugh. "The baby is the size of a sweet pea. I'm good. Thanks."

"But you might have bloating." Her nose scrunches. "I read that."

"No nausea. No bloating. All of my clothes fit. I'm eating well and not drinking any alcohol."

"And you're not working too much or under any unnecessary stress. Right?"

If she only knew. "Nothing I can't handle." I slip on my panties and lower my cotton skirt before sliding on my sandals.

"What about cravings? I can bring you anything you want, any time of the day. If it's two in the morning and you're craving something that you don't have, promise you'll call me."

"Chloe." I press my palms to her face, brushing my fingertips along the short hair by her ears. She's always had a pixie cut for as long as I can remember. "I know you wish this were you. I know you feel indebted. I know you worry about me and what may or may not

217

happen in the coming months. But I'm good. Your baby is good. If I need anything, I promise you'll be the first to know."

Gah! Such a lie. I need Jimmy out of my house and Shep out of my head. I have imaginary sex with him at least a dozen times a day.

CHAPTER
Twenty-One

SHEP texts me the time and place. I go through six outfit changes, three hair styles, and five shades of lip gloss. After settling on a gold shift dress with a lace hem and lace neckline, I bolt past Jimmy, ignoring his "where the hell are you going in that" comment. Arriving at the restaurant twenty minutes early, I request a table for two.

The waiter brings me a lemonade and an order of caramelized brussels sprouts with garlic and honey pistachios. After a few minutes of taking small bites followed by a swish and swallow of water to ensure I don't have anything green stuck in my teeth, Shep and his parents pass my table as the hostess leads them to their table.

"Sophie?" Shep stops.

I stiffen and smile, making a quick glance at his parents who have turned to look at me. "Hi."

"How are you?" he asks in a well-rehearsed tone, perfectly infused with inflections of surprise.

My gaze continues its nervous ping-ponging between Shep and his parents. "Fine." I'm really good at one-word answers because we didn't work out any specific dialogue.

"Sorry ... Sophie, these are my parents, Hillary and Gordon. This is my friend, Sophie. I met her at the store. And it just so happens that she's a really skilled golfer. Had her dad not suffered injuries from an accident, he would have qualified for the PGA."

My smile gets faker with each passing second. This is too weird. Why did I agree to this? Can we go back to our exclusive little bubble?

Gordon perks up. "Is that so?"

I nod. "It is."

"What's his name?" Gordon asks.

"Dalton Ryan. It was many years—"

"Oh yes. I've heard of him. I remember the accident. It was in the news. He was a very promising player. So tragic. How is he now?"

"Good. Some arthritis in the joints where he has hardware, but he plays almost every day. And he's as good as I remember him being when I was younger."

"That's great," Gordon nods.

"Are you alone?" Shep asks.

Here we go. Am I playing the loner, the loser, or the boyfriend-is-saving-a-life dreamer?

"I am. My plans sort of ... fell apart. So here I am, having dinner by myself." Vague. There's a fourth option.

"You should join us." Shep glances at his parents as if he needs permission. Now it's just awkward. But the awkwardness doesn't last because they quickly agree.

"Perfect. Is a booth okay?" the hostess asks as I

realize she's been waiting during the entire conversation about my dad.

Shep nods. "That works." He grabs my lemonade and my appetizer as I stand. His gaze shows complete appreciation for my dress. "You look ... tempting." He smirks, whispering his words so his parents don't hear him.

I bite my tongue because what I want to tell him is that I heard the heartbeat of the baby in my tummy. I'm still reeling from the morning in the doctor's office.

The hostess waits for us to file into the booth before handing us menus. Shep grabs his menu with one hand and my leg with his other hand, sliding it from my knee to halfway up my thigh.

I suck in an audible breath. His mom glances up at me from across the table. My smile attempts to cover up my reaction.

"I'm glad we ended up at the same restaurant tonight," I say before sipping my drink as everyone else scans their menus. The heat from Shep's hand leaves a singe mark on my leg. "I don't know if Shep passed it along, but I really enjoyed staying at your house in Sedonaaa!" I clamp my mouth shut so I don't disrupt the entire restaurant as Shep squeezes my leg harder than necessary.

His parents narrow their eyes while I gulp down the rest of my words. *Oops ... that was supposed to be a secret.*

I knew that. I just forgot. This ... this is the reason

we shouldn't be together in the presence of people from our real lives. Things get too jumbled.

"Oh?" Hillary eyes Shep.

He loosens his grip and clears his throat. "Yeah. Last week, Howie had to skip out on our trip, so I invited Sophie to golf with me in Sedona."

"You did?" Hillary asks with so much hidden suggestion in her voice it makes me blush. "We had no idea you were seeing anyone."

"Oh! We're not seeing each other." I push my black-framed glasses up my nose. "I mean, not in a romantic sense. We're just friends who have dogs and like to golf."

Shep inches his hand up my leg as if I need a reminder that we've done more than play a few rounds of golf and hang out with the dogs. I don't need the reminder. It's on constant replay in my head.

"I see." She nods slowly. "Are you married? Do you have a boyfriend?"

"Mom, really?" Shep cocks his head to the side.

"I'm just asking." She shrugs and returns her attention to the menu.

"Well, anyway…" I feel the need to make things better "…it's a lovely house with stunning views. And I had a wonderful weekend. So thank you for your generosity."

Gordon lifts his gaze to Shep and narrows his eyes a bit. Shep returns a barely detectable headshake, but I don't miss it.

"Well, Marcus loves Sedona and golfing, so I'm sure

the pleasure was all his." Hillary closes her menu and sips her water.

"Marcus?"

Shep removes his hand from my leg and closes his menu too. "My last name is Shepherd. Everyone ... except my mom ... calls me Shep. My best friend in high school was also Marcus, so I went by Shep, and it's just stuck all these years."

How has he not told me that? Jesus ... I close my eyes for a brief second. How have I not asked for his last name, which would have revealed his true first name? I had sex with a man I've known only as Shep.

It's fine.

It's called Shep World for a reason, and that reason is because I didn't know his name is Marcus.

And we're not real.

And there's a lot he doesn't know about me.

And ... there are too many "and's" to list.

"Shepherd is a good last name." I spoon more brussels sprouts onto my plate and mumble. "German would be a cool first name."

His parents must not hear me. I don't mean for them to hear me, but Shep (Marcus) chuckles and mutters, "It really would be."

After they order their food and drinks, Hillary wastes no time diving into all things me.

What do I do?

Where do I live?

Have I ever been married?

And my favorite ... do I see myself having children someday.

Why yes ... yes I do.

"Probably" is the answer I give her.

Shep offers me a sad smile when I make that comment. I'm not sure why.

I give generic answers to everything. If I'm not sharing my reality with Shep, I'm also not sharing it with his parents.

"Marcus wants kids. He's so good with them. We were waiting on Millie and him to have kids, but that clearly didn't work out. Marcus, have you told her much about Millie? You know ... I'm just going to shut up now." She covers her mouth and leans into Gordon's shoulder.

This seems to dissolve the awkwardness. Everyone laughs.

Shep had to know this might happen. Kids know their parents well enough to predict their thoughts and blunders.

"I met Millie just this week. She's an excellent sales person." My comment draws suspicious looks from his parents.

"Full court press on Sophie." Shep shakes his head.

"We really don't know what happened to her." Gordon frowns. "Millie went from being the best daughter-in-law you could ask for to a relentless maniac always trying to make a sale. She was even hell-bent on getting me to try the men's line of wrinkle cream like I give two cents about my wrinkles."

"They make you look mature and distinguished." Hillary leans toward him and plants a kiss on his cheek. He returns such an adoring expression. I could watch them all night.

Shep has a good family. I didn't need to know this. Things start to feel less fictional when we open our imaginary world to other people. I learn all about them as the night stretches into desserts and coffee.

His dad is retired after forty-five years of selling insurance. His mom was a nurse in the ER for twenty years—five before starting a family and fifteen more after Shep and his sister graduated high school.

"Marcus missed out on his college years. That's how he ended up with Millie. Online dating was his only option." I think his mom is buzzed. I like her buzzed. She's even more chatty, aka revealing, after a few glasses of wine.

"It wasn't my only option. I had friends willing to fix me up, and bars were an option as well. I could have gone to college and still met someone online."

"Marcus is dyslexic. He could have gone to college, but he didn't want to deal with asking for special accommodations. It's not severe dyslexia, so I honestly think he would have been fine." His mom prattles off more information than I'm sure he cares for her to share with me.

"He's done fine." Gordon for the save. "Life isn't about certificates and merit badges. There are a lot of happy and successful people who don't have a college degree. Hell, some don't even have a high school diploma."

I love how proud Gordon is of his son who works in a pet shop.

"Who's calling me?" Hillary pulls her phone from her purse and Gordon leans over to look at the screen.

Shep's mouth gets as close to my ear as he can without touching it. "Are you wearing panties under that dress?"

Really?

Right in front of his parents he has me flustered. I'm sure they can see it on my cheeks.

"Yes." I grit my teeth and fake a smile in case they glance up at me.

"That's a shame." He sits up straight.

"What are you two talking about?" Hillary glances up from her phone, having missed the call.

"Shep asked me about a concert, but I've already seen it. And I don't usually see the same performance more than once."

He downs the last few gulps of his beer and sets his bottle on the table. "Unless you really like them and you know that no two performances are exactly the same. And maybe you get backstage passes."

"Oh, Marcus knows a lot of people. I bet he could get you backstage passes." Gordon nods several times. "You should do that for Sophie. It might be fun. Concerts are great."

Shep dips his chin into a sharp nod, his grin on the

verge of cracking his whole face. "They really are. A good concert is unforgettable. So intense and satisfying. It's like you're in another world, and you don't ever want it to end. You want to relive it over and over again."

When the two men finish their big concert sales pitch to me, I shrug. "Sorry. I'm a one and done girl. I need variety. Life is too short to experience the same thing twice."

"I agree with Sophie. Try something new." Hillary comes to my rescue.

Shep rolls his eyes. "Says the person who's been vacationing in the same three spots for twenty years. Says the woman who married her high school boyfriend. Says the woman who only buys one brand of purses."

Gordon laughs. "He's got you there, sweetheart."

"Fine." She fakes a pouty face. "Maybe you should see the same performer more than once, Sophie. If you like them, it's a safer bet than trying another one and them not living up to what you've already experienced."

"That's likely. Probable. Nearly a one hundred percent guarantee." Shep's enjoying this a little too much.

After his parents insist on paying the bill, Hillary stands. When I scoot out of the booth, she hugs me. "It's been so much fun. I really hope we get to spend more time with you soon."

"Yes. I'd love that."

"The four of us should play golf sometime," Gordon suggests.

"Be careful what you wish for, Dad." Shep nods for me to follow his parents to the exit.

"Bye, Marcus. Bye, Sophie." They give us a final wave before heading toward the parking lot.

"Are you parked on the street or in the lot?" Shep asks, turning toward me and standing too close for me to breathe properly.

"Street."

"What's your address?"

I shake my head. "Depends on the night. Remember? I'm homeless."

"Have it your way. I'll follow you."

Why does he have to play this way? He can't follow me. I'm not ready to explain my roommate situation until I no longer have a roommate situation and therefore don't have to explain it.

"Why don't you give me your address, *Marcus Shepherd*? God ... I can't believe I didn't know your real name. How did it never come up in conversation?"

He winks. "Because you weren't thinking about my full name. You only needed one to scream when I made you—"

"Just ..." I cover his mouth. "Stop. You're obnoxious."

He grabs my wrist and kisses my hand and up my arm. I pull it away from him because it tickles and because it's giving me that fuzzy headed, intoxicated feeling.

"I'll follow you to your place *just* to converse for a while before I go home. We'll do the real friend thing tonight."

His eyes widen, brows peaked. "The *best* friend thing?"

"No. The-only-two-people-at-a-party-not-making-out thing so we talk about the weather and count down the minutes until it's cool to go home."

"Sophie, did you just give me a glimpse of your college life?"

"Ob-nox-ious ..." I squint at him.

"Follow me. I'm the red car over there." He nods toward the street.

CHAPTER
Twenty-Two

"NICE PLACE," I say with a little apprehension as we meet at the front door to his house. It's a very small house. I'm sure he's renting it. But I'll give him credit for having his own place and keeping a job to pay for it.

"Thanks." He unlocks it and opens it for me. "Hey, kids." He greets Julia and George.

I bend down to pet them. Kids. He calls them kids. There he goes again, being completely obnoxious one minute and endearing the next. I'm getting whiplash. He ushers the dogs to the kitchen and the sliding door leading to the backyard.

His place appears to have two bedrooms, a shared bath, and a dinky living room and kitchen. But ... he has a place. I'm kinda proud of my progress in men. It's nothing to brag about since I'm not telling anyone (except Jules) about him, but it's something.

"I know what you're thinking."

I lift my eyebrows. "Oh? What am I thinking?"

He plops down onto his sofa and pats the cushion beside him. "You're thinking I have a small house. I used to have a bigger house, but Millie has it now."

I shake my head. "It's fine. You have to live within your means."

He shrugs. "I don't need anything bigger. Can I get you something to drink?"

"No. I'm good." I ignore his invite to sit next to him and opt for keeping a safe distance, finding every painting on the wall and every family photo quite interesting or at least a good distraction from him.

"Millie took the house. You should have at least gotten full custody of the dogs."

He grunts. "Millie tried to take everything." He stands and prowls toward me, a lion toying with a lamb.

"Do you want to play a game?" I wring my fingers in front of me, taking refuge behind his sofa next to a fig plant.

"Strip poker?" He smiles.

"I was thinking board games, but if you only have cards, we could play Crazy Eights, Speed, Kings in the Corner, Slap Jack ..."

"Or we could check out my new sheets. They're a bamboo blend. I just put them on this morning. They feel like silk."

On a nervous laugh, I shake my head. "Not a good idea."

"Why?" He unbuttons his shirt without taking it completely off. Instead, he remains on the opposite side of the sofa in faded jeans, his white button-down open and rolled at the sleeves, and the most wolfish grin ever. No single woman in her right mind would say no to *this*.

Now I just need to figure out if I'm in my right mind.

"What are you afraid of? I've said I wouldn't ask to move in with you. I just want to do things ... really good things to your body because it feels so fucking good. Are you opposed to feeling good? Do you worry that your massage therapist might fall in love with you because he or she relaxes you and makes you feel good?"

I snort a tiny laugh. "Where are you getting your massages? I've never had one make me feel that kind of good."

Shep unbuttons his jeans, and I try not to stare, but it's like someone telling me not to blink and now I *have* to blink. He slides his hand down the front of his boxer briefs and strokes himself.

"Shep ..." I lose my voice halfway through his short name.

"Yeah?"

Gulp.

"What are you uh ... doing?"

"Touching myself. Do you touch yourself?"

With a nervous laugh, flames shoot out of my cheeks. "Not uh ... not usually on a full stomach. You know ... muscle cramps and other physical dangers associated with rigorous activity after a meal. One time I made a batch of cookies late at night and overate." I lift my gaze to his when his hand stops moving.

He bites his lips together, fighting his grin.

My head shakes slowly. "Got a little frisky with myself after like ... six cookies, and two of my fingers cramped up so badly I had to stop. I went to sleep that night horny and crippled."

Shep twists his lips, fighting it so hard as his hand inches out of his briefs and he turns his back to me, fisting a hand at his mouth and clearing his throat. Then his shoulders shake, and I know I got him. I got the grin. The silent laughter. Dare I say I won the moment?

This is the version of me that's truly *me*. The woman who loves life, friendship, and laughter. I *love* to laugh. I don't like taking life too seriously unless I'm forced to play that part. With Shep, I don't have to play it.

"Jesus, Sophie ..." He coughs again, continuing to stifle his laughter as he turns.

I swear his eyes are red with tears.

"You are one weird chick."

I smirk. "You love it."

He nods. "I do love ... *it*."

My gaze shoots in another direction. That was a weird moment. Did I tee that up? I didn't mean to.

"Speaking of cookies," Shep says, "I didn't eat much dessert tonight on purpose. Because I knew I'd fill up on your—"

"No!" I cover my ears and start giggling. "You are terrible. Just terrible, Marcus Shepherd. A fucking drug dealer. And you know all of my weaknesses."

He sighs, letting his smile wilt into a frown. "I have Scrabble. My mom bought it for me, hoping it might help my dyslexia. It didn't. We can play. You will win. How does that sound?"

This is not fair. He's playing the dyslexic card, which I didn't even know was a card to be played until just now. One of the dogs scratches at the door, and Shep heads to the kitchen to let them inside.

I don't know what my angle is at this point. There's no stopping the clock. I will start to show a baby belly. Our friendship will, at best, change into a true, non-sexual friendship, or it will end altogether. Having sex ... not having sex ... won't change that fact.

A few minutes later, he and the dogs return. "Bed," Shep says to his dogs. They ignore him, opting to hump each other instead. Twisting his lips and watching their behavior, he shakes his head. "Animals just know. They know what feels good and they do it. It's not that complicated. Why do humans make it so complicated?"

I rub my hand over my mouth to cover my smile. George and Julia are really going at it. "If humans were as uninhibited as dogs," I say, "we'd hump all the time. In public, just wherever. There's a reason we're considered the most evolved species."

"George, Julia, bed."

They head straight toward one of the bedrooms. Shep slides open a drawer to his coffee table and pulls out a deck of cards.

I notice his jeans are buttoned and so is his shirt.

Doesn't he know how to give a girl a few seconds to overthink everything and land on the right decision, only to say "fuck it" and do the wrong thing after all?

"Kings in the Corner?" He holds up the deck of cards, wiggling it a few times.

"I can't. I have to get to bed."

He deflates. "It's Friday, Sophie."

"I know." I unzip the side of my dress and let it fall to the floor.

Shep's lips part a fraction as his eyes flare.

"Soft bamboo blend, huh?" I grin.

"Fuck you, Sophie ..." He drops the cards and takes three huge strides to get to me. "You just always have to be on top." Our mouths connect in a hard kiss. He grabs the back of my legs and hoists me up, wrapping my legs around his waist.

He carries me to his bedroom and dumps me onto his bed.

I bite my lower lip and giggle as he quickly discards his shirt. "I'll let you be on top, Shep. Just this once." I'm asking for it. I don't know what *it* even is yet, but I have a feeling *it* will involve me not having an orgasm anytime soon. *It* will involve me pleading. *It* will involve me on the verge of self-combustion as he takes his time getting back at me.

"Are you claustrophobic?" He twists his lips to the side while he slips off his sneakers and socks.

"No. Why?"

"Well, my new bedsheets..." he saunters to the

closet "...came folded and tied with these matching sashes." He turns, holding said sashes. "I'm going to tie your wrists to the headboard before I fuck you."

This is new. Not new as in Shep just invented a new way of having sex, but new to me. I've never had anyone ask to restrain me. Now that I think about it, Shep's not asking; he's telling.

"Why?" I have to ask. I'm curious by nature. Not curious about his full name, but sexual positions and restraints pique it for sure.

"Why not?" He shrugs.

That's not the response I anticipated. I'm not sure why. Silly me, I forgot to ask the OB this morning if pregnancy was a contraindication for being restrained during sex. Might it cause me to feel unnecessary stress and therefore stress the baby? I don't know. What are the chances anyone has studied this with great detail? About zero, I'm sure.

"Have you tied other women to your bed?"

"Not this bed."

My eyebrows lift in response.

Shep chuckles. "No. I have not. I'm unclear as to when the appropriate time is to suggest tying a lover to the bed, but we're just friends. And friends do weird and stupid stuff together. Right?"

Sure, I think to myself, when they're fifteen or maybe during a second round of Stupid Things College Edition, but I'm not sure the same could or should be said of grown-ass adults like us. I lift onto my elbows and give it some more thought. Does love get in the way of being sexually adventurous? Have we, as friends, already reached a level of trust and comfort with each other that surpasses anything between lovers? At this point, should we just hump in public because it feels good?

"What if I tie you to the bed?" I suggest.

"You said I could be on top. How is the top person supposed to be tied to the bed?"

Trapping my lips between my teeth, I fight the laughter bubbling in my chest, the sheer joy this new friend of mine gives me. I can't believe we're having this conversation. Yet, I *love* that we are so easily having this conversation—like two friends deciding on whether or not to go to a club for the night.

I lie back, stretch my arms above my head, and smile. It's just me, my panties, and my submission for the night.

Shep scrapes his teeth along his lower lip several times. He can hide his grin, but he can't hide the victory in his eyes. With deft hands, he ties my wrists to his headboard and steps back to inspect his handiwork. "Tomorrow, I'm sending out emails to all of my other friends, cutting ties. I have no need for anything more than this. You are the only friend I need."

"Shut up and take off my panties, *Marcus*."

Shep obliges, dragging them slowly down my legs.

"Now kiss me."

He rests a hand on his hip and stares at the floor.

"Really? Are you *really* trying to be on top from the bottom?"

"Sorry." I close my mouth and grin.

As if he needs to make his point that he's on top and in control, he doesn't kiss me. He teases his lips along my legs, my inner thighs, and right down my middle, causing me to buck. That pulls an evil grin from him. His fingers find all of my sensitive spots, and he tests that line between pleasure and torture.

"Shep ..." I sigh on a harsh breath. "You're not naked."

"So?" His thumb circles my clit while his gaze remains glued to said clit and his fingers teasing me there.

"What are you doing?" All of my words come out a little breathy.

"Admiring you because I can." His fingers relocate, gripping my knees, bending them more and spreading them wider.

I'm so intoxicated by him right now, I can hardly see straight. And that's where my mind goes crazy, feeling more than it should, feeling possessive. I don't say it, but it makes me a little twitchy to think of him with another woman, to think of him kissing someone else the way he's kissing me, looking at someone else the way he's looking at me. My psyche begins to crumble, obliterating Shep World. A snow globe shattering on a tile floor.

"I gotta go. Untie me."

Shep pauses. "What?"

"Untie me. I have to go home."

"Now?"

"Yes, Marcus. I have to go home now."

"Why?"

I bring my bent knees together, forcing him to back up, kneeling at the end of the bed, hands on his jean clad thighs and bare shoulders curled inward.

"Because I can't have sex with you."

He coughs several times, more like a laugh of disbelief. "What changed?"

"It doesn't matter. A woman has a right to change her mind, even if it's at the last second. A man could too …" I twist my lips. "I wonder if that happens very often? Anyway, I don't have to give you an answer. And as my friend and a non-rapist gentleman, you need to honor my request."

With narrowed eyes and lips parted, he remains idle. A sponge absorbing everything I just told him. "Honor your request …" Curling his lips between his teeth, he makes the slightest nod. "Okay."

Okay.

That's it?

No more questions?

I'm fully prepared to hold my ground, plead the Fifth. I'm ready for his childish fit and desperate pleading.

He does none of that. Instead, he unties me and slips back on his shirt while I scurry to step into my panties and power walk toward the sofa to retrieve my dress and shoes.

"Thanks for inviting me to dinner. I had a great time. Let's do it again ..." I head toward the door just as he emerges from the bedroom, silent and unreadable. "The dinner part." I smile, nose scrunched before shooting out the door.

CHAPTER
Twenty-Three

"Mind telling me where you've been?" Jimmy asks as I shut the door and toe off my shoes.

I glance up at him hogging my sofa and monopolizing my television.

"I was on a date." I smile, shoulders back and head held high as I make my way to the kitchen with Cersei on my tail waiting for my attention. Maybe this is a new direction that I never thought about—showing Jimmy I'm moving on.

"Excuse me?" Jimmy says slowly as I fill a glass with water.

"A date. You know ... when two people go out to dinner because they like each other, and sometimes they take things further if the night's going well. We dated, Jimmy. Don't you remember back when I liked you? Back when you had a sliver of self-respect left in your body? I know time flies, but it wasn't actually that long ago."

"Are you fucking kidding me?" He sits up slowly, at the same pace that my words must be sinking into his damaged brain.

"I'm serious. Like how serious I am about you moving out of my house. Like how serious I was when

I said we were over. I'm flattered you think I have such a rich sense of humor, and I did before you moved into my house, but if I'm not laughing, then I'm probably serious, Jimmy." I drink the whole glass of water and set it down with a little more force than necessary.

I'm mad, but for reasons I can't explain. Today started off so good. The baby. The heartbeat. My sister and her husband in tears because I'm giving them something they want more than anything. Even work went well. Dinner was amazing. Then … Shep.

Shep happened.

And Jimmy.

One of them I want and can't have. The other I don't want and can't seem to shake.

I'm completely drained of all sympathy for the two hundred pounds of dead weight on my sofa. It's terrible, but I think I'd have a weak moment of happiness if he said he had some terminal illness because it would mean that he's leaving my house, even if on a gurney with a sheet covering him. Again … ninety-nine percent not serious about that. Okay. Maybe seventy percent.

I blame these morbid thoughts on pregnancy hormones. They're making me sick, but not in a physical way.

"So now what?" He stands like his joints won't bend properly, like an eighty-year-old man instead of the spry twenty-nine-year-old I found on a dating app. He had sex appeal and vigor for days.

"Uh … what do you mean *now what*?"

"Clearly we have more issues to work out now."

It's rare, but not unheard of for young adults to experience dementia. Maybe he's schizophrenic, and I'm dealing with multiple personalities. Brain tumor? Stroke? Really ... what am I missing? "When's the last time you had a physical?"

He presses his hands to his lower back and stretches like it's painful to stand fully erect. "You mean with my doctor?"

"Yes."

"A year or two. Why?"

"No reason."

"I don't qualify for health insurance with my new job until I've been with them for thirty days. And I'm not sure if it will cover couple's counseling, but I'll check. It would probably be easier if we were married."

Je ... sus ... really? I left my tied-up position in Shep's bed, and this is my reward for having a conscience? For not letting our physical relationship go too far? (Too far *again*) For doing the right fucking thing!

"What if I were pregnant? What if I were pregnant and it wasn't your baby?"

"W-what the hell are you talking about?" His words rush out like I just punched him in the gut.

"Would you still act like the world's biggest asshole? Would you still act utterly clueless and pretend that what we had can be salvaged?"

His slack jaw snaps shut, teeth clenched, and a

little vein in his forehead pops out. "I'd be fucking pissed off."

"Pissed off enough to leave? To move the hell out of my house?"

"The fuck ..." He runs his fingers through his hair. "I just bought a new driveway."

"And I bought that desk and computer." I point to his "office" in the corner of my living room. "Take them. Go. We'll call it even."

"Who? Who have you been screwing behind my back?"

"Jimmy!" I clap my hands together in front of me several times—the adult in the room, trying to capture a child's attention.

"We."

Clap.

"Are."

Clap.

"Not."

Clap.

"Together!"

Clap.

"So if I were screwing someone, it wouldn't be behind your back. It wouldn't be cheating. It just simply wouldn't be any of your business."

"If ... you said *if*. You're not really screwing anyone else. Are you?"

"Yes. That's where I was last weekend. I was in Sedona with a guy I met. And we screwed. And it was amazing because he's not a squatter." Okay, he's not a squatter at my house, but Jimmy doesn't need the finer details. Shep could be one missed paycheck away from being a squatter at his parents' house. I have no idea.

"Informal settler." He frowns. "Squatter is so belittling."

"If you feel belittled, may I suggest you move out so I no longer offend you?"

"You're not pregnant." He ignores my suggestion. "You wouldn't know this early if you were pregnant."

That's his takeaway? I confess to sleeping with another guy, and all he cares about is the possibility that I'm *not* pregnant? No self-esteem. No standards. He's belittling himself. It's time to consider the real possibility that this is not Jimmy, but rather an imposter. Maybe there was an alien situation and this extraterrestrial person, who has taken over Jimmy's body, doesn't fully understand how human relationships work. That would explain so much—everything really.

"You're right. It would be too early to know, but it's not too early for you to move out. What do I owe your mom for the new driveway? Will she take a check? Do I need to get her cash?"

Then, as if a switch flips (again lending credence to the alien hypothesis) Jimmy narrows his eyes. "You'd like that, wouldn't you? Well, I'm not ready to move. I have equity in this house now. So you and your new boyfriend can just deal with me until I'm good and fucking ready to move."

This is progress. It probably wouldn't seem like

progress to anyone else, but Jimmy just took a big step. He acknowledged we're over by getting angry. He's gone from an asshole in denial to a vengeful—well, still an asshole—with the realization that he's no longer welcome here. I'm reminded of why Shep has to be a friend. Only a friend. It's nearly impossible for lovers to end and still be friends. Casually falling out of love is as likely as finding a unicorn at a petting zoo.

"I'm evicting your ass, so your days are numbered. It didn't have to be like this." I whistle and jerk my head toward the bedroom for Cersei to follow me.

"What does it say about you that you can't handle the rough times, huh? I lose my job and we're over? I lose my job and you jump into some other guy's bed? Really, Sophie? I thought you had more depth than that."

Great. Letting a jobless guy live with me, who showers twice a week, and uses my credit card without my permission is the new "deep?" And here I figured it was the classic doormat scenario. The answer to my problems is to purge all men from my life and focus on the little pea in my uterus. Maybe going through the stages of pregnancy and giving birth will change me in a way that allows me to see men differently.

CHAPTER
Twenty-Four

To my disappointment, and no one's fault but my own, I don't hear from Shep for days ... and more days. Maybe it's for the best. I can't stop this train that's already left the pregnancy station. Still ... I miss him.

I miss my friend and our world.

Jimmy makes me miss Shep even more. Maybe Shep doesn't own one damn thing, and maybe he's as penniless as Jimmy, but he's not Jimmy. God ... I hope he's not Jimmy. What if the reason he hasn't called is because he's pissed off at me, just like Jimmy?

After work, I pop into the pet store before they close. No big deal. Cersei needs more treats.

Okay. She doesn't really.

A couple exit with their dog just before I step into the refreshingly crisp air. I straighten my white pencil skirt and smooth the front of my floral ruffle-sleeved blouse.

Pink wedges.

Pink glasses.

Hair straightened and in a sophisticated ponytail, as sophisticated as a one-inch-long ponytail can be.

"Hi." Shep glances up from the register, the store empty besides us. He's unfairly handsome. I instantly notice he's had a haircut since I've last seen him, but it's still a little wavy, and he's clean shaven. It's the first time I've seen him without any facial hair. I have mixed feelings about it because I like the memories of his stubble rubbing along my skin.

"Hi." I smile and clear my throat. "Just needed some treats." I grab the first bag of treats that I come to, barely taking my gaze off Shep for more than a second.

"Did you get a cat?"

My eyes narrow. "No. Why?"

"Because those are cat treats."

I glance down at the bag in my hand. "Oh." This isn't going as planned. Why am I such a nervous wreck? Oh that's right ... the last time I saw him I was tied to his headboard, and I chickened out because I started to feel something too real. "Long day," I say on a nervous laugh as I return the cat treats and scan the area for anything with a dog on the packaging.

"Busy day here?" I ask, browsing the shelves, suddenly feeling the urge to thoroughly inspect them before making my choice.

"Not bad for a Wednesday. How was your *long* day?"

I shrug, reading the back of a package, but not really reading the back of it. "The usual. My days are pretty monotonous. How are your parents?"

"Good. How are yours?"

Chuckling, I glance over at him. He's never met them, but it's nice of him to ask. "They're good."

"And Cersei?"

"She's good."

"You didn't bring her. She'll be upset when she finds out." Shep leans against the back counter and crosses his arms over his chest. His sex appeal is so effortless. It's simple really. The hair. The way he smiles and it reaches his eyes. Always a simple tee, jeans, and tennis shoes. Expensive shoes. I'm pretty sure the shoes he wore to dinner with his parents were Yeezy's, close to four hundred dollars.

I try not to think of him as a sixteen-year-old boy whose parents pay for nearly everything, therefore he can blow his whole paycheck on stupid expensive shoes, but I can't *not* think it either.

Friends … I remind myself. So it's none of my business. Temporary friends at that. I'm obviously a terrible temporary friend. I got all weird on him at his place, then he didn't call. That should have been my clean break, but here I am … stalking him.

"I just came from work. Had I gone home to get her, you would have been closed since you close early on Wednesdays."

"True."

I take the dog treats to the register. "Are Julia and George with Millie this week?"

He nods, scanning the bag. "Seven thirty-five."

I pull a ten out of my purse. "Want to meet at the park sometime?"

Before he can answer, the door opens behind me. A young woman with flowing brown hair smiles and waves at him as she heads to the back room.

"New employee?" I ask.

"Yes. Riley. She started last week. She's working weekends and every Wednesday night after closing to help me do inventory."

The leggy *young* woman is spending Wednesday nights alone with Shep to do inventory. Well ... that's awesome.

He gives me my change. "Two sixty-five."

Riley emerges from the back room and reaches to open the drawer next to Shep. "Scooch." She gives him a playful nudge.

I hate her.

No!

I inwardly cringe as my thoughts run amuck. Of course, I don't hate her. I don't know her. And Shep is my friend, just my friend. And I'm pregnant. And ...

He eyes her with a fake scowl. "Ask nicely or I'll make you inventory all the frozen food from the inside of the freezer."

She bites her bottom lip and bats her eyelashes. "Pretty please, Your Highness."

Again, he smirks like he's enjoying their banter. "That's better." He steps to the side and lets her open the drawer.

She retrieves a box cutter and stabs him in the side: of course, the blade is not out.

"You'll pay for that," he says as she saunters to the back room.

"I'm sure," she replies just before disappearing behind the door.

"Hope Cersei enjoys the treats," he says, returning his attention to me.

I push through a pile of jealousy and irrational hate toward a person I just met (we haven't officially met) to unearth the version of myself I need to honor. The altruistic pregnant woman.

The friend.

The mature woman.

The professional.

But it's *really* hard because jealousy is dense and heavy. It's suffocating and sticky. It can't easily be discarded or shook off.

"I'm sure she will." I take the bag and carve a smile into my stiff face. "Have a good night."

I know ... I just *know* he's not sleeping with Riley. That's not Shep. And while it's ridiculous to think I know him well enough to believe it with such certainty, I do. There's something about him that I've *known* since the day we met. That undeniable feeling.

"You too. Just call me when you find an evening that works to let the dogs play."

With my fake smile, I return a sharp nod. "You bet."

"It was good to see you," Shep says as I partially open the door.

I give myself five seconds ... five seconds to pretend I never met Jimmy which means I'm not in the middle of evicting him.

Five seconds to pretend Chloe's baby is inside her uterus and not mine.

Five seconds to pretend I can be more than friends with Shep.

Then I ram my foot into the mouth of those crazy ideas and continue out the door, leaving them in a pile of beat-up dead dreams behind me.

✳✳✳✳✳

"WHEN'S THE last time you ate dinner at home?" Jules asks as we catch the last few rays of the sun, and her kids burn off the last twenty percent of their energy for the day.

"I don't remember. How ... *how* did this happen? Jimmy should be the one holed up in his bedroom. Well, *my* bedroom because it's my house, and all of the bedrooms are mine. He should be the one hiding from me. I want my house back."

"Speaking of house ... how's pet store dude?"

"You know his name is Shep ... technically Marcus, but I'm sticking with Shep. And he has nothing to do with my house. What do you mean 'speaking of house?' Don't change the subject. I'm mad and I want you to do the BFF thing and agree with me. Feed my anger. Validate my emotions whether they are rational or not."

Her lips twitch as she shifts her attention to the kids in the pool. "You're absolutely right. What was I thinking? Jimmy is Satan. He needs to leave. And until then, he needs to stay out of your sight so you can invite pet store dude over to play hide the bone."

"You're being demoted. You're no longer my best friend."

Jules laughs. "What's your deal? You said you're just friends. You are *just* friends, right?"

It's tempting to stare at the sun until I go blind so I never have to look at Jules again.

She clears her throat. "I mean ... friends who play hide the bone."

"Not anymore. No bones. No boning. I'm as boneless as a chicken sandwich."

Jules snorts. "Oh dear ... did you manage to mess up your imaginary world? Is that even possible?"

"I didn't mess up ..." I bite my tongue for a few seconds. "Gah! Okay, he tied me to his bed. I was onboard. Like, yeah ... let's get kinky. Then my mind ran away, a racehorse out of the gate. And I decided it might crush me if I knew he was tying someone else to his bed. Hello feelings! And I bolted, sprinting after some sort of self-preservation that I'm certain no longer exists. Radio silence followed."

"You are a hot mess. Legit, Sophie. If I Googled 'hot mess' your profile pic would appear."

"I know," I say on a defeated sigh.

"Look at the bright side. It's a clean break. You knew the time would come. I realize you probably thought that time would involve your belly expanding, but this works too."

"When I didn't hear from him, I stopped by the shop."

"Sophie ..." Jules runs her hands through her hair and grumbles. "Shep World must be amazing."

I cringe. "It kinda is."

She stops pulling her hair and gives me the side eye. "He tied you up?"

Biting my lower lip, I nod.

"What's the admission into Shep World? Are we talking daily passes? Monthly? A punch card?"

I giggle. "Oh man ... why? Why did I have to meet him now? Why didn't I wait a year to pop into Wag Your Tail? It's not fair."

"Screw it. Tell him you're pregnant ... well, when you're allowed to share that news bulletin. And I'd say tell him about Jimmy, but really I think you should just ..."

"Dispose of Jimmy's body?"

Jules's jaw drops and she covers her mouth and her grin. "Sophie!"

I smirk, taking a sip of my drink. "It's the pregnancy hormones. I'm not thinking clearly. And I don't want to tell him I'm pregnant. I like how he looks at the non-pregnant version of me. And again, I do *not* regret being Chloe's surrogate."

"Some men find pregnant women quite sexy."

"Uh ... I think that's when said pregnant woman is pregnant with said man's child. It's pride that's channeled into lust. This isn't Shep's baby. I wouldn't be that adored pregnant woman in his eyes. I'd be his fat fuck buddy."

"Shh ... oh my god ..." she whisper-yells at me before giggling. "Hello! My kids are ten feet away."

"They can't hear me." I don't know this. Chances are they're hearing everything, but Jules won't know it for sure until they're in the middle of a family dinner with all the relatives packed around the table ready to pray. Then one of the kids will blurt out, "What's a fuck buddy?"

Oops ...

"Then it's over. You walk away now. Forget about him. Have Chloe's baby. Start dating again. No big deal."

No big deal ...

Is Shep no big deal? Is that why I fled his bed while dragging my undecided heart behind me? Do "no big deals" rent so much space in your head that you fear losing vital information like how to breathe, to not drool, and to complete sentences?

"He *is* no big deal. Right, Sophie?"

I give her my best "duh" smile and roll my eyes for added effect.

"Oh, god ... no, no no. Don't tell me you have feelings for him? Real feelings."

"What does that even mean?" I give her no more than a quick glance. Nope. She'll see right through me, and it's not pretty. "Feelings ... I have feelings for you. I love you. We're best friends. I have feelings for the people who work for me. And my patients ... I have feelings for them too. Humans feel all the time. It's impossible not to have feelings."

I *feel* her gaze on me, heavy and unblinking. "Was that fun? Concocting so much BS so quickly? Word sparring with me? You're a total politician. It's actually a little scary how easily that came to you. Which means ... you've been thinking about these 'feelings' for a while now. You've been building a defense for them. You should have been a lawyer instead of an eye doctor."

Tipping my chin up a fraction, I drum the pads of my fingers on my lips, keeping a close watch on the kids because they are not the ones judging me right now. "I might like him a little. So what?"

"You like him a little? Well, that's good to know. I think you should like a guy at least a little before you let him put his D-I-C-K inside of you."

I snort a laugh. "Your kids are eight and ten. I bet D-I-C-K is in their spelling vocabulary."

"I don't think their brains are in spelling mode. At least ... I hope not." She chuckles. "Parenting is nothing more than mind games. I say to my husband 'Don't be a Richard' when I'm upset with him. The girls ask what that means, and I tell them people named Richard are often silly. So they think I'm telling their father not to be so silly."

"Mom of the Year, Jules ... Mom of the Year." I chuckle.

"Shut up. You can't judge me until you've been a parent."

"I have Jimmy. He's a Richard. And he acts like a toddler. Doesn't that count?"

"Fair. I'll give you that."

"Here's the thing with Shep …" I sit up and turn to face her.

Jules grins, silently gloating like she knows me so well, and she probably does.

Yes, there's so many *things* about Shep.

"I'm sure he's emotionally scarred by his failed marriage, even if he'd never admit it. Yet, he's … easy. He's the person you like to be around. You know? That person who makes everyone around him feel comfortable and accepted. He's a smiling baby, a puppy or a kitten. I can't be with him and not feel joy. Effortless joy. He's the guy who shows up at the park with a pack of dogs because he can't imagine dogs at the shelter not getting to explore and play with other dogs just as much as his own dogs. He's the random phone call in the middle of the day with nothing all that important to say … he just wants to have a conversation because he likes the sound of your voice."

Jules mouths the word "wow" before whistling. "Dang, Sophie. Just … dang. You're—"

"I have pregnancy brain. I'm delusional. I'm dealing with Jimmy, and he makes absolutely any other guy seem amazing. Gray is white when you've been in the dark for so long. It's highly likely that I don't see the real Shep. He could be awful. I mean … he's divorced. What if it was him as much as her?"

Jules shrugs. "Let him go."

I frown. "I just … really like him."

Jules stands and wraps her towel around her waist.

"I suggest you *unlike* him, stay out of his bed, and walk away sooner versus later."

Unlike him.

Stay out of his bed.

Walk away.

Good plan.

I'm screwed.

CHAPTER
Twenty-Five

FIVE DAYS without a call or text from Shep feels like the perfect opportunity to *walk away*.

Done.

Over.

Problem solved.

Unfortunately, he's not my real problem. I'd rather deal with Shep than deadbeat Jimmy. I gave him notice. He's not gone. Jimmy has doubled, tripled, and quadrupled down on this. Now I have to make time to officially evict him, which, according to my attorney, could take *months*.

In my self-defeating mental state, I opt for the lesser of two evils as if avoiding both isn't an option.

"Roll over," I tell Cersei as we stand in a patch of dirt near my new driveway. They botched up my landscaping while replacing the driveway, and Jimmy didn't care to fix it. Maybe I can sue him for that. I make a mental note. For now, I'm taking advantage of the exposed dirt ... if my stubborn dog will roll in it.

Cersei stares at me; she shakes her head, actually her whole body. She rolls in dirt and shit all the time when I don't want her to, but now that I actually want her to do it, she wants nothing to do with it?

"Treat? Do you want a treat?" I hold up a treat. "Roll over."

It's a no-go.

"Fine. Have it your way." I grab a few dry clumps of dirt and rub them over her fur. When that doesn't seem to make a big difference, I retrieve my watering can and get the dirt wet. "Now we're talking."

After I sufficiently get her dirty, I dip my hands into the rest of the water and rinse them before wiping them on the sides of my denim shorts. It wouldn't hurt for me to look a little dirty and disheveled as well.

It takes us fifteen minutes to walk to Wag Your Tail to wash my dirty dog. There are a few other customers and dogs milling around the store. Two of the three dog wash stations are occupied. It's nice to know my dog isn't the only one that gets *so* dirty.

"Sophie." Marta smiles from the register as she helps a customer.

I return a smile and an easy nod.

"Looking for Shep?" she asks, swiping the customer's credit card.

"No ... I'm ..." I stutter for a few seconds, answering her honestly in my head. Yes, I'm looking for Shep. Yes, I dirtied my dog on purpose just for an excuse to come in here and take my sweet time washing her while giving Shep a chance to ... what? I'm not sure. I clear my throat. "Cersei got into some mud. I just need to wash her. If he's not here or if he's busy, it's no big deal. I really just came to wash her."

I no sooner start washing Cersei and Shep's

laughter fills the room. It gives me goose bumps. However, I pause a minute before glancing over my shoulder because I know that laughter isn't for me. Someone else is the lucky recipient of that level of happiness and the smile I'm sure accompanies it. As if my head is on a squeaky swivel that I don't want anyone to hear, I turn ever so slowly until I see Riley (the perky new employee) clinging to Shep's arm like it's the only thing keeping her standing as she cries in silent laughter.

Really, she should take a breath. I can't imagine what could be *that* funny. Unless they're talking about my life. It's hysterical. A tragicomedy.

A pickle.

A quandary.

A muddle.

"You kill me, Shep," Riley says as she peels herself from his arm and floats three feet away to assist a customer.

What's she doing here? I thought she was working weekends and every other Wednesday night. It's a Thursday.

"Your friend is here, Shep," Marta says, and I whip my head back around and focus on my dirty dog.

"Look what the cat dragged in," he says.

Dog. And Cersei hardly dragged me in here. It's really the other way around. Thank god she can't tell him that.

"Oh, hey." I smile when he positions himself on the opposite side of the wash bay.

"What happened? She looks like she rolled in mud? Where'd she get into mud? Did it rain when I was in the back room?"

Why does he have to be such a detective? Does it matter where she got into mud? Does he ask all the other customers twenty questions regarding the location and circumstances that led to their dogs needing a bath? I think not.

"I see Riley's working Thursdays now." That's my answer to his line of questioning.

"What?" Shep narrows his eyes. It takes him a few extra seconds to catch up to my shifting of the conversation away from my dirty dog antics to his new employee being here on a Thursday. My mind goes wild, like a pack of dogs off leash.

What were they doing in the back room?

Why must she lean on him when she's laughing?

Does she have a boyfriend squatting at her place?

Is she carrying someone else's baby?

Would she run out on Shep if he tried to tie her to his bed?

Am I losing my fucking mind?

So many good questions. Maybe I don't have a classic case of morning sickness driving me to stay in bed or remain within feet of a toilet, but something wonky is going on with my thoughts.

"Nothing." There's no need to repeat my Riley observation since I have no point in making it.

"Are you..." his confusion turns into a smirk "...jealous of Riley?"

"Do I look jealous of Riley?" I soap Cersei. It's an honest question because yeah, I feel jealous of Riley, and I'm curious if that really shows.

Shep helps me suds my wiggly dog. "I thought you were going to call me to meet up at the park."

"I thought *you* were going to call *me*," I say.

"The park was your idea. And I told you to call me when it would work for you."

Keeping my gaze on Cersei as I rinse her off, I shrug. "Well, clearly you didn't care to meet me since you weren't going to call if I didn't call."

"Really. What's going on here? I detect an angry tone. Have I done something wrong? After dinner with my parents and what happened following that, I assumed you needed some space. Was that not correct?"

I squeeze the excess water from Cersei's front side as he works on her backside. Shep has been doing all kinds of wrong things.

Smiling.

Laughing.

Flirting.

Looking sexy.

Existing on the same planet as my pregnant and unavailable self.

"I have a friend going through some ... *things*." I pause, eyeing him for a second as he works the towel over Cersei. "She broke up with her boyfriend, but he won't move out. Now she has to go through an actual eviction process which could take months to get him out."

Shep sets the towel aside and takes Cersei to the drying station. "Sounds about right." He nods.

"Right? No. There is nothing *right* about it. It's her house. The mortgage is in her name. She makes the mortgage payments. He hasn't even had—" I bite my tongue before my rant goes into overdrive.

"Typical." He shakes his head. "By 'right' I meant typical. I agree. He shouldn't have a right to stay there, but the law seems to allow good people to live on the street while protecting freeloaders."

"What should she do?" I ruffle Cersei's coat while Shep continues to dry it.

A smirk bends his lips. "She should have better taste in men."

Okay. I deserve that. *She* (imaginary friend) deserves that.

"For the record, the guy had a job when they met. And he was handsome and charming. My friend is a sucker for love; she simply has the worst luck with men."

"Maybe it's a sign."

"What do you mean?"

He shrugs. "Maybe she needs to figure out *why* she has the worst luck with men."

"It's luck, Shep, for which the whole mysterious concept implies lack of human control."

"I realize this. Meeting the wrong guy might be bad luck but allowing him to move in with her sounds more like a poor decision on her part."

"You know what I think it is?"

"I don't," he says. "But I'm sure you're going to tell me."

"I think she's too nice. And people take advantage of nice people, and then they make it seem like it's the nice person's fault, absolving themselves of any wrongdoing in the matter. I hate that ... you know? I hate when being nice becomes a flaw."

Shep's eyebrows lift a fraction. Does he think I'm losing it? I may have gone too far defending my "friend" and her niceness.

"So I guess my point is this ..." I have no point. Well, that's not entirely true. My silent point is that I'm attracted to Shep. I know I can't have him, nor should I want him even if my life weren't in a little disarray. However, I don't like watching him flirt with Riley. Or is he just being Shep?

I blow out a long breath. "We went from strangers to *conversing* friends to friends who golf and spend the weekend in Sedona. Then that crossed over into a new kind of best friend category. And I'll admit ... I had the 'when in Vegas' mentality. But now we're home. And you know I only offered you a temporary friendship, but ..."

But what? I have no clue.

Cersei buries her nose in the corner of the drying station. She wants nothing to do with my ridiculous antics to get Shep's attention.

"Okay." He nods slowly. "I keep forgetting about your arranged marriage, criminal activity, and homelessness. My bad. How about this ... you tell me exactly what you do and don't want from me. I endured the mind-fuck thing with Millie, and I'm kinda over it."

That's easy. I want Jimmy out. I want the gestational period for this baby to be six weeks instead of forty weeks. I want Riley to find a different job. And if I'm going big ... I'd like a tiny peek at Shep's retirement portfolio to calculate the chances of him needing free housing in the future.

"I like golfing. And spending time at the dog park."

Shep offers another slow nod, eyes slightly squinted. "So you want to be friends, the kind that golf and take their dogs to the dog park?"

I nod and Shep refocuses on Cersei's fuzzy butt.

"I like talking to you on the phone too," I add.

He grunts a laugh without giving me his gaze. "It would have been easier for you to have simply said you don't want a friends-with-benefits relationship."

He's so wrong. I want *all* the benefits.

"Can we do that? Can we go back to friends without benefits?"

"It's like you read my mind." He turns off the dryer when Cersei decides she's had enough.

"I read your mind?" I put Cersei's collar and leash around her neck.

"Yes." He saunters to the wash bin we used and begins to clean it.

"You wanted to go back to just friends again?"

"Yes." He sprays the basin.

"Why?"

"I don't know ... I think the company has been great. And I agree, talking on the phone is fun. Even the golf is enjoyable despite your unfair talent." He glances over his shoulder and winks at me before returning his attention to the basin. "But the *benefits* part was not up to par. And I've never been one for beating a dead horse, so I feel just as relieved as you do."

As soon as I can pick my jaw up from the floor, I will have a few words to say to Marcus Shepard. But for now, I'm utterly speechless. The sex? He doesn't think the sex with me was up to par? What the actual fuck?

Just as I start to unscramble my brain and the words make their way to my lips, Riley interrupts. "Are we out of the dehydrated duck feet?"

I am in the middle of a secret relationship crisis and she's asking about dehydrated duck feet?

Shep wipes his hands on a towel. "No. There's another box in back. I'll grab it." He gives me a smile. It seems a little generous for someone who is unhappy with my sexual performance. It must be the friend smile, not the *best* friend smile. "I can meet you next Monday night at the park. Or I can call you later to chat. Or we can golf this weekend?"

I have no clue how to respond to him. That's it? I'm a bad lover, but how about we get nine holes in this weekend? No. I don't accept this on the principle that I AM NOT BAD IN BED!

This is my ticket. A free ticket to get out of explaining why I will need to go approximately six months without seeing him in person. Before long, I'll have a little bump and our friendship will be over or put on a long pause. I'll need a good month after the birth to wrap my midsection like a heroine in a Victorian romance novel. It's not clear yet whether my vaginal region will be noticeably lax to someone who had once ventured into the tighter canal. And if I'd end up having a C-section, how would I explain that scar? What are the chances of Shep knowing the difference between a C-section scar and one left after say ... an appendix removal? But then ... Jesus ... what if I use the appendix excuse and then actually need my appendix out? Surely Shep knows humans only have one appendix.

These are moot points because Shep will never have sex with me again. I am the dead horse he won't beat.

"I have plans tonight," I say, even though I don't unless I can count plotting Jimmy's death as plans. "The dog park Monday sounds good."

Shep bites his bottom lip and nods. "Sounds good. You should go get a massage or something. I still sense a lot of pent-up anger."

I return a tight smile. "I'm good. See ya."

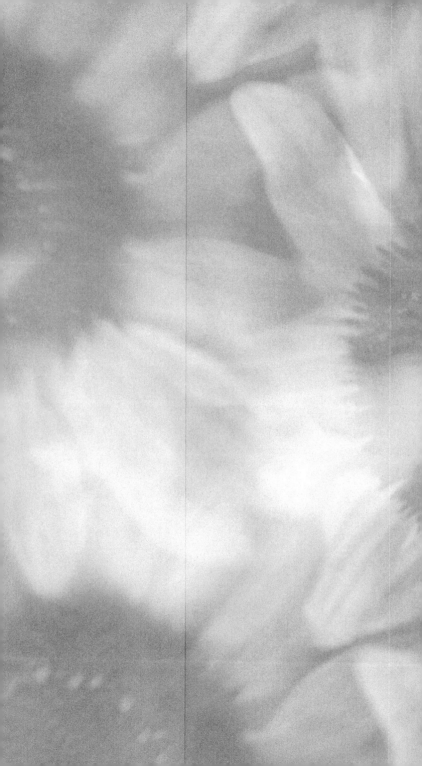

CHAPTER

Twenty-Six

"JUST GREAT ..." I mumble upon returning home from my disastrous planned encounter with Shep.

There's an Accord parked in the new driveway. Jimmy's entertaining someone at *my* house.

"There she is. You must be Sophie. I'm Kora, Jimmy's aunt. It's nice to meet you." She shoots me a grin as she trims Jimmy's hair in my kitchen.

Jimmy keeps his gaze on the television, totally ignoring me.

I grit my teeth. "Hi ... Kora." My attempt to keep from acting like a disgruntled bitch fails.

"Jimmy said you've been pretty busy lately, so he didn't want to burden you by asking you to give him a trim, so since I'm in town for a few days, I agreed to get him fixed up."

Burden me? Could she be more delusional?

"I see." I release Cersei from her leash and toe off my shoes. "I'm glad it worked out, especially since he's been dying to ask you if he can move to Tennessee and live with you since we broke up."

Jimmy shoots me a scowl.

"Oh ..." Kora pauses her trimming. "Jimmy, you

didn't say anything about that? Your mom said you and Sophie were working things out."

"We are." He returns his attention to the TV. "Sophie's been a little moody lately. I think she might be bipolar. One day she's all over me, and the next day she's screaming at me to move out. This must be a move out day. It's best not to engage with her today."

"Kora ..." I grab the scissors from her hand and slap them onto the counter. "I'm not bipolar. Your nephew is in denial. I've taken legal action to have him evicted. You should be embarrassed for him. He's the one who needs help, psychiatric evaluation or maybe an MRI to rule out a brain tumor. He either leaves on his own free will, maybe with your help, or the sheriff will physically remove him from my property. Is that what you want?" I rip the towel from around his neck and shake it before shoving it into Kora's chest.

"See what I mean?" Jimmy stands and brushes off his shorts. He's not wearing a shirt. Muscles. Tattoos. All the things that used to do it for me. I don't think I can ever date a guy with tattoos again. Jimmy has ruined it.

"Have you two looked into therapy?"

"I suggested it, but Sophie won't pay for it, and I don't have health insurance with my new job until I've been with them for thirty days."

"Kor..." I clap my hands once "...a." I clap them again, accenting each syllable of her name. "I don't need therapy. I need Jimmy to get the fuck out of my house."

She frowns. "Sweetie, that language is a little unbecoming of a lady."

"I'm not a lady. I'm a foul-mouthed bitch. And you should not want your nephew to be anywhere near me. I'm anxious. Stressed. And borderline *fucking* rabid!" I ball my fists. I feel rabid. Surely, I look it as well.

Baby. Baby. Baby.

I take a few deep breaths.

Kora flinches, but just barely. "Have you considered trying 5-HTP? I'm not a fan of prescription meds for depression and anxiety, but I take 5-HTP and it's helped me tremendously."

"I don't need 5-HTP. I need your nephew out of my life! I need both of you out of my house!"

Kora's frown deepens as she turns her head to the side a bit, eyes narrowed like my words slapped her. "You don't deserve Jimmy. But he loves you. And I know this because if he didn't love you, he wouldn't put up with you and your moods. So I suggest you take some time to get ahold of yourself and show a little gratitude for the man in your life who has done so much around your house, including the new driveway, taking care of your dog, cleaning, yard work, and when I showed up, he was dusting off that ceiling fan. And he could have fallen and broken his neck. Have you ever thought about that? I bet not. I bet you haven't stopped for one single second to think about anyone but yourself. I really don't understand what he sees in you, young lady, but I love him, so I support him and respect his heart's decision."

His heart's decision?

I close my eyes and slap my palms against my cheeks.

Wake up. Wake up. Wake up!

This isn't real life. This is too ridiculous to be real life. It's just one of those eerily real dreams where you try to wake yourself up, but you can't. And eventually, when you do wake up, you're in shock because everything felt too real. And it leaves an uneasy feeling in your stomach for days.

"Baby, stop. Let's get you to bed." Jimmy grabs my wrists to stop my incessant face slapping.

I yank my arms out of his grip. "I'm not your baby. I'm a victim in your stupid game—a gullible woman who fell for your synthetic charm. And now I'm stuck with you because your own family doesn't want you."

"That is not true, Sophie." Kora has the audacity to act offended.

"Then take him and leave!" I pound my bare feet to my bedroom with Cersei right behind me, and slam the door and fall onto my bed, screaming into my pillow.

In the middle of my tantrum, my phone rings. It's Chloe.

"Hey." I clear the anger from my throat and roll onto my back, staring at my ceiling fan, the one Jimmy didn't risk his life to dust.

"I'm on my way. I'm bringing you some clothes that Sarah gave me. I know you're not showing yet, but when you do, I don't want you to have to spend a bunch of money on maternity clothes. And you and Sarah are the same size."

Sitting up, back ramrod straight, I blow my bangs out of my face. "No. Don't come over. I'll stop by your house tomorrow and pick them up."

"Don't be ridiculous. I'm literally three blocks from your house. I was just making sure you were home; otherwise, I was going to get your garage code and leave them anyway."

"Actually, Chloe ... it might be a good idea to just leave them on the front porch. I'm just getting ready to jump in the shower."

"Well, unlock your door. I'll wait for you. I want to talk about some other things. Like the birthing classes. Mason and I want to attend them with you."

"Yep. Fine. No problem."

Chloe laughs. "Why are you acting so weird?"

"I'm not."

"Yes, you are. I'll see you in a few minutes." She disconnects the call.

"Shit. Shit. Shit!" I toss my phone aside and open my bedroom door like I'm trying to rip it off its hinges.

Jimmy's back in his spot on the sofa, and thank god Kora is gone.

"I'll give you fifty dollars to go to your room, not make a sound, and not come out until I tell you it's okay to come out."

He gives me a lifted eyebrow. "Let me guess ... you've invited your boyfriend over here. I want to meet him."

"No. Chloe's on her way. And she thinks you've moved out."

"Why does she think that?"

"Because I told her."

"Why did you lie to her?"

"Jesus Christ, Jimmy! Just go to your room."

"What do I get in return?"

"I just said I'd give you fifty dollars."

"I don't need your money."

Just my house and a death grip on my sanity.

"What do you want?"

"I want to stay and work things out."

"No." I cross my arms over my chest.

"Then I want a blowie."

"I'm not sucking your dick."

"Then I'm not getting off the sofa."

Everyone has a limit, maybe not the same limit, but *everyone* has one. I march into the kitchen and grab that gifted butcher knife. "I'm going to cut off your testicles."

"No you're not." He scoffs.

Gripping the knife tightly, I make a beeline for him, cock my arm back, and plunge the knife forward between his spread legs.

"The fuck?" He jumps back, covering his junk with one hand while eyeing the knife I just stabbed into the sofa cushion where his left testicle was just seconds earlier. "Are you insane?"

Yes. I'm officially insane. A docile optometrist by nature. My non-confrontational demeanor is what got me into this Jimmy situation. I need something bolder to get me out of this situation. Maybe that's destroying a sofa that I plan on burning after he leaves. Maybe that's removing a testicle. I'm not sure yet, but I'm going to figure it out.

"Not insane Jimmy ..." Okay, I can feel my wild eyes on the verge of busting a blood vessel or two; they might look deranged. "Fed up. I'm fed up with you and your assholiness. I'm spending way too much time thinking about all the ways I could make you leave my house and at least half of them involve your body being unresponsive and lacking a pulse." I remove the knife from my sofa cushion and rest it gently at my side while taking a slow breath and an easy step backward.

Jimmy releases an audible breath.

"It's not a threat. Don't think you can twist my words and use them against me. It's just a natural reaction to you fucking with my life. *You* are responsible for all of this. *You* are the culprit. *You* are the reason I feel twitchy and violent. If you poke a bear, bang a stick against a beehive, or step on a rattlesnake, you will get a violent reaction that is not the fault of the bear, the bee, or the snake. Do you understand what I'm saying?"

Jimmy's wide-eyed gaze ping-pongs between me and the hole in the sofa just inches from his man parts. "I'll move out tonight for fifty grand."

I have the knife. He should be paying *me* fifty grand not to kill him, maim him, castrate him. "Sleep with one eye open, asshole."

The doorbell rings.

My grip on the knife handle tightens again.

His gaze flits to the knife. "I'll go to my room." He slowly stands, throat bobbing. "It will cost you."

With Chloe at my door, I don't have time to negotiate any sort of cost. As he makes his way to the bedroom, I quickly return the knife to the block and hide his shoes and hoodie by the door before opening it.

"Hey." I smile.

Chloe eyes me a second before stepping inside, a bag in each hand. "You okay?"

"Yeah. Absolutely."

I'm not okay. When Chloe calls me complaining that her newborn baby is unsettled and colicky all the time, I'll know it's Jimmy's fault.

CHAPTER
Twenty-Seven

"ORANGE FRAMES. I think they're my favorite," Shep says when I get about ten feet from him and release Cersei to play.

I instinctively adjust said orange glasses and smile. "Thanks. How are you?" I'm so good at small talk and really proud of myself for not starting the conversation with, "Why do you think I'm bad in bed?"

"Better now." He grins.

I want to walk right into his arms and rest my cheek on his chest. I want to tell him that my friend with the squatter boyfriend is me and that I'm thinking, saying, and doing the most awful things. Who was that woman who tried to skewer a man's testicle? In high school, I was voted Most Likely to Join the Peace Corps. We didn't have a Most Likely to go to Prison, but that would have been Robbie Hartgrave or, come to find out, more accurately, Sophie Ryan.

"Want to golf this weekend?"

I nod.

Why do you think I'm bad in bed?

I smile.

You seemed to enjoy it. You said "fuck" and you sweated and ... why? Why? Why? WHY?

I clear my throat.

"Are you okay?"

I nod ... and smile.

"Can you speak?" He laughs.

I bite my lips together and take a deep inhale. "Sorry," I say on the exhale. "It's weird. I've never taken a step back like this, so I'm trying to figure out how to act or what to say. There's an order. Friends. Flirting. Lovers. Break up. Going in reverse is weird. Lovers to friends. What's the protocol? Do I ask you about your dating life? Do I tell you about mine?"

"Oh ..." His eyebrows lift. "You're dating?"

"No. Of course not. It's been two seconds since we stopped..." my nose crinkles "...doing whatever we were doing. I was just using it as an example. I don't know what to talk about."

"How's your mom been since her cat died? Are you nervous about your arranged marriage?"

I grin. How does he make it look so easy? Oh that's right ... he wasn't the bad lover. "I'm a little nervous about my *arranged* marriage. And my mom is fine, I guess. I haven't talked with her lately. My dad called and wants me to go to California and golf with him in two weeks."

"Sounds fun."

I nod. "Yeah, it should be fun. What about you? Any plans to travel?"

"Nah. Just working. Unless my new friend invites me to California to golf with her and her famous dad."

Averting my gaze to the dogs chasing each other, I

give him a nervous laugh. "I'm sure my dad would love to play golf with you, but he wouldn't understand our friendship."

"Now see ... that's the problem. When did it become so unnatural for men and women to be just friends?"

"Since you didn't want to tell your parents you took a woman to Sedona instead of your male friend. *And* since we had bad sex in Sedona." There. I slip that in there. He pitched the perfect ball; how could I not hit it out of the park?

Shep smirks, rubbing the pads of his fingers over his mouth. He can't erase his amusement no matter how hard he tries. "Well..." he glances at the dogs instead of holding my gaze "...now that we got that *experience* over with, we can be friends who go to California to golf instead of having bad sex."

WHY WAS IT SO BAD?

"I'm not inviting you into my world."

"I invited you into my world."

"Yes, but I didn't ask to be invited. In fact, I fought you on it."

"I didn't ask to be invited into your world. I suggested you invite me into your dad's world. At this point, I don't even care if you go. I'm good with playing golf with just your dad."

"Are you seriously trying to hijack my golfing trip with *my* dad?"

"Why are you making this so difficult?"

I roll my eyes. "Because I can. Because I should."

"You worry too much."

"I worry an adequate amount."

Shep smirks. "So that's a yes to me going with you?"

"What would I tell my dad?"

"We were best friends, but that didn't work out, so now we're just friends—the really mature kind who *can* go reverse in relationship status."

I shake my head slowly. This is a bad idea. Everything about Marcus Shepard has been a bad idea. Why can't I say no to bad ideas?

"Are you flying or driving?" he asks.

"Driving."

"Great. If I go, you won't have to drive the whole way. You can kick back, read a book, take a nap ..."

I shake my head, but I can't help but grin. "I don't know."

"Think about it and let me know. If you don't want me to go, I get it. I'm sure it's nice to spend time alone with your dad."

I grunt. "It's never time alone with him. His wife Taryn is always with us. She's a shitty golfer."

"Worse than me?"

I smirk and giggle. "Just barely, but yes."

"Is she younger than your dad?"

I roll my eyes. "She's younger than me, by a year."

"Ouch."

I shake my head, watching the dogs chase the ball that Shep throws. "I'm not bothered by her age. He adores her; that's all that matters. It's not like I hate her.

She's a yoga instructor and her family owns a winery. My dad hates wine, but it's a secret. He's never had the nerve to tell her that. I think he's hoping it's an acquired taste, but he has yet to acquire it. So if you like wine, then she will love you."

"So..." Shep slides his hands into his front pockets "...that's a yes. Right? You said she'll love me, that means I'm invited?"

Shit ...

I shake my head. "Hypothetically. That's what I meant. I haven't decided yet." Too bad I can't say that without grinning.

"Oh ... I'm *so* going." He takes a step closer, keeping his hands in his pockets. "You want me to go because I'm your favorite friend."

I shake my head. "Jules is my best friend."

"Yes, but I'm your favorite."

"Favorite and best are the same thing."

He shakes his head slowly. "No. They're not. George Clooney is my best dog. He's better behaved and knows more tricks. But Julia Roberts is my favorite dog because she's a lovable daddy's girl. So Jules can be your best friend because you've been friends for so long, but I'm your favorite friend because I golf and I'm available at a moment's notice."

A little uneasy in his close proximity, I clear my throat and lift my gaze to his. "Funny, for a short bout of time you said *we* were best friends."

"No. We were *best* friends—accent on best. Think of it like a two-year-old being a naughty girl and a twenty-five-year-old being a *naughty* girl. See the difference? Hear the difference?"

"For someone with dyslexia, you sure do have a lot of opinions about the English language."

Shep barks a laugh, throwing his head back. "Touché."

CHAPTER
Twenty-Eight

SHEP

"WHAT'S CAROLINE DOING?" I ask Howie as I take a seat at the bar he's tending tonight. He's owned this sports bar for almost a decade. I've occasionally filled in as bartender like he's doing tonight. It's a fun gig.

"Working late." He eyes me while mixing a drink, daring me to suggest his darling wife might be screwing her boss.

I say nothing.

"Beer?"

I nod.

"How's the eye doctor?"

"Depends on the day." I wrap my hand around the cold mug of beer. "She's a little too mysterious for my taste. At first it was fun, but now it's just confusing. I've been stripped of my benefits."

"Benefits?"

I grin before taking a swig of beer. Then I nod. "Friends with benefits ... now without benefits."

"Then what's the point?"

I chuckle under my breath. "Good question." I

shrug. "She's the female version of me. And I never imagined saying this, but I kinda dig female me."

Giving me a lifted eyebrow, he runs a transaction through the register. "That's messed up."

"She's ... fun. Sexy. Competitive. And she makes me laugh like no other. I'm talking laughing until I have tears in my eyes. And I haven't found a good explanation for it other than to say that the days I get to see her or talk to her are really incredibly good days. And the days I don't ... well..." I take another swig of beer "... they're a little less ... everything."

He nods while wiping the bar beside me, an intent expression on his face. "Millie's pregnant."

Squinting at Howie, I wait for him to repeat himself. It sounded like he said Millie's pregnant, but that's ridiculous.

Biting his lips together, he gives me a slow nod.

I grunt, a stabbing feeling in my chest making it hard to breathe as an onslaught of emotions collide, unearthing resentment I thought I'd laid to rest many months ago.

"Random hookup guy. Caroline said it just happened. A few too many drinks. Hell, they didn't even make it to her place or his. She's keeping it. I guess the guy thought he was sterile. It's the reason his previous marriage ended. Caroline said he's elated, and Millie's not exactly bummed about it either. Sorry, man."

"I..." my head inches back and forth. "...I don't ..."

"Millie was messed up, Shep. Hell, I think she's still messed up. She's changed. It was never you. It was her. Millie changed so much from the person you married. Call it a midlife crisis, call it ... whatever. You weren't going to please her."

"She didn't want a baby," I whisper, unblinkingly staring at my beer. "I ... I wanted a baby. Not ... her."

"I know," Howie says just above a whisper. "Caroline says it's sometimes hard to know what you want until you just ... have it. The best things in life come without warning. But I'm not sure that's true. I think her saying that to me, under the illusion that she's explaining Millie's behavior, is actually a warning to me."

I lift my gaze to his.

Howie tries to smile, but it's not working. I see his pain. Hell, I *feel* it. "And I don't think what's coming my way is good."

"Howie ..."

He shakes his head. "She works late. We don't have sex. When I touch her, she pulls away and blows it off like I'm being obnoxious or something. And sometimes I can be, but lately, I've just wanted to touch my wife. You know?"

"Yeah ... I know all too well."

After one beer, I head home, calling Sophie on the way. It's been several days since we've talked. I just need her voice. That's all.

Her phone goes straight to voicemail. "You've

reached Dr. Sophie Ryan, please leave a detailed message." It's not her, but it's her voice ... and for now, that's enough.

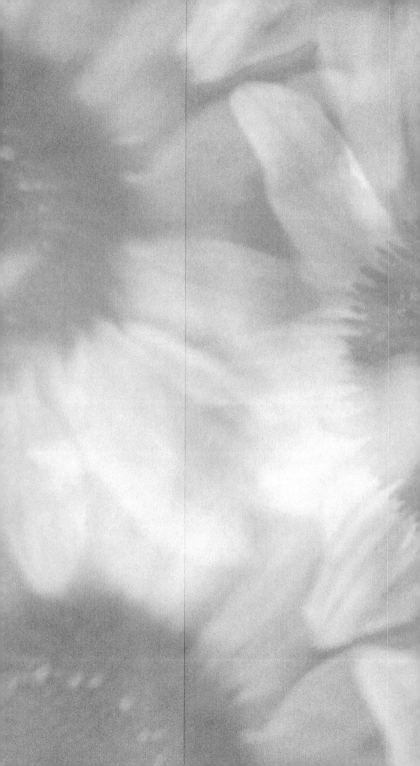

CHAPTER
Twenty-Nine

SOPHIE

WE DO IT.

We manage to digress back into the friendship category—conversing on the phone several times a week about work, current events, and our dogs.

We take the dogs to the park. Shep shows me his brewing setup in his garage. And we golf twice before our trip to Santa Monica.

However, Shep's been a little different, a little less than his usual jovial self. It's subtle, but noticeable. As much as I want to ask him about it, I don't know if I want the answer. Avoiding personal details, *reality,* is what makes this friendship work.

Jimmy? Oh, he died. That's what I tell myself. In actuality, he's been residing in his room when I'm home. He doesn't leave the house for work. He has groceries delivered. And he's stopped walking Cersei while I'm at work. I'm certain he's scared of me, yet vengeful. He's not a telemarketer; he's a full-time asshole living only to ruin my life. And he knows ... he *knows* I will change the locks on the house if he leaves for so much as a trip to the end of the driveway.

I'm biding my time. Waiting for the justice system to do its job.

Since we're taking my car to Santa Monica, I pick Shep up, which means I don't have to make up some excuse for him to pick me up at work instead of home.

"Where's Cersei?" Shep asks as he tosses his bag in the back of my car.

After he gets into the passenger's seat, I smile. "She's with my sister and her husband."

I can't give Jimmy any more ammunition. He's already declared himself the primary caregiver for *my* dog.

"Is Millie keeping Julia and George?"

"Yes. I'll have them next week and the following week while she's in Florida for more training. There's a new product line they're launching next month, and she wants me to mention it to you in case you're interested. So there, I told you. You're not interested. And I think you look nice today."

I giggle. "Thanks. You look nice today too."

He glances down at his basic white tee and gray shorts. "Ya think?"

"I do."

After two hours, we swap and Shep drives the rest of the way to Santa Monica. He seems content listening to music while I crochet and try not to think of all the things Jimmy might do to my house while I'm out of town. What other things will he "update" to use as evidence that he deserves to stay indefinitely?

"Soph!" Dad pulls me into his arms as soon as he opens the door.

"Hey, Dad. Good to see you."

He holds me at arm's length. "You look different."

I stiffen. There's no way he notices I'm pregnant. My stomach is still flat.

"Uh ..." I return a nervous laugh.

"You're glowing, baby. Life must be treating you well." He releases me.

I nod several times. "Something like that. This is my friend, Shep. Shep, this is my dad, Dalton."

"Nice to meet you." Dad shakes Shep's hand.

"The pleasure's all mine. Sophie's told me all about you."

"All lies, I'm sure." He winks at me and steps aside to let us inside his single-story, three-bedroom, mid-century style home. It's filled with solid wood floors and contemporary furnishings, stained glass windows, and French doors leading to a nice sized lot enclosed with greenery in every direction. It's not the family home I grew up in, but I've always felt welcomed and at home here.

"So what do you do, Shep?" My dad dives right into the important questions as he leads us toward the bedrooms.

"I work at a pet store in Scottsdale," Shep answers without any sort of hesitation.

"So ..." Dad turns. "I'm not as old fashioned as my daughter has probably led you to believe. Just be straight with me. Are you friends who sleep in the same bedroom or separate bedrooms? I'm fine with whatever."

"Separate," I blurt out so quickly it elicits raised brows from both men. Clearing my throat, I offer a sheepish grin. "Just friends, Dad. Nothing more."

"Okay, baby. Then you know where your bedroom's at." He nods to my room on the right. "Shep, make yourself at home in here. I think the bed has been slept in less than a dozen times. You can use the bathroom two doors down on the right. Taryn ran to the market to get something to throw on the grill."

"Thanks, Dalton. I really appreciate your hospitality." Shep gives my dad a polite smile and nod before taking his bag into the guest room as I deposit my bag in my room just opposite his.

"It's not as fancy as your parents' place in Sedona," I say, slipping back into his room and plopping down on the bed as he opens the blinds and peers out the window at the yard. "But it's close to the pier, the beach, and so many great restaurants and shops. I know how much you love to window shop."

Shep turns toward me, slipping his hands into his pockets. "Only with you."

"Liar." I giggle.

"Everything's better with you."

"Liar," I say again, but in a whisper.

He gives me the most cryptic expression. A half smile. An intensity in his brow and eyes.

"Sometimes, I wish I could read your mind," I say.

And just like that, his expression morphs into one

hundred percent mischief. "I don't know if you're mature enough to read my mind."

"Mature enough?" I sit up straight and fold my legs in front of me.

"Mature enough ..." he echoes, taking a few steps toward me and pushing my glasses up my nose even though they're up plenty far. "Have you always looked this cute in glasses?"

I laugh. "No. And I'm not sure I look cute in them now."

"Speaking of spectacles ... are you going to make a spectacle of me tomorrow when we golf with your dad?"

"You mean am I going to let you beat me?"

"I'm pretty sure golfing with a great like your dad will elevate my game. On the off chance that you have a lucky day, are you going to gloat?"

My head cocks to the side. "I don't elevate your game?"

He shrugs a shoulder.

"Shep, I will beat you tomorrow. I will likely beat my father as well. Pretending otherwise is just ... beating a dead horse. And I know how much you don't like to beat a dead horse."

A funny expression steals his face. Does he honestly not remember saying it?

I stand and straighten my T-shirt before folding my arms over my chest. "If you can't hold your own tomorrow, physically or emotionally, then you shouldn't have invited yourself on this trip."

"I can hold anything I need to hold or that you need me to hold. Thanks for your concern."

"Hey!"

Our attention goes to the doorway and Taryn's bleached smile with red lips. I catch my nose crinkling into something distasteful while eyeing her black braided pigtails wound into two buns on the top of her head like a young girl in middle school. She looks too young for my dad. Hell, she looks like she could be my daughter.

"Hi, Taryn." I pad my way to her and submit to her open arms. She's decorated like a Christmas tree in necklaces and bracelets.

Nose ring.

Half dozen earrings in each ear.

A full sleeve of tattoos on her right arm.

"Taryn, this is my friend, Shep."

Taryn eyes Shep a little too long before shifting her gaze to me. "*Just* friends?" She holds out her hand, all the while giving me a conspiratorial look.

I think she's salivating, seconds from sprinkling a little salt onto him and devouring him right in front of me.

"Just friends," Shep says while taking her hand and giving her his best smile. "Nice to meet you, Taryn. Thanks for allowing me to stay in your beautiful home."

"Mi casa es su casa," she says without releasing his hand.

"What's for dinner?" I ask, forcing the lingering handshaking to end.

"Fish and wine." Taryn smiles. "Good for the heart. In fact, let's open a few bottles now. Shep, did Sophie mention my family owns a winery?"

We follow her to the kitchen, where my dad is already opening a bottle of wine that I know he hates. She has him trained quite well. As much as that thought disturbs me, it's amazing what a guy will do when he's thoroughly pussy whipped.

"She did. My ex and I used to visit wineries all the time."

That's right. How did I forget that?

"Shep's an expert brewer," I say.

He coughs, shaking his head. "I'm not. To put it in my sister's words, I'm a man child conducting science experiments in my garage."

Everyone laughs. He's probably right. After seeing his setup and all the bottles of failed attempts, I now realize his brewing talent is about as well-honed as my crocheting talent.

"We should go to the winery," Taryn says. "If you're not into golfing, I'd be happy to take you there tomorrow while Dalton and Sophie golf. They are so competitive; it's not exactly an enjoyable outing." She winks at my dad and takes the glass of wine he offers her.

"As tempting as that is ... I actually love golf. I think I elevate Sophie's game. Without me, I'm certain Dalton will win." Shep is so full of shit.

"Then you should go with Taryn tomorrow," Dad says to Shep while smirking at me.

I roll my eyes at the absurdity of everything that's being floated in the air to get a reaction out of me.

"Sophie?" Taryn tries to hand me a generous glass of wine.

"I'm uh ... off alcohol for a bit."

She and my dad eye me with suspicion because I love wine. It's really what won me over with Taryn. I hated that he chose someone young enough to be his daughter, but since her family owned a winery, I was willing to overlook it.

"Are you cleansing?" Taryn asks.

I smile and shrug. "Uh ... yeah."

"Oh! I did one last month." Taryn sets the glass of wine down on the counter. "I'll make you a green juice."

"Water's fine. Really."

"No. You need to keep things moving. Since you've been in the car all day, I bet you haven't pooped much. Have you?" She breaks out her juicer and retrieves a head of kale and a lemon from the fridge.

Through the corner of my eye, I notice Shep's hiding his grin behind his glass of wine.

God ... I miss wine.

I also miss having dinner with my family and not talking about my bowel movements.

"I had to incorporate a little smooth move tea to keep things going. Ya know?"

Shep can't hold it. He sniggers and so does my dad.

"I'm good, Taryn. Really. It's not a hardcore cleanse. It's really just … no alcohol, less salt and processed sugar …"

"And no fish." Shep feels the need to add that.

"Of course," Taryn flicks her wrist. "I'll throw some things into a pot for a detox soup. You can basically eat that for all your meals. Easy peasy."

"Thanks," I mumble. Why did I come here? It's simple to hide the baby belly I don't have or the morning sickness I don't have. It's harder to hide my special pregnancy diet.

"Yum …" Shep whispers in my ear while also succumbing to the unnecessary pinching of my side just before following my dad out to the patio and grill. Men have it so easy. Give them a drink and a grill, and life is good.

If a man says he's not drinking, a collective "awe …" fills the air. He's clearly a recovering alcoholic. Everyone decides to go dry for the night in a heroic act of solidarity. But when a woman says she's not drinking, it means she's pregnant or on a cleanse. Why did no one assume I'm an alcoholic? Or pregnant for that matter? I could get knocked up as easily as the next chick.

It's the glasses. Boring optometrist. Cute glasses. Basic to the bone.

I'm going to slaughter Shep's ass on the golf course tomorrow.

✳✳✳✳✳

UNDER A STRING of lights with Alexa playing my dad's favorite Sinatra hits, we eat the catch of the day, empty bottle after bottle of Collymore wine, and listen to a play-by-play of my dad's brush with stardom as an almost-PGA player.

And by we ... I mean them.

I have to get up every ten minutes to pee. I don't laugh at everything that's said like it's a joke when it's not. Being the only sober one is like being the only one on the bench that never gets put into the game.

This is the first time I've seen Shep kinda tipsy. It's in his eyes. Drunk eyes can't lie. He's thinking really inappropriate things about me and wetting his lips like Cersei after a spoonful of peanut butter. The wine must have blurred his memories of our subpar sex.

During my fifty-seventh trip to the toilet, I text Chloe. It's not her fault I'm here on a freaking juice cleanse. And I don't ever want her to feel like this pregnancy is inconveniencing me—except tonight. I want her to know my level of dedication to this baby.

Me: Taryn is forcing me to drink gallons of green juice and eat vats of detox soup because I'm not drinking wine, which means I'm on a cleanse.

I take a selfie on the toilet and send it to her.

Chloe: Don't tell them!

I roll my eyes. Did she miss my point? I'm not

telling them. I'm drowning in piss and my tummy is churning in the worst possible way.

Me: If I were telling them, I wouldn't be camping on the toilet!
Chloe: Don't detox too much. You shouldn't detox while pregnant. Eat a potato with butter. Apple with peanut butter.

"Jesus ..." I bend forward as my stomach cramps up. I need to fart or shit or something. It was the soup. What did Taryn put in that soup?

Me: Gotta go.
Chloe: Love you. Xo

"Yeah, you'd better love me," I mumble as my stomach muscles cease up rock hard.

Just as my anal sphincter starts to relax to let out ... god knows what, there's a knock at the bathroom door.

"You okay? I need to take a piss."

Just the sound of Shep's voice makes my hole squeeze into a tight fist. I have never been this miserable in my life.

"Um ..." I wipe, flush, and wash my hands. I can't even stand straight because my stomach hurts so much. I'm sweating, and my glasses are fogged up. "All yours," I manage to say without my voice straining too much as I squeeze past him, avoiding all eye contact.

"You okay?" He grabs my arm.

I'm a water balloon at capacity, the slightest squeeze to any part of my body might cause a catastrophic explosion. If that happens, I will never *ever* be able to look Shep in the eye again. I will have to change my name and move to someplace like Tanzania, where I'll hire a stork to return Chloe's and Mason's baby to them after I give birth standing up, dancing with a birthing pole, and moaning like a cow until it just drops onto the ground. I'm pretty sure I saw a video where that happened—maybe not the dropping onto the ground part.

"Fine," I squeak, doing something between a waddle and walk to the kitchen in search of the most absorbent food I can find.

No apples.

No potatoes.

They have rice, but I don't think my bowels will hold out for twenty minutes while it cooks. In the fridge, there's a loaf of gluten free bread. I steal a slice and squat in the corner by the lazy Susan, eating the dry, cold, piece of cardboard.

And then I pray.

Please don't let me shit my pants.

Please don't let me explode.

Please don't let anyone hear me if I do.

Please don't let it stink up the whole house.

Please just let me die if you can't prevent the aforementioned from happening.

Yours truly, regards, sincerely, amen,

Dr. Basic Sophie Ryan, OD

The bathroom door opens, and I wait to hear the click of the guest bedroom door shutting. It's bedtime. We have an early morning. Everyone just needs to go to bed.

"Sophie, what's going on?"

I glance up at tipsy Shep as he crosses his arms over his chest, looking down on me in what feels like a literal and proverbial way.

Forcing myself to swallow the dry, bland bread, I grab the edge of the counter and pull myself up. "It's late. I'm going to bed. Night, Shep."

"Too much juice?" He narrows his glossed-over eyes.

"Too much juice ..." I murmur, making a beeline for the bathroom.

I barely get my pants to my knees before Shep knocks on the door again. "Sophie, are you sure you're okay?"

"Fine!" I cringe at my sharp tone. "I'm showering. Go drink." I reach for the exhaust switch and turn it on for some noise, but it's not enough so I turn on the faucet.

That's still not enough. Next, I turn on the shower.

The first explosive burst releases. I suck in a big breath and freeze, willing my ass to cooperate and hold it in a little longer until I can find more ways to drown out the sound. My last option is my phone, so I turn on a song. Any song. And I turn the volume all the way up.

For the next sixty seconds, I thoroughly detox to AJR's "Burn the House Down."

Since the bathroom is filled with steam anyway, I go ahead and shower. How is this my reality? What did I do to deserve this? I am a vessel for life—the ultimate gift and what feels like the ultimate sacrifice at the moment.

Wrapping a towel around my body and hugging my clothes to my chest, I slowly open the door. Lucky for me, if I can call anything "luck" at this point, it's that they are still outside. Bolting into my room, I shut and lock the door.

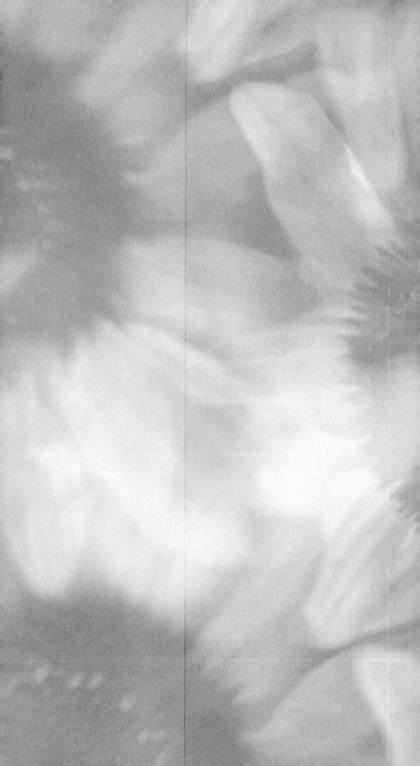

CHAPTER *Thirty*

"FEELING BETTER, PEANUT?" Dad asks as I round the corner to the kitchen. Shep's door is closed, and Taryn is nowhere in sight.

My dad only calls me Peanut when he thinks I need to be coddled.

I shrug, grabbing a mug and pouring my one allotted cup of coffee. "Fine." I act as though it's a silly question.

Dad sips his coffee as I lean against the counter and sip mine. "You really tore it up in the bathroom last night."

"Daaad!" I turn my back to him and stare out the window to the patio. I don't care who it is. Mom. Dad. Best friend. It's embarrassing to talk about explosive diarrhea with anyone, even a doctor. It's the most unflattering thing a human does. My face burns with embarrassment.

"Maybe you should ease off the cleanse. Are you going to be able to golf today? It could be a trek to the restroom if the urge hits."

"Jeez ... just ..." I shake my head and pinch the bridge of my nose. "I'm fine. Can we not discuss this like ... *ever again*?"

"I'm just saying we were a little concerned about you last night."

"We?" I cringe, slowly turning back toward him.

"It was a little ..." He smirks behind his steaming mug of coffee. "Loud."

My heart sinks into my stomach. "Who heard?" I whisper past my dying breath.

Dad rubs his lips together, and that's my answer. Everyone heard.

"Dad, I need you to take Shep golfing. I'm going to drive home after you leave. I'll buy him a one-way ticket back to Phoenix if you'll kindly drive him to the airport."

"Soph, it's nothing to be embarrassed about. It happens to everyone at some point. When Taryn did her cleanse, she was a little bloated and gassy for a few days while everything worked its way out."

"You *heard* me," I whisper yell. "I wasn't 'a little gassy.' I was a goddamn volcano. Taryn and her stupid green juice and detox soup. I'm not on that kind of cleanse. I'm not really cleansing at all. I'm simply temporarily restricting a few things from my diet. Is that okay? Can I do that without some long explanation as to why I'm doing it?"

My dad is the best. Really. I have to hand it to him; he's doing a phenomenal job of holding back his reaction as he clears his throat. "Sorry, Peanut. You're right. Taryn went a little overboard. I'll tell her to let you do you, and no one will say another word. Okay?"

I frown. "I'm going to get ready."

"Here." He tosses me a banana. "This will help slow things down."

"Why me?" I mumble, sulking toward the bedroom.

Before I can close the door, Shep's door opens, and we make eye contact for a full second before I avert my gaze to the floor. "Morning," I murmur while closing my door.

He jolts forward, pressing his hand to it so I can't close it. "Sorry I had a little too much wine last night. That was bad on my part since you're not drinking right now."

I wait, inspecting my toenails painted black.

I wait awhile longer. Nothing.

Slowly risking a glance up, Shep greets me with a smile, a normal smile. Did he really not hear me last night? Impossible.

Maybe he drank so much he doesn't remember. That would be an acceptable gift from God. Or is he being nice, really nice to me, by not bringing it up?

"It's fine. I'm glad you had a fun evening. I'm going to get dressed. Help yourself to coffee." I shut the door without giving him a chance to respond.

Taryn doesn't mutter a word to me about cleansing on our way to the golf course. Dad must have said something to her. Shep plays the role of the drunk who forgot the night before or maybe the really nice gentleman role. I'm still not sure which one. Occasionally, my dad glances at me in the rearview mirror and gives me a look. It's the fatherly pride look. Daddy dearest saves the day by silencing everyone from mentioning my explosive diarrhea episode.

"The banana help?" Dad whispers in my ear as soon as I get out of his Lexus sedan.

I give him a quick nod and grab my clubs from Shep, murmuring a clipped "thank you." I wish I knew for sure what he does or doesn't remember. Not knowing is its own kind of torture. But what am I supposed to say? *Do you remember that explosion that came out of my ass last night?*

"We're good at this," Shep says as he drives the cart to the first tee.

"At golf?"

He shakes his head, a secret hidden in his grin. "Living."

"As opposed to dying?" I snort.

"Well … yeah. It's not a holiday. You have a job. I have a job. Yet, here we are in Santa Monica playing golf on a regular ole Tuesday. I didn't have to work that hard to talk you into inviting me, and my guess is your dad didn't have to twist your arm to plan this visit. We're good at the good stuff in life. Ya know?"

I nod slowly. "Was Millie not good at the good stuff? I thought you golfed with her and visited vineyards." *And had six-thirty a.m. sex that wasn't like beating a dead horse.*

"We did. But she wasn't good at it. With Millie, I always felt like every moment was spent planning the next one, like she always lived five steps into the future, which meant she never really lived at all."

Living in the moment is good. It means we don't have to think about the previous night that involved cleansing or the future that involves my belly expanding.

"Have you talked to Jimmy lately?" Taryn asks as we come to a stop at the first tee. "I never asked if things ended amicably between the two of you. I assumed so since you don't have a mean bone in your body."

Taryn doesn't know about Shep World, where Shep doesn't know about Jimmy. She met Jimmy a month after we started dating. I'm not sure why they hit it off, but they did. Maybe she and my dad will adopt Jimmy, let him move in with them, and rehabilitate him before releasing him to the real world where things like holding a job, paying rent, and valuing a little dignity matter.

"I heard he's working as a telemarketer." I shrug, avoiding eye contact with Shep. I feel his gaze on me. "And his grandma died not that long ago." Look at me being honest. Not a mean bone in my body. Nope. Never once have I thought of doing bodily harm to Jimmy.

"Oh, that's too bad." Taryn takes a practice swing. "If you see him, give him my condolences."

I mumble a quick "sure" while slipping on my glove.

"Jimmy ..." Shep says just above a whisper as he hands me my driver.

I lift my gaze to his, waiting for him to elaborate. Jimmy what?

No, Shep. You don't need to know about Jimmy.

He doesn't elaborate. All I get is two seconds of Shep's contemplative gaze on me before he pushes my white-framed transition glasses up my nose until I have to wrinkle my nose to let them slide back down a bit. Sometimes I think he pushes them up so far just to annoy me.

This is where I'd normally ask if he's jealous of this mysterious Jimmy guy, but his bad sex comment has my ego in a bit of a chokehold.

"Why do you insist on messing with my glasses?"

He smirks. "Just getting in your head, Dr. Ryan. Just ... getting in your head ..." he says before following my dad and Taryn to tee off.

"Nice, baby," Taryn verbally applauds my dad's long drive after she shanks it five yards.

"After you." Shep nods for me to go.

As my ball sails through the air, headed straight for the green, my dad and Shep whistle together.

I bite back my grin and saunter toward the cart.

"You and your smooth stroke," Shep says, returning his club to his bag.

"It's not everyone's taste," I murmur as I take a seat on the driver's side.

Shep eyes me, a half grin stuck to his handsome face as he scoots in next to me. *Yes, Shep, I'm driving. I'm winning. I'm going to dominate your ass for the next four hours.*

"Are we still talking about golf?" He adjusts his black baseball cap. "Or are you talking about other kinds of strokes?"

I stomp on the accelerator, forcing him to grip the dash. "Golf, of course."

"Are you sure?"

"Stop beating a dead horse." I slam on the brakes, pluck my iron from my bag and wait for Taryn to hit two more times so I can head to my ball. Shep's long fingers cuff my arm, tugging me toward him.

I give his cocky grin one second of my attention before averting my gaze to the fairway over his shoulder.

"Are you … upset over what I said at the store?"

"No."

"Bullshit."

My head shakes a half dozen times.

"You've alluded to it before. You're upset. But why? Why would you care what I think when you don't want to be more than friends?"

I don't have to look directly at him to see all the creased lines of satisfaction on his face.

I yank my arm from his hold and march my cleated shoes toward my ball … and I. SHANK!

"Whoa … what happened?" my dad asks on a chuckle.

"It's my fault," Shep chimes from behind me. "I got in her head a while back. I said no one person can be great at everything. I mentioned something that she's a little subpar at. I'm not sure what that was." He scratches his chin and narrows his eyes. "I'll think of it. Anyway, it's really bothered her since that day. My bad."

My bad?

Is he joking? He damn sure remembers what he said.

Ignoring him, I march to my shanked ball and hit it again.

SHANK!

"Peanut ..." Here comes the coddling. "I've never seen you so off your game. What did Shep say you were subpar at doing? I'm sure he's wrong. You're always successful when you try your best."

Again, I take ten full strides to my ball, line up, breathe ... breathe some more, and manage to pull off a decent stroke.

"Attagirl," Shep says, following me back to the cart.

I don't talk to him for the rest of the morning. By the eighteenth hole, I'm ready to bury him six feet under next to Jimmy.

Men are evil creatures. And while I'm not saying the world would be a better place without them, I'm not saying it *wouldn't* be a better place without them.

*****

"Shep, I think you're my good luck charm." Dad squeezes Shep's shoulder as we take a seat in the clubhouse for lunch. "I haven't beat Sophie so badly in years."

"Me neither." Shep barks a laugh, feeding my anger toward all men in this world.

"I'm going to the restroom," I mumble, rolling my eyes and eliciting a giggle from Taryn.

As I exit the restroom, Shep's unfairly sexy grin greets me from his spot, leaned against the opposing wall, hands in his front pockets. "Rough morning?"

For two full steps, I take the high road. Then I turn and retreat toward him.

"You're kinda in my space." He cocks his head while tipping his chin toward me.

"It's not your space. It's *my* space. We're in California with *my* dad, playing golf on *my* turf. My trip. My idea. It's all mine. Got it?"

"Someone's a little ripe."

My nose scrunches as I take a step away from him, slowly lowering my chin while lifting my shoulder to take a whiff of myself. I put on deodorant.

Shep clamps his lips between his teeth and clears his throat. "I'm not talking about your body odor."

"Then what are you talking about?"

"You're ripe for angry sex."

I scoff. "With whom? You? Never. Not in a million years."

Shep's eyebrows slide up his forehead. "A million years is a long time."

"Let's eat." I deflate and sulk to the table with him right behind me.

"The cheesesteak is perfection, Shep," my dad says as soon as we're seated.

"Sounds perfect."

This seems to please my dad as he sets his menu aside and grins at the man next to me.

Ripe for sex ... what does that even mean? Who says that? And why can't I forget he said it?

"Dalton and I are thinking of taking Shep up on his offer, Sophie. If we come a few days early, can we stay with you?" Taryn asks.

My head snaps up from my menu. "What?"

"His parents' place in Sedona. He invited us to golf with you two. He said there's plenty of room. Sounds amazing, but I thought it might be nice to go a few days early. I have friends in Tempe, and we'd love to see Chloe and Mason."

My head inches to the side, allowing me to shoot a million daggers at Shep. "How nice of you to invite them. When exactly did this happen?"

"Last night while you were ..." He presses his lips together.

When I was suffering from over-cleansing. He wasn't that drunk. He remembers. Fantastic.

"I see." I don't make him finish. "I'm sure Shep will love golfing with you. His parents' house is amazing. But I'm not taking off any more time for a while. And I think it's best for you to stay with Chloe and Mason if you come for a visit. She'll get jealous if you stay with me."

"Did they get a spare bed?" Dad asks.

No. They got a crib. I frown.

"I'm sure they can figure something out."

Taryn laughs. "Do you not want us to stay with you?"

"No. It's just that uh ..."

I have a Jimmy infestation. I'd rather have an over-population of termites or ... snakes. Yep. I'd rather live with snakes than with Jimmy. I think I've always preferred snakes to men.

"My house is a little torn up. I've been repainting." I shrug.

"Didn't you repaint last year?" Dad asks.

God ... why can't he have dementia?

"I have a spare bedroom. You're welcome to stay with me," Shep offers.

"No." I cringe. "Just ..." Massaging my temples, I shake my head. "Of course you can stay with me. Just wait a few weeks. Next month would be awesome. Okay?"

Again, I've drawn unwanted attention to myself. After a few seconds of silence, Shep nods. "Next month it is."

On the way home, my mind reels. I have a month to get Jimmy out. It shouldn't be a problem, but his middle name is Problem, so I have to formulate plans B, C, D, E, F, G, and H-omicide.

"What's up with all the traffic?" Dad says as we wait in a long line at the light.

"You always say that." Taryn plays with the graying hair at his nape.

"Yeah, well it's true. It's rush *hours*. Twenty-four to be exact. It's taking forever to get home."

"Mmm ..." Shep nods slowly next to me, keeping his gaze out his window. "Feels like a million years."

"Not a million years," I reply on reflex.

"No. It's definitely a million," Shep says.

"It's taking twice as long to get home, and it didn't take five hundred thousand years to get there." I roll my eyes.

"I think it did."

"No. It did not."

Taryn glances over her shoulder at me and laughs. "You two sound like children fighting over something completely nonsensical."

"That's because my *friend,* Shep, is a nonsensical person."

He smirks, but he still doesn't look at me.

"Oh, Dalton, you should swing by the dry cleaners and pick up my dresses," Taryn suggests.

"Sure. I'll drop them off first, then we can run to the post office too. I need to pick up some flat rate boxes."

"We can run errands with you," I say.

"The house is on the way. Go take a nap, Peanut."

Peanut.

This is Dad's way of telling me I played like shit today because I had so much shit last night, and I could use a nap.

"Well, you can let Shep run errands with you. Give him a tour of Santa Monica."

Shep chuckles. "I've been here many times. Actually, I could use a nap too. It feels like it's been a million years since I had the chance to take a midday nap."

He's *so* nonsensical and ... obnoxious.

"Okay, Peanut. Get some rest." Dad stops in front of the house.

"Thanks," I mumble, hopping out without giving Shep a second thought.

Not true.

I give him way too many thoughts. He's like a cancer or a fungus, slowly spreading out of control in my brain.

CHAPTER
Thirty-One

"IN A HURRY?" Shep calls as I speed-walk into the house.

"Just uh ... getting my nap in before they return home."

"I enjoyed being under your skin today."

My pace slows to a stop just before I reach my bedroom.

"I crawled under your skin," he continues, "that day at the store when I implied sex with you was subpar. And I've been there ever since, keeping you on edge. The jealousy in your eyes when you think I'm screwing Riley—it's my favorite appetizer. Watching you shank ball after ball today ... it's all so fucking perfect."

"Perfect?" I whisper, making a slow turn toward him.

"Perfect," he mouths, prowling toward me.

"I'm not a game."

He grins. "Oh, Sophie ... you're the *best* game."

"We are never having—"

"Yeah, we are." He grabs my face and kisses me, obliterating every single protest on my lips.

Jimmy. Baby. Jimmy. Baby. Jimbab ... jiba ... j ...

I push Shep away, breathless. Flustered. *Really* turned on. "I am un ... unavailable."

"Because of the nap?" Shep doesn't have a serious bone in his body. I'm trying to be serious about not being serious with him, and he's making jokes.

"Stop. I need you to get what I've been telling you since the day we met."

"No dating. The arranged marriage. I'm not your reality. You're on the run from the police. Maybe you're homeless ..." He rubs his lips together. "Got it."

Mirroring him, I rub my thoroughly kissed lips together and nod. "Yes. All of that."

"I'm not allowed to fall in love with you. I'm not allowed to stalk you. I'm not allowed to plaster photos of you all over my dream board." There he goes again, making me grin when I need to be serious.

I clear my throat. "Correct."

"I don't want to marry you, Sophie. I just want to fuck you before your dad and Taryn get back here."

Gah! When he puts it like that...

"It's probably not going to happen." I tip my chin up, shoulders back.

"I've waited a million years."

"Shep," I snort. "No."

"Yes." He grabs my face and kisses me again.

Again, I push him away. "No."

He wipes the back of his hand along the corner of his mouth as defeat settles into his eyes.

"You..." I point a stiff finger at his face "...don't get

to call me subpar in bed, flirt with that chick at the store, weasel your way on this trip with me, and press all my buttons until I play the worst game of golf I've ever played, *then* think I'm going to spread my legs and let you climb on top of me. No. Fuck no."

He blows out a long breath and lowers his gaze to the floor.

Checkmate.

"*I'm* going to be on top," I say.

It takes a few moments for him to lift his gaze back to mine, a slight wrinkle of confusion on his face until I relinquish a grin.

"I'm going to be on top," I repeat, taking my time getting to him, pressing my hands to his chest, and backing him into my bedroom.

Shep tosses his hat onto the floor as I work his shirt up his torso. He grabs it and peels it off in one quick motion.

We kiss for a few seconds, and I shove him backward onto my bed.

He chuckles, lacing his fingers behind his head as I remove my shirt and shorts. My hand brushes down my belly like I need to make sure it's still flat. Shep's gaze follows my hand, so I cover up my belly check by letting my hand navigate down the front of my panties.

"Sophie ..." His grin swells and he draws in his lower lip, gnawing at it for several seconds.

I close my eyes and touch myself for a few more breaths.

"Christ, Soph ..." He groans. "Careful, you just ate."

I have to bite my lips to keep from laughing. A grin cracks my face the second I open my eyes. "I like being under your skin." I set my glasses aside before leaning forward. My fingers make precise movements opening his fly and pulling his shorts down his muscular legs along with his briefs.

Keeping his hands behind his head, his grin swells as I shimmy out of my panties. I crawl up his body and straddle him, teasing my fingertips along his abs just as he jackknives to sitting. It happens so quickly, I gasp. The intensity in his eyes makes it hard to release my breath, to surrender, to stay focused on my mission which is to be on top, to stay in control of him, of us, of my emotions.

"Crawl under my skin, Soph ..." he whispers before brushing his lips over mine. "It will never be close enough."

I lower onto him, ensnared in his gaze, fingers curling into his shoulders. "Shep ..." I close my eyes.

Don't say that.

Don't mean it.

Don't ... just ... don't.

I lose control. So does he.

I'm on top. He's on top.

I touch him; I touch us where we're joined, drawing a slow moan from him.

He touches me, his mouth on my breasts, his hands in my hair, ghosting down my back, gripping my ass as he moves inside me.

This is messy. We are tangled in every way, and it's going to be hard to untangle from this mess we're creating without pieces of my heart ripping, without exposing all the parts I don't want him to see.

"Sophie ..." He moves over me, eyelids heavy.

I press my palms to his face, framing it, taking a mental picture of the way he's looking at me—a snapshot of truth in a bed of lies.

As he reaches his release, he drops his head to my shoulder, I grind my hips into him.

"God ... Shep ..." My fingernails dig into his flesh as my lips brush his ear, my labored breaths whispering to him just how much I've let him under my skin, inside of me in every way possible.

Silence envelopes our naked bodies; the slow rise and fall of our chests pressed together is the only sign of life. I don't know what to say. That ... what just happened ... it's not what friends do. Not like that.

It's what lovers do.

I've had enough sex to know *that* wasn't sex.

Shep slowly lifts his head from the crook of my neck, and he kisses me. It's undemanding and sensual. His fingers feather up my leg and over my hip while his tongue makes lazy strokes against mine. This is intimate. It's way on the other side of a line we weren't supposed to cross. When the kiss ends, our gazes lock. Right there in his eyes. Those eyes that can't lie. He knows.

"Sophie ..."

I shake my head a half dozen times as emotion stings my eyes. Feeling it is bad enough. He can't say it. Sometimes words mean nothing, but sometimes they change the course of a life. If he says it, those words will shake me like an explosion. I will lose my way, and it's no longer just my journey. I have a passenger.

Right now, it's not solely about me.

"I'm sorry you had to beat that dead horse."

Shep's eyes narrow. He's not getting the humor in my comment. "Why can't you get pregnant?"

"What?" Where did that question come from?

"In Sedona, you said you had a procedure. Like an IUD placed?"

"Shep ..." I wriggle my way out from underneath him and sit on the edge of the bed. "No." I shake my head, a little frustrated that he's taking this conversation in that direction. I get it. He wants to know that I'm not going to show up on his doorstep with a positive pregnancy test. "It's not an IUD. It's ... nothing to worry about." I glance over my shoulder, but my words don't seem to erase the worry from his face. "It's a hundred percent. I *guarantee* you can't get me pregnant. Okay?"

He stares at the mattress between us, worry clinging to every tiny crease along his brow and at the corners of his eyes. "Are *you* okay?"

I laugh a little. "I'm fine, Shep. Now, get dressed before my dad and Taryn get home." Gathering my clothes, I hug them to me, peek out the door, and dash to the bathroom.

When I emerge, Shep's in a lounge chair out back

with a glass of wine in one hand, head back, eyes closed.

"Taryn will be thrilled that you're drinking the wine," I say, taking a seat in the hanging egg chair.

"No wine for you, though," he murmurs.

I shake my head, but he doesn't open his eyes to see me.

"Can I ask why?" Now, he opens his eyes.

Tell him. Just say it. Lay it out there and let him decide what to do with everything.

I can't. He's not Jules. And we're at my dad's house. Chloe would hate me if Dad found out before she told him.

"My doctor doesn't want me drinking for a ... while."

"You're sick?"

"No. I'm ... it's ..." I press my lips together. "I'm not ready to talk about it, but I'm fine. I just ... I'm fine. Really."

"Does your dad know?"

I shake my head.

"Your mom?"

Another headshake.

"Are you going to tell them?"

"Yes."

"When?"

"When I'm ready."

"Jesus." He sits up, setting the wine glass on the table before running his hands through his hair, elbow on his knees. "Would you tell me if it were serious?"

I'm not sure how to respond. I'm not dying. Is that what he thinks?

He grunts a laugh. "Of course you wouldn't tell me."

"No. That's ... that's not true. I'm fine. Really. Not dying. Just ... not ready to discuss my situation, yet. But soon. I promise."

"Does Jules know?"

I nod.

"So she can know, but your own family can't know?"

He's *upset*? I think. I'm not really sure.

"It's complicated."

"Is it cancer?"

"What?" I narrow my eyes and shake my head. "No, Shep, it's ... I'm fine. It's not cancer."

"Fuck, Sophie ..." Shep stands and blows out a long breath while resting his hands on his hips. "Just tell me."

"I will, just not—"

"Dammit, Sophie! I'm so tired of your wishy-washy crap. It's no longer cute. It's fucking frustrating. You're all over the damn place. You're not drinking, not eating certain foods, you don't want me to know about your *real* life, but you won't tell me why. And I'm done playing the arranged marriage, jail, homeless, *whatever* game. It's no longer funny. We just had the best sex of my whole damn life, and you nearly cried when you thought I was going to actually get personal with you.

And now you're admitting something is wrong with you, but it's *fine*. It's not fine! It's driving me—"

"I'm pregnant," I say in a calm voice.

Shep's head inches back, his eyes unblinking. After a few seconds, his throat bobs. "W-what?"

I shrug. "I'm pregnant."

"Your ex's?"

"No," I whisper.

Then something ghosts over his face, erasing the anguish with something else ... something less terrifying.

Oh, god ...

Does he think I'm pregnant with his baby?

"Sophie ..." He exhales a long breath as though he's ... relieved?

But that doesn't make sense. I'm reading him all wrong.

"Not yours." I clear my throat, and before I can finish, he deflates like a bullet impaled his chest. Why is he reacting this way?

"It's Chloe's and Mason's. I agreed to surrogate for them before I met you. They made me promise not to tell anyone until I'm a little further along, just in case ..." I give him a sad smile. "And Jules knows because, well, she's Jules and she managed to drag it out of me. But my parents don't know. And if I tell them, Chloe will be so angry with me. I'm not dying. I don't have cancer. I'm carrying a tiny human inside of me. So yeah, I'm not eating fish or drinking alcohol, and I can have sex and not get pregnant because ..." I shrug. "I'm already pregnant."

As he turns his back to me, he runs his hands through his hair again and blows out a slow breath. Shep has this mix of shock and relief on his face, yet there seems to be a storm of pain in his eyes.

"Please don't say a word to my dad or Taryn."

His head inches side to side, but he doesn't respond.

"Are you mad?"

He releases a stifled laugh. "Mad ..." he says it like an echo more than a declaration or an answer to my question. "No, Sophie. I'm not mad. I'm ... I don't know what I am." Scrubbing his palms over his face, he grumbles something incoherent.

The best sex of his whole damn life. His words. What does one say to that when this particular *one* is pregnant with her sister's baby?

"Shep ..." This wasn't the conversation I imagined having on this trip. I'm not ready. I feel like all the wrong words are tumbling off the tip of my tongue. "This pregnancy was carefully thought out and meticulously planned. And I haven't had one moment of regret since I agreed to do this for them. Not one. I think I didn't prepare for all the unexpected things, the unexpected people. I just thought I'd take a year off from dating. Grow a baby. Let my body heal. And get back in the game. I mean ... what's one year to give your only sister the one thing she wants more than anything else in life?"

Shep nods several times. "I'd expect nothing less of you, Sophie. It's selfless. And generous. It's ... you." He smiles, but it's such a sad smile.

My heart aches. He's feet away, but it feels like he's untouchable.

CHAPTER
Thirty-Two

SHEP

"YOU'VE BEEN REALLY QUIET," Sophie breaks a long stretch of silence, her delicate hands working the crochet hook and yarn as I drive us back to Scottsdale.

"Sorry. What do you want to talk about?"

She shrugs a shoulder. "Well, I disclosed my health status to you. Thank you, by the way, for not letting it slip to my dad and Taryn. But you haven't been yourself since I told you. If you're not mad, then do you want to tell me how you are feeling?"

"How am I feeling ..." I chew on the inside of my cheek while focusing on the road. "I'm uh ... suffering from a bad case of irony."

"Irony?"

I nod. "A few years into our marriage, Millie thought she was pregnant. *I* was elated. I never hid my desire to have a family. We didn't discuss a family in great detail before we got married, but she knew my feelings. I wanted kids. I said those exact words. Her lack of saying otherwise is the reason I never questioned her more. So we married. I worked. She didn't.

It's not that I didn't want her to work; she just wasn't sure what she wanted to do.

"I told her I could support us, and maybe it was a good idea anyway if 'we' wanted her to stay home when we started a family. She said nothing, again, leaving me with assumptions. So I worked, and she stayed home. Doing what? I have no idea, and I didn't care. I loved her. I worked for us, for our family. The family I thought we were trying to have together. As time passed, and she didn't get pregnant, I started to wonder if something was wrong with her or with me. She assured me it was that we were trying too hard."

Sophie nods a few times, her lips pressed tightly together.

"Millie was beside herself with grief when she missed her period. It made no sense. We had been trying for so long. Only ... *we* weren't. She had never stopped taking the pill. She didn't want kids. When she thought she was pregnant, the truth came out. I felt betrayed beyond words." I grunt a laugh. "She took a dozen pregnancy tests, went to the doctor for another negative test, and finally got her period."

"And then you divorced?"

"No. I was 'for better or worse.' No kids? Well, that sucked, but I loved my wife. I married her. End of story. Only it wasn't. Her relief was short lived. A long streak of unhappiness followed. I worked too much. It was my fault she wasn't happy. So I quit my job. Took some time to reconnect with her. That's when she decided she couldn't be around me so much. That's when she said she wanted something for herself. Again. Fine. Get a job. We weren't having a family. Why not at that point? And from there … it all unraveled. She took a job with her current company and turned into a monster as I've alluded to before and as you've seen for yourself. I could do nothing right in her eyes. So here we are."

"Shep … I'm sorry. That's …"

"No pity or apology needed. I've accepted things. We're *amicable.* Parents to two dogs. That's good, mature of us, right?"

A nervous laugh escapes her. "Sure. I guess. I'm clearly not an expert on relationships." She shoots me a quick sidelong glance. I'm not sure if she's referring to her previous boyfriends or to me.

Miles of roadway pass in more silence before I feel brave enough to take another step. "Can I ask about Jimmy?"

At first, I'm not sure she hears me. She doesn't move a muscle. Finally, she wets her lips and draws a long breath in through her nose. "He was my ex."

Again, I wait. We have time. I gave her a big part of my previous relationship. Is she really not going to give me more than what I already gathered from Taryn's conversation with her?

"Annnything else you want to share about him?"

With her focus out her window, she shakes her head several times. "No."

"Did your relationship end because you offered to be a surrogate for your sister and her husband?"

"No."

This is a great conversation. I'm learning so much about her.

I'm done. She has nothing to say. I have, at best, a shaky grip on the news of her pregnancy. We seem to have nowhere to go at this point. And I do get that our relationship seemed to be going nowhere from the beginning. But things in life change. I thought we had changed.

When we get to my place, I shut off the engine. "Thank you for letting me tag along. It was great meeting your dad and Taryn. You're a ... good person, Sophie Ryan. I'm lucky to have you as my friend." I give her a quick smile and climb out of the car to retrieve my things from the back.

"I had a nice time too. Even if you did beat me this time." She moseys to the back of the car and slips her hands into her shorts' pockets, rocking back and forth on her feet as I lug my clubs and duffle bag over my shoulder.

There is *so* much I want to say to her. I have all these feelings and no place for them to go. I don't want to upset her or make her feel bad. So I do the right thing. The unselfish thing. "Listen. Your secret's safe with me, and I get it now. I understand why you've tried to keep me at arm's length. Taking care of yourself and the baby should be your number one priority."

She nods a few times. "The baby is pretty easy right now. I'm up for walks. Golfing. Whatever. I mean, we're still friends, right?"

I hate this. How did my life end up here? And why can't I just pull it together and ... and what? Hell, I'm not even sure.

Sophie presses her lips together, puffing out her cheeks for a moment before blowing a long breath out her nose. "This is it, isn't it?"

"Sophie—" I deflate a bit. I need a minute. Maybe a day or two. Maybe longer.

"No. It's fine. I mean, it was supposed to be me, you know ... ending things when I could no longer hide the pregnancy. It was supposed to be me walking away when I didn't want you to think I was being dishonest for any other reason than I made a promise to my sister before I met you. Now it's easy, right? You do you. I'll do me. It was fun while it lasted. All that good stuff, right?"

Every time she says "right," I feel like something inside of her is breaking or maybe I'm feeling something breaking inside of myself.

"Right," I manage, just above a whisper.

"Well, I'll uh ... see you around."

I nod. One. Fucking. Nod.

Sophie drops her head and shuffles her feet to the driver's side door. Before she gets a chance to look up at me, I head up my driveway. I'm not sure where I saw my relationship with Sophie going, but it wasn't here. This isn't an ending I could have ever imagined.

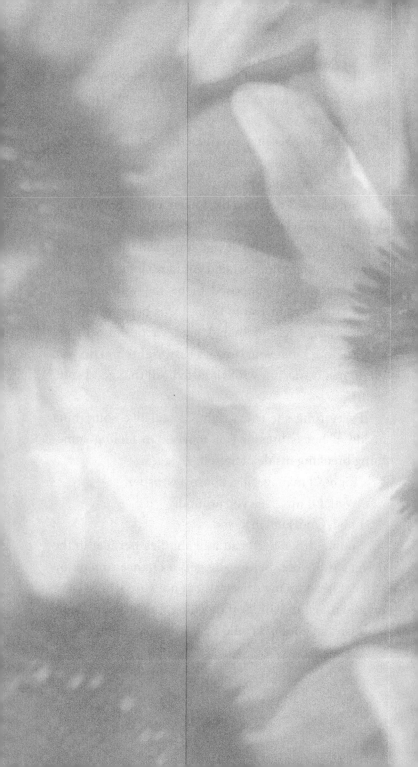

CHAPTER
Thirty-Three

SOPHIE

I HAVE a good pregnancy hormone cry on the way home after leaving Shep's place. When I open the door, I don't hear Jimmy. I need to pick up Cersei from my sister's house, but first, I need to gain a little more composure.

When I reach my bedroom, passing all the other rooms in the house, I realize Jimmy is not here.

Jimmy. Is. Not. Here.

"Jimmy?" I turn on his bedroom light and then the bathroom light. I don't have any messages from him, and he didn't leave a note. But his belongings are still here.

I don't even think. What's there to think about? My attorney said I could change the locks if he ever leaves. And you better believe I've been prepared for this day. I have new deadbolts in my garage along with the tools I'll need to swap them out.

If he wants to take me to court over a new driveway, that's fine. I'll counter sue for destruction of property. But he's not living under this roof another day.

My shaky hands hustle to get the locks swapped

out. After the new locks are secured, I change the garage door code and head straight to Jimmy's bedroom—*my* bedroom. All of the rooms are mine.

One armful after another, I carry his stuff to the end of my driveway, where he will either take it or I'll have it hauled off to the landfill.

When the door with the new lock is shut and latched behind me, I exhale a long breath. Today, I lost two men in my life. Is this Karma? Did I have to lose one to rid my life of the other?

And where is Jimmy?

"Not my circus. Not my monkey," I repeat several times. In the morning, I'll call a security company and arrange for cameras and an alarm to be installed. If Jimmy comes into my house again, it will be breaking and entering. That's the only way he's stepping foot in here again.

Pulling my phone from my pocket, I call Chloe.

"You home?"

"Yes," I say.

"How are Dad and Taryn?"

"Good. They want to come for a visit. I managed to hold them off until next month."

Hmm ... will that still happen if we're not going to Sedona with Shep?

"Thank God. We can tell them together."

"Yeah."

"How are you feeling? Did you quit cleansing?"

I roll my eyes. "Yes. No more cleansing. I'm uh ..."

I'm sad. So very sad.

"Sophie? Is everything okay?"

"I'm good. Really. I'll be over in a bit to get Cersei."

"Okay. See you soon."

✳✳✳✳✳

I GET Cersei and make it home and still no sign of Jimmy. It should be a relief, but he'll return. I'd rather just get that over with now. He can have his little tantrum and take his stuff to a hotel or move to Tennessee. Or I can call the police if he gets too irate.

Just when I give up on him coming back, assuming —hoping—he's with someone else, the doorbell rings.

I glance out the window. It's him. The door handle rattles as he tries to open the door.

"Soph ..." he says in an agonizing tone. "My key doesn't work. Open the door."

I stand right next to the door, hugging my arms to myself. He had to see his stuff at the end of the drive-way. He knows what's happening. "Go away, Jimmy. You no longer live here. I changed the locks. If you don't leave, I'm calling the police."

"Soph ..." He sounds like he's in pain, a little broken.

Now he knows what he's done to me for weeks and weeks. Now he knows what it feels like to be worn down, mistreated, and helpless.

"It's over, Jimmy. I'm going to bed. Go away."

"Soph ... m-my ... my mom ... d-died."

I stop after taking several steps away from the door.

Nope. I'm not falling for that. He just wants me to open the door. I can't do that again. I have a baby inside of me. That's my priority. Period.

And I already miss my friend, Shep. I want to crawl into bed and forget about so much of this day.

"Sophie ..." he cries. An actual cry.

I grimace. "You're lying."

"I'm not lying! S-she died ... a h-heart attack ... Soph ... s-she's gone ..."

Nope. Nope. Nope.

I skitter to the bedroom and close the door. He sounds like an injured animal. I open my suitcase and start unpacking. Then I take a shower and get ready for bed. Before I call it a night, I glance out front. Jimmy's on his side, curled into a ball, shaking, sobbing.

No. I can't. It was the last straw ten straws ago. Every time I think I have the courage to rid Jimmy from my life, something happens in his life, and I cave.

No more caving.

I shut off all the lights and crawl into bed. It takes me forever to get to sleep, but eventually, I do. Waking early in the morning, too early, I peek out the window.

"No ..." I sigh and rub my temples.

He's still there.

His mom died. I let him sleep outside all night. I can't win. I can't find that balance between doormat and raging bitch.

I slowly pad my way toward the front door. Before opening it, I have a moment. Everything hits me all at the same time. Leaning my back against the door, I hold my breath to keep from making a single noise, but my body vibrates as emotions shake me, the earthquake I knew was coming.

Sniffle.

Wipe my tears.

Repeat. Repeat. Repeat.

The look in Shep's eyes when he thought I might be pregnant with his baby. It slayed me once then again when I told him it wasn't his.

And the story about Millie not wanting kids.

It's so much.

Jimmy ...

His mom who I knew and cared about too ...

It's *too* much.

I slip outside, my feet at Jimmy's head. "I'm very sorry, Jimmy."

He sniffles, lifting his head just enough to gaze at me through red, swollen eyes. I've never seen Jimmy cry.

"I have nowhere to go, Sophie." His face scrunches, and he begins to cry again. Shoulders hunched. Body shaking in silent sobs.

Fuck my life.

If heaven exists, I want wings. Crowns. A parade in my name. Something really special because I'm being a saint. I'm giving people babies. I'm taking in the homeless. Caring for abandoned dogs in my own way.

"Come on." I hold out my hand.

Jimmy stares at it for a few seconds before taking it.

We go inside to the bedroom. *His* bedroom. After he crawls onto the bare mattress, since I threw out the sheets, I grab a blanket and cover him. Then I make a dozen saintly trips from the driveway to the house, returning all of his belongings to the bedroom.

"Sophie," his gravelly voice stops me just as I shut off the light to the bedroom and start to pull the door shut. "You're too good to me ... too good *for* me."

Jimmy ... who knew he would be the one to humble me at the end of a long couple of days?

I'm not too good for him. I'm not better than anyone else, just different. Just not the one for him. He deserves what we all deserve: to be loved, to be desired, to be wanted.

As I get dressed, and do my hair in the bathroom mirror, I let a few tears make a slow descent down my face. I don't know if this round of tears is for me, for Shep, or for Jimmy. I'm just incredibly sad.

The image of Shep looking at me in bed—the moment I knew he was about to say something that I wasn't ready for him to say—it takes front and center in my mind.

So I call him.

Setting my phone on the edge of the vanity, I wipe my tears and pull out my makeup to fix my blotchy face before I have to go to work.

"Hey," he answers in a somber tone.

"Hey," I echo him.

What I wouldn't give for him to ask me what I'm wearing.

356

He doesn't.

"Everything okay?"

I nod, dragging in a shaky breath. "Yeah. I just ..."

Miss you. Want you. Love you. Yeah, I love you, Shep.

"I feel like things are weird, and they don't have to be. I didn't think I needed another friend beyond Jules. But I think I'll miss you if I don't see you. And that's unnecessary. I mean, I'm pregnant. So what? Really, why can't we talk, golf, take the dogs to the park? Maybe catch a movie or ... anything. Before we were *best* friends, we were normal, regular, run of the mill friends. Can't we go back? I ... I thought we agreed to go back to that before the trip to Santa Monica. What happened?"

Silence.

I start to question if he's still on the line.

"I'm walking the shelter dogs Friday afternoon. Meet at the park?"

"Sounds perfect."

"Bye, Sophie."

"Bye, Shep."

CHAPTER
Thirty-Four

"No. Just ... no, Sophie." Jules looks as devastated as I felt when I caved two days ago. I get it. I really do.

I nod to the waitress when she holds up a pitcher of water. After she refills my cup, I frown at Jules. "I realize it seems so simple right now, sitting here in a cafe with upbeat music playing. But there was no upbeat music. The sun had set. It was just the heart-breaking sobs of a man grieving the loss of his mom. I didn't cave. I waited all night. I let him sleep at my door because I didn't trust him, and I didn't think he'd still be there in the morning. But he was. Really, you can't honestly say you wouldn't have done the same thing in my shoes."

She deflates, rubbing her hands over her face. "I know. I do *know*. It's just that he had left the premises. You changed the locks. Gah!"

My nose scrunches. "Yeah. It's like two big steps forward and fifty steps backward. He doesn't leave the bedroom. I set food just inside the door. He eventually eats a few bites, and later I replace it with the next meal. And Cersei ... Jules, I swear Cersei feels his grief because she spends all her time with him. All day and all night. I have to drag her out for walks. She hasn't been eating well either."

"Jesus."

I nod, sucking on my water straw.

"When's the funeral?"

"No funeral. She was cremated. I don't think she has friends or family beyond Jimmy and her sister who can't get off work to come be with Jimmy or get the remains because she visited right before his mom died."

"What a shit show."

"It's sad. I mean, my family is far from perfect. But we're there for each other."

"Not true. No one went home for Prince Harry's funeral."

I grin. "True. I'm a terrible daughter."

"How was California?"

My cheeks puff out as I hold a big breath for several seconds before blowing it out in one big *whoosh.* "Unexpected."

Her eyebrows lift a fraction. "Unexpected good or unexpected bad? Did your dad love Shep?"

"Yes. Of course. Everyone loves Shep. But I had to keep the pregnancy a secret, which is hard to do when they're used to me downing bottles of wine on my visits. There was a forced cleanse. The most embarrassing GI issues in the history of mankind. A terrible game of golf. Incredibly intimate sex. And a pregnancy confession."

Jules opens her mouth, but nothing comes out.

"My dad and Taryn don't know about the baby, but I had to tell Shep."

"Was he mad?"

"Mad? No. I don't think so anyway. Definitely surprised. I think he's not sure where that leaves us. And that should be fine. I wasn't going to let things with him go on forever. But after the Jimmy fiasco, I broke down and called Shep, basically begging him to keep being my friend. So we're meeting at the park with the dogs tomorrow. And honestly, I'm feeling stupid for being so weak and calling him."

Jules eyes me for a few seconds, a cheesy grin on her face. "Incredibly *intimate* sex, huh?"

I shake my head. "Just my luck. My sister and her husband knock me up and weeks later I meet *the* guy."

"I think you're forgetting that he could be Jimmy in a prettier package. Jimmy was the shit until he moved into your house."

I sigh. "Shep's different."

"Jimmy was different."

I frown. "I know. Shep wanted kids; when he was married, he really wanted kids. His wife didn't. And I swear, I just swear, Jules, that when I told him I was pregnant and it wasn't his baby, he looked disappointed."

Her painted eyebrows slide up her forehead. "That's ..."

I nod slowly. "Yeah ..."

✳✳✳✳✳

On Friday, Cersei and I meet Shep at the park. Once again, he has a whole pack of dogs, and my heart goes all aflutter because I love Shep with his huge heart and his pack of dogs just looking for someone to love them.

"Wow. Ten? Shep, that's mighty brave of you. Hope no one starts a fight."

He grins, releasing every single leash, sending them running.

"Eek!" I squeal and stiffen as they rush past me. "Why do you do that every time?"

"Because I like the look on your face."

"Horror?"

He chuckles, sliding his hands in his back pockets instead of around my waist where I want them. "How are you feeling?"

"Fine. How was your week?"

"Boring. Any morning sickness?"

"Shep…" I shake my head "…we don't have to do this. I'm not showing. I'm not sick. You wouldn't know I'm pregnant had I not told you. So let's just be friends and not think about it."

"How do you not think about a human growing inside of you?"

"Because this baby is supposed to spend nine months inside of me, and life around me doesn't stop. Right now, you and those three billion dogs you brought with you are far more interesting than the little sweet pea that I can't see or feel."

It's hard to read the expression on his face. It's new. I thought I'd seen all of his expressions, but in the past week, he's shown me a few new ones, and it makes me think that I don't know my good friend Marcus Shepard as well as I thought I did.

The creepy part is the way his eyes keep going to my belly. I don't have a bump. Nothing yet. There's nothing to see.

"I'm free next weekend if you want to get in eighteen holes," I say, trying anything.

"Millie's pregnant."

Whoa. Okay, where did that come from?

Eyeing him for a few seconds, I return a slow nod of acknowledgment.

"Hooked up with some guy she met on a dating app." He stares past my shoulder at the dogs, unblinking with a blank expression. "He's happy. Thought his dick was broken or he had weak swimmers that ended his marriage. Something like that."

I'm not touching this. No way. He needs to be the one to keep this conversation going.

"She's ... happy."

His story on the way home from California? It makes sense now.

"That must sting, Shep. I'm really sorry."

"Yeah. It's life. Sucks that it's mine. Well, I guess it's really not, is it?" His attention returns to me. "I loved her. She's pregnant. And it's not my baby. Not my life. I'll get to show up at her house, *my* old house, every week to pick up or return the dogs while she's growing some other dude's baby. Like a weekly gut punch as her belly expands over the next nine months."

"That does suck."

He nods again. "I can't do this, Sophie." His eyes look different, misted over with emotion I'm certain he'll never release.

My stomach twists as a heavy ache settles over my chest.

"It's selfish of me. I know this. I wish I had militant control over my thoughts and emotions, but I don't. I bleed just like everyone else. I fall victim to irrational thoughts and random musings of my life before now."

I return an incremental nod, but I don't know why because I don't understand where he's going.

"In a matter of days, I found out that Millie is pregnant and so are you. And I can't do it. I can't watch you go through this pregnancy with someone else's baby. And before you state the obvious, I know it's not your baby either. But my stupid, unreasonable brain will self-destruct seeing you pregnant, wishing it were mine because I want that life. I just can't seem to find the right person at the right time in my life to have that."

It takes everything I have to keep from begging him to just wait. Wait for me to churn out this baby. Then I'll give him one too. An original baby machine.

One for you.

One for you.

One for you.

Everybody gets a baby!

He's waited long enough. It's his turn. He deserves to find the right person who is in sync with him now, not later, not after a divorce when it's too late, not after having someone else's child.

My mom's favorite line to Chloe and me when we were young was "there will be another."

Another toy because the one I want is sold out.

Another friend because the one I had no longer wants to be my friend.

Another chance next year to try out for drill team.

Another dress since my best friend just bought the prom dress I wanted.

There will always be another.

Except, there won't. There will never be another Shep.

"So this is it? Like a forever goodbye? No more outings. I stop shopping at Wag Your Tail. We just end it forever?"

"I can't tell you where to shop. And I won't say forever."

"True. But if you could, would you tell me to shop at some other store?"

"Sophie ..." He bows his head and closes his eyes.

I shake my head and take a few steps back. "That's a yes."

"Sophie ..."

"No. I got my answer."

"It wasn't an answer."

"Cersei!" I call her, keeping my focus on Shep. "I didn't pursue you. I didn't call you first. I didn't invite you to Sedona. I didn't ask to be your friend. And I definitely didn't ask to be *best* friends. I told you I could give you one day at a time. I never promised to share everything with you. I did not mislead you. Just friends. You could have said no, but you didn't."

"I know."

Why? Why does he have to be agreeable? He has no fight in him. I'm not wrong, but god ... just fight me on it. Fight with me. Fight *for* me.

"It's me," he says. "It's the fact that I could not have envisioned this situation. Not Millie. Not you. And I definitely could not have predicted or even imagined how I would feel, how the emotions I've suppressed would come to the surface and suffocate me. It's an awful feeling, and no one is to blame. Still ... I'm sorry. Even if you weren't expecting anything from me, even if you didn't want anything from me, I'm still sorry."

I remain unmoving for several breaths, wordlessly telling him that I hear him. I acknowledge him and his feelings. With a slight nod, I accept his apology and turn. Taking a few more steps, I stop. "For the record, you were easy." Swallowing hard, I blink out more tears. "The good kind of easy. You were what I n-needed when I didn't know what or ... w-who that was. So ... thank you."

CHAPTER
Thirty-Five

SHEP

"I'M GETTING A DIVORCE."

I line up my putter. "You don't have to copy everything I do," I say to Howie.

He uses his putter to do some side to side stretching as I replace the flag. "I think it's a trend. I think one woman does it and the rest follow suit after they see the first friend who did it made it to the other side in one piece. Financially stable. Feeling the rush of freedom." He grunts. "Completely delusional that they will find something better than they had."

"Caroline will never find another Howie." I glance over at him as we make our way to the cart.

"Are you being sarcastic?"

I grin. "Nope. I'm serious. You are a good man. A good father. And it really sucks for Simon. I know he's only three, but he's going to feel it even if he doesn't fully understand."

"She wants everything."

I drive us to the next tee. "Everything?"

"The house. The minivan. Custody of Simon."

"Did she fuck her boss?"

"Yes."

I laugh. "She's got balls. What are you going to do?"

"I'm going to give her the house and the minivan, but not Simon. I'm going to give her the house and minivan *for* Simon. But I'm going to be with my son as much as she's going to be with him. She's not quitting her job, so I'm making sure that I have daytime coverage at the bar so he doesn't have to go to daycare, and so I can be with him more than she's with him."

"Good plan." I take my driver to the tee. "He's a daddy's boy anyway."

"He is. How are you doing? I felt like you took the news of Millie's pregnancy pretty hard. And totally understandable, dude. Really. I'd give the eye doctor all of my attention and forget about Millie."

Focusing on the teed-up ball, I release a long breath and a smooth swing. It's a great shot. "The eye doctor is pregnant." I grab my tee and turn toward an unblinking Howie.

"Holy shit! You're going to be a dad."

Rolling my lips into my teeth, I shake my head. "I am *not* going to be a dad. It's not my baby."

"Fuck. That's … jeez, I'm sorry, Shep. Who's the other guy? Do you know?"

"Her brother-in-law." I return my club to my bag.

Howie quickly drives his ball, a terrible shot into the water. "That is seriously fucked-up. Her brother-in-law?"

"It's actually her sister's baby too. Sophie is their surrogate."

Howie's eyes widen as he makes his way to the cart. "That's ..."

"Generous?"

He nods. "Understatement. She doesn't have children of her own yet, does she?"

"No."

"So you're dating a really generous woman who loves to golf and has babies for other people. Shep, are you dating out of your league?" He climbs into the cart beside me.

"No. I'm not dating her, but if I were, then yes, I'd be dating out of my league."

"You're just screwing her without a fear of her getting pregnant."

"Nope." We speed off. "Not doing that anymore either."

"So ... what happened?"

I slam on the brakes and angle my body toward him, blowing a quick breath out my nose. "I had a moment."

"A ... moment?"

I nod. "Millie's having the baby she refused to have with me. The woman I loved ... with somebody else's baby. Right after you broke that fantastic news to me, Sophie told me she's pregnant. I asked if it was her ex's baby. She said no. And honest to god, I thought it was mine. Millie? Millie who? The woman who has been living rent free in my head for many weeks ... pregnant with my baby. For a few indescribable seconds, I was on top of the fucking world. And then she brought me back to reality, and I felt so low. Rock bottom."

Howie grimaces.

I sigh. "And as if that's not fucked-up enough, I told her I can't see her anymore because I can't watch her develop a belly, grow a baby inside of her that's not mine. Dickhead? Absolutely. I'm not claiming anything short of Dickhead Status."

"We're having a chick talk. You know this, right?"

"Yes. It's yet another new low for me."

He laughs. "For *us*, buddy. For us."

"I adopted two more dogs from the shelter after we broke up ... or whatever it was we did."

"Wow. Okay. Instead of eating or drinking or hooking up with three women in two days, you're filling your emotional void with shelter dogs. That could get out of hand, buddy."

Facing forward again, I drop my head back and close my eyes. "I don't know what I'm doing anymore."

"Do you really like Sophie? Or does her pregnant state remind you of Millie and that's what you can't handle?"

I lift my head and shoot him a sideways glance. "You know the answer to that."

"Uh ... I actually don't. Do you?"

I don't know the answer to anything right now. I'm tired of being held at arm's length from the life I want.

✳︎✳︎✳︎✳︎✳︎

"CAN you keep the dogs next week too?" Millie asks at our weekly dog swap. The one where she doesn't let me in the house I bought while she was pretending to get pregnant with my baby.

"Millie, I'll take both dogs every week," I say from the porch; not even, more like the end of the sidewalk leading to the porch.

She gives me a bratty eye roll. "Nice try. I'm taking a trip. I've uh ... met someone."

"Yes. I heard. You found a virtual stranger to impregnate you. Congratulations."

For an unguarded moment, Millie gives me a glimpse of the woman I married. For an unguarded moment, she shows me something resembling an expression of true regret. And in the next breath, it's gone.

"It wasn't planned."

"Maybe keep that to yourself. No child needs to know they were unplanned. Unwanted." I whistle for the dogs to come with me.

"Shep ... you have to know that I would have had your baby had I been pregnant when we had that scare."

"Jesus, Millie. What is wrong with you? How generous of you to say that you wouldn't have terminated a pregnancy had you really been pregnant." I shake my head, opening my car door. "I loved you. I loved you as much as any man can love a woman. But now … I don't know you. I don't see that woman. I'm *embarrassed* to say that I fell in love with you and married you."

She quickly wipes her eyes. Her tears don't touch me. I don't feel them. I don't understand them. Not now. Not ever again.

"You were this larger-than-life person, Shep. Everyone loved you. Everything you did turned into a huge success. And I lived in your shadow. I think you liked it. The woman behind the man. Can you imagine what it would have been like for me had we had children? I would have been Shep's children's mom. Millie? Millie who? Oh, yeah. Millie the stay-at-home mom. And suggesting I wanted anything less would have made me into some ungrateful monster. An unfit mother and wife who chose a career over her family. So even if I managed to escape the shadow of you, I'd always live under a cloud of shame for wanting something else, something more."

I hold my tongue, not because she's right. I'll acknowledge that she's had many *feelings* about us, about her future, her dreams, her goals. But all the scenarios she's played in her head never happened. Our marriage crumbled because she predicted our future on assumptions that weren't based on anything but her fears and insecurities. If two people speak at the same time, nothing is heard. If two people listen at the same time, nothing is spoken.

I listened, but she didn't speak. So I spoke. And sometimes my words were my feelings, and sometimes my words were guesses as to what she was thinking. It's unfortunate, just incredibly sad, that when she finally found her voice, she used it to end our marriage.

I don't hate her. I'm numb to her, too disconnected to feel anything, to feel *her*.

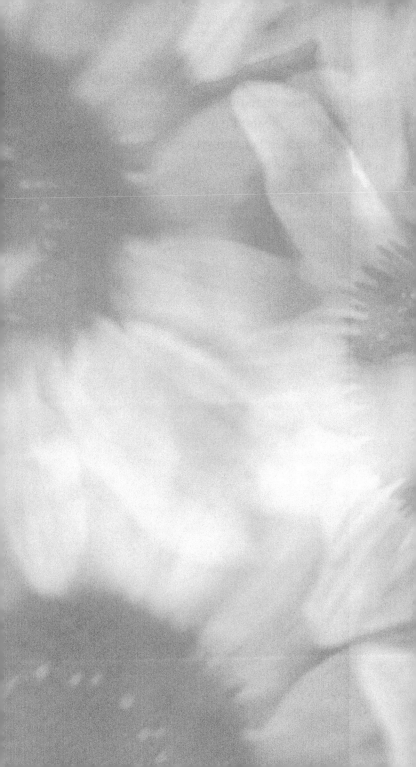

CHAPTER THIRTY-SIX

SOPHIE

DEFINE FAILURE. Well, I'd define it as the security company installing cameras and a security system to keep my ex-boyfriend out of my house *while* he's still in my house.

"Where should we put the urn?" Jimmy asks, staring at it on my coffee table next to his bare feet.

He showered this morning. It's a small victory. I'm celebrating all small victories in an effort to keep the baby healthy. I've been reading more books on pregnancy, and they all stress the importance of not stressing.

Oops ...

Now my ex *and* his dead mother are "informal settlers" in *my* home.

"So ... I assume you'll inherit some money, which will allow you to get your own place?" I'm trying not to be insensitive, but I need some answers.

"Mom didn't leave me much, but how do you feel about a swimming pool? I've always wanted one. I love the water. Did you know I was on the swim team in high school? I still hold the record for the two hundred butterfly. I could have been the next Michael Phelps, but we moved, and my new school didn't have a swim team."

I glance up from my crocheting, gently rocking in my swivel chair. "No. I didn't know about your swimming career. You've never mentioned it. But if you've always wanted a pool, and you can afford a house with a pool, then I think you should go for it. I'm sure your mom would have wanted that for you."

"Sophie, I'm talking about putting in a pool here. For us."

Don't stress. Don't stress. You've got this. DON'T STRESS!

"Sophie?"

I bite my lips together so hard, I taste blood. "Hmm?"

"I'm kidding." He grins. "I know you want me gone."

I don't confirm or deny it. I don't move. I wait. That's my new game.

"You didn't have to let me back inside. I know that. And while part of me wanted to believe you did it because you love me like I love you, I remembered a story you told me. When you were a child, your dad injured a garter snake with a weed eater and you insisted your parents let you nurse it back to health. And you did. Then you released it. A snake, Sophie. A measly garter snake. You didn't let me back in the house because I'm special. You did it because *you're* special."

I have ... nothing. Nothing to say. Not a word.

I forgot I told him that story. And he remembered. I feel a little less stupid for temporarily falling for Jimmy. He's a lot of things.

A lot of awful things.

A lot of disgusting things.

A lot of annoying things.

And he's sometimes sweet. Sometimes sexy. Sometimes funny.

"Hercules. Right? That's what you named him."

I feel my face losing the fight. I grin. He remembers the name of my snake.

"Miss?" The guy from the security company pokes his head into the living room. "Do you want to set a code?"

Jimmy sticks his fingers in his ears and smiles. That. Right there. It's the Jimmy that I said "yes" to one date. And another. And another.

I'm not losing my mind. Swoon-worthy Jimmy *did* exist.

✳ ✳ ✳ ✳ ✳

As THE WEEKS PASS, Jimmy's the perfect roommate. He works. Cooks and cleans. Walks Cersei and takes daily showers. He buys all the groceries and spends his evenings searching online for homes in the area.

I stop the eviction process, and he promises to make himself scarce if my family comes to visit. Luckily, my dad and Taryn postpone their visit by another month. I haven't told them I'm no longer golfing with Shep or seeing him at all.

I miss him. I have yet to go a full day without thinking about him. Without contemplating calling him just to hear his voice.

"Dr. Ryan." Jules smiles when I enter the exam room.

"Do you need reading glasses? Last I knew, you had twenty-twenty vision."

She messes with the controls to the chair like a child. "Nope. But feel free to charge me for an exam. I decided it's the only way you'd give me more than two seconds of your time. You've been avoiding me."

I sit on my stool and cross my legs. "I've been busy."

"Liar. Jimmy's still living with you. I'm not stupid. Are you two back together? Is that why you've been avoiding me? I'm sure it's embarrassing. And it will be quite the story to tell your kids someday. 'Hey, kids. Mommy used to hate Daddy and she tried to legally evict him.'"

Rolling my eyes, I chuckle. "It would be quite the story. But no. That's not happening. Yes, he's still living with me. But I'm good with it. I don't actually see him. He did buy a house, but he's renovating it. So he's doing his phone sales thing during the day, and right about the time I get home from work, he's heading out the door to work on his house. And I'm asleep by the time he gets back to my house."

"And he knows you're pregnant?"

"No."

She glances at my stomach. "Do you have a bump yet?"

I lift my coat and blouse. "Barely."

"Bitch."

I laugh. "Dad and Taryn were supposed to visit last month. And we were going to tell them about the baby, but they had to reschedule. They were going to come visit this month, but we're making the rounds instead."

"Making the rounds?"

"Chloe, Mason, and I are going to see my mom and grandma and tell them. Then we're making a stop at Mason's parents' house to tell them. And our last stop will be Dad and Taryn's. Then ... I will tell everyone here at work and Jimmy too."

"And Shep?"

"He knows."

"Yes. But have you talked to him lately? Does he know about your roommate?"

"I haven't talked to him in over six weeks. I don't shop at the store or take Cersei to the park where we used to hang out. He doesn't want to see me. And I'm respecting that."

"I think that's terrible of him."

I shake my head. "No. It's not terrible of him. We were never meant to be anything more than friends. It sucks that we're not really even friends now, but that's life. I'm not asking him to fall in love with a pregnant woman. I'm not asking him to wait until my life, my body, and my house are mine again. It's a big ask. It's too much. If he loved me, he'd ..." my train of thought falls off a cliff because I don't know what I think he would do if he loved me. Just because you love someone doesn't mean you make all the right decisions.

"He'd wait forever. That's what you do when you love someone. You wait forever."

I shrug. "I don't know. There has to be something in the middle of selfless and selfish. Right? Lord knows my luck with men has taught me that lesson. I think it's time for Shep to think about Shep. He's been through a lot with his ex-wife. It's okay to choose yourself sometimes."

"Says the woman carrying her sister's baby and housing the homeless."

I smirk. "Do you know how many times I've had to talk myself off the ledge? How many times I've felt on the verge of completely losing it? I did actual internet searches on ways to kill someone without evidence. And then I hear Shep talk about his pregnant ex-wife. I witness Jimmy lose his job, then his grandma, then his mother. And do you know what I've come to realize?"

Jules eyes me with her full attention.

"We are all one event away from losing. Losing our minds. A job. A loved one. A marriage. A dream. We are all one event away from losing *ourselves*. Stability and sanity are not human qualities. They are not genetic traits. They are a state of mind. Now, do you want your eyes examined?"

Jules inches her head side to side like she's

processing what I said before the eye exam offer. "Did you tell Shep you love him?"

"He knows."

"How? Did you say it?"

"Not in words."

"Then it doesn't count."

I frown. "When we were in Santa Monica ... having sex, it wasn't sex for pleasure. Well, it started out that way, but it was more. Like you know when it's more, when you're done, words you can't take back are exchanged? There's a look you share that acknowledges what just happened went way beyond sex?"

"Yeahhh ... so words *were* exchanged?"

"No. I stopped him, stopped us short of saying anything because that was before he knew I was pregnant. And I knew our time had an approaching expiration date."

"Then he doesn't know, Sophie! You have to say the words. Five seconds ago, you spoke such profound words about humans losing themselves and stability and sanity being a state of mind, which means it's fragile and ever-changing. He doesn't know you love him. And if you didn't let him say the words when he wanted to, then he thinks you stopped him from saying them because you don't feel the same way!" Jules is really worked up. Scooted to the edge of the chair. Hands making all sorts of gestures as she pleads her case.

"It's a moot point now."

"Moot schmoot. Go to him. Say, 'I love you. I don't

383

want to lose you because I'm a surrogate for my sister and her husband. If you can't handle watching me go through this pregnancy, I understand. But wait for me because I'm worth waiting for, and I'm not done loving you. I will never be done loving you.'"

I press my hand to my chest. "That's so romantic."

She smiles, slowly sighing after that performance.

"But no. I'm not doing that."

"What? You just said it was romantic."

"And it is. But ... *but* ... I've pleaded my case twice. I've suggested we stay friends. And my case was good. But twice he rejected my offer. I really have to muster a little dignity."

Jules rolls her eyes. "You had Jimmy out of your house and you let him back inside. Don't try to feed me the dignity line. You have no dignity."

I cringe because it's a little true.

"And suggesting Shep be friends with you is *not* the same thing as declaring your love. He needs the promise of an endgame. Commitment. Marriage. A baby that's *his*. How can you be so smart and so stupid at the same time?"

Giving her words some thought, I nod slowly. "I'll tell him."

The most triumphant grin overtakes her face.

"If he rejects me a third time, I'm done. Maybe I lost my dignity, but it's time I find it again."

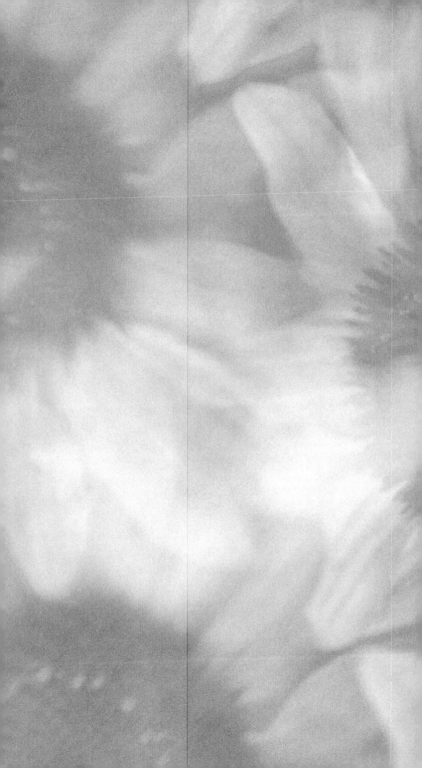

CHAPTER
Thirty-Seven

SHEP

Marta has knee surgery, so Riley takes as many extra shifts as she can. However, it's mostly just me running the store. Me and my growing pack of dogs. Being short staffed is not a problem unless there's an issue with one of the wash stations or a customer wants to talk forever about freeze-dried treats versus dehydrated treats while five other customers wait at the register.

Today is one of those days.

After I fix the leaky hose and end the unnecessary treat debate with a "just buy both," I get back to the register.

"Dude. Are you the owner? If so, you need to hire some help," some smart ass says as he waits at the back of the line.

I don't have time to look at him. "I am. And thanks for stating the obvious," I mumble.

The woman first in line laughs at my reply.

By the time I get to Mr. Smart Ass, I'm no longer focused on him. "Cersei?" I pull out a treat for her.

"You've met Cersei?" The guy with tattoos covering one of his arms eyes me with suspicion.

"Yes. She uh ... used to be a regular. Are you her dog walker?" I scan his items.

He chuckles. "No. I'm her mom's boyfriend."

"Sophie's boyfriend?" I ask without sounding shocked, but I am.

"Yeah. And I was totally kidding, man. I'm sure being the only employee on a busy day isn't exactly easy." He hands me a debit card before I give him the total.

Jimmy Houser.

I swipe his card. "How long have you known Sophie?"

He shrugs, entering his PIN. "I don't remember. It's been a while. I'm trying to remember when I moved in with her?" He twists his lips and narrows his eyes. "Can't remember. Anyway, what's your name?"

"Shep." I hand him his receipt.

"When I get home, I'll tell Sophie that Cersei and I saw you today."

I nod, unable to muster so much as a fake smile. "Yeah, you do that."

After he leaves and things die down a bit, I grab my phone and download several dating apps. Either I hook up with someone ASAP or I adopt more dogs. I'm not sure if there is any sort of group therapy for people who use pet adoption to soothe their grievances in life. Can I "find a meeting" around me?

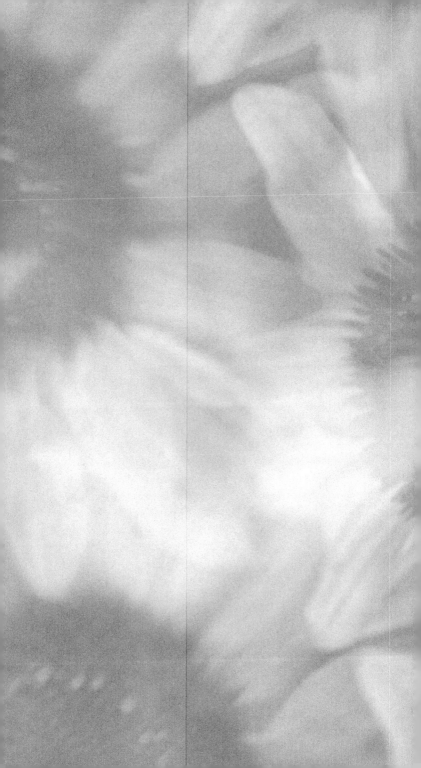

CHAPTER
Thirty-Eight

SOPHIE

I DECIDE it's time for a heart-to-heart with Shep, but not until we tell the rest of the family. Not until I have a bigger bump. I need him to see me, really see me. Pregnant me. Then he can make a decision. We can no longer pretend reality doesn't exist in Shep World, even if I miss that escape.

Mom loses her mind. She's overjoyed.

Mason's parents are a little more reserved. After all, their grandchild is in the womb of a woman who is not married to their son. They need reassuring more than once that I did not have sex with Mason. The egg was Chloe's. The sperm was his.

Dad and Taryn share the same sentiment as Mom, but not without the light bulb going on. Yes, it's why I wasn't drinking or eating fish.

A month later, I'm showing with a fitted tee. A cute little bump. I decide it's time to visit Shep, but not before telling Jimmy. He's close to finishing his place. I never imagined us reaching this level of amicability, yet here we are.

"Hey," I say to Jimmy as he packs a sandwich for

his dinner before heading off to his house. He's finishing the entry tile. The carpet gets laid next week. Then ... he's moving out of my house.

He glances up and smiles, glances back down, then does a double take. Zeroing in on my little bump, his lips part.

"It's not yours," I say before he jumps to any conclusions.

His eyes flit to mine, and he nods slowly. I'm proud of him. The Jimmy who riffled through the trash, searching for tampons, would not have given me a chance to say anything before jumping to conclusions.

"When I knew things weren't going to work out between us, which was long before you accepted it..." I smirk and he can't help but concede with a smile "...I offered to be a surrogate for Chloe and Mason. I've been sworn to secrecy, but now family knows, so it's no longer a secret."

He returns his gaze to my stomach. "Jesus ... I've been the biggest asshole ever."

"You have." I chuckle. "I'm going to walk up to Wag Your Tail. I'll be back later. I'm sure you'll be gone by then. So I'll see you tomorrow."

"Oh!" He fills a big bottle with water. "That totally reminds me. It was probably a month or two ago, but I met the owner when I stopped in there with Cersei to pick up treats."

"Oh?" I say cautiously. "Was anyone else working that day?"

"Nope. Just him."

"Her," I say. "Marta, the owner, is a woman."

Jimmy shakes his head. "No. It was a man. Shit, what was his name?" He squints for a second.

"Shep?"

"That's it!"

"He's not the owner."

"Said he was."

"No." I shake my head. "You must have heard him incorrectly."

"I didn't." Jimmy shrugs. "Maybe he was lying."

Why would Shep lie about that?

"Did he recognize Cersei?"

Please say no.

"Yeah."

"Did he uh ... ask about you?"

"Yeah."

"What did you say?"

"I ... I don't remember. It's been a while."

"Well, try, Jimmy."

He shakes his head. "I don't know. I probably said I was your boyfriend. And before you get upset, I just said it because I wasn't sure what to say. He asked if I was the dog walker."

"Jimmy ..." I press my palms to my cheeks. "Why?" I mumble, dragging my hands down my face.

"What was I supposed to say? I'm sorry. Really."

"Just ... never mind. I'll ... I ... I have to go." I grab Cersei's leash, attach it to her collar, and bolt before Jimmy can say any more. He's said and done enough.

A month or two ... Shep's been thinking I'm with

Jimmy for a month or two. I feel sick, and it has nothing to do with the baby.

When I get to the store, it's crowded. Just my luck. Riley's at the register and Shep's showing someone how to work the wash station. In a matter of seconds, my bravery is crushed. What am I supposed to say when he has a store full of customers?

Hey, just wanted you to see my belly before I tell you that I love you and ask you to wait for me. Oh, and I heard you met Jimmy, my ex-boyfriend who's still living with me. Did I totally forget to mention that when we were friends having sex? Sorry, my bad.

While rehearsing what I'm not going to say, I miss Shep finishing up at the wash station and sneaking up behind me. "If you need help, you'll just have to ask Riley or me."

I turn. Shep looks at me like I'm a stranger. He's offering assistance like he would to any customer. And he doesn't let his gaze fall to my little bump. Not once. That hurts the most. I used to feel seen with Shep. Seen in a way that made me feel nervous and vulnerable, yet completely understood. Now, it's like he doesn't want to see me. He doesn't care to see me.

"Hi." I manage one word.

"You good?"

"Yeah, things are good."

He gives me a blank expression. "I meant, do you need help with anything or do you know what you're looking for?"

Jesus. This is it? This is where we're at?

"Can we talk?"

He glances around the busy store before returning his attention to me like I just suggested the dumbest thing ever.

"Can we talk later?" I try again.

"I'm going out with friends later."

"Tomorrow?"

"Sure. Do you want me to come to your house? Or do we need to meet some other place so your *boyfriend* doesn't find out?"

Pressing my lips together, I nod several times. "He's not my boyfriend."

"Doesn't matter. I have work to do." He turns and heads toward the checkout.

I grab a few items that I don't really need and get in line. When it's my turn, Riley smiles. "Find everything you were looking for?" She clearly doesn't recognize me. We were never formally introduced.

"Not really," I say. "Is the owner in today?"

"Yeah." She nods toward Shep standing behind her, retrieving treats out of the glass display.

"He's the owner?"

Riley nods. "Shep, she wants to speak to the owner. Let's swap," Riley says, taking the bag of treats from him and moving so he can stand at the register to help me.

"You're the owner?"

He types my name into the tablet and scans my items. "Yeah," he mumbles like it's no big deal, like I knew that.

"You called Marta your boss."

He shrugs, refusing to look at me as he bags my items. "She's bossy."

I toss my credit card onto the counter. "Is it weird that you never told me you owned this store?"

"No." He slides the credit card back to me. "We weren't real."

I deserve that. And I'm not mad. I'm surprised. Here I thought the lack of transparency was one-sided. I stare at him until he looks at me, holding my bag out for me to take it.

"I ... I thought you were ..."

"Broke?" He cocks his head to the side.

I shake my head.

"I thought you were single," he says.

"You thought I was getting married. Then married with kids. Homeless. On the run. You thought a lot of things that you knew weren't true."

He shrugs. "We needed a narrative, and you weren't providing one. But cheating on your boyfriend? Gotta say, that I didn't expect from you."

"He's not my boyfriend. I never lied to you." It's a stretch, but it's true.

"I never lied to you either."

"Shep ..."

"Thanks for stopping by. Hope you enjoy your purchase."

"Shep ..."

"Next." He leans to the side to see past me to the person waiting behind me.

I pivot, pulling Cersei toward the door. After partially opening it, I turn back around and let it slowly shut behind me.

Shep glances up as if to check that I'm gone. When he notices I'm standing at the door staring at him, he can't seem to look away.

"You're a terrible friend, Shep." That was supposed to come out as an "I love you." That was the plan. Why do my plans always go to shit?

I love you, Shep. Just say it!

A few people in line turn to look at me. I'm sure there's more than just a few staring at me, but I focus only on Shep.

"I didn't ask for you to be in my life. You weaseled your way into it. For a moment, maybe several moments, I let you be my *best* friend. Friends have to be more ... friends have to be a safe place to share your fears, your dreams, heartaches, and the embarrassing things that make you feel *less*. Friends have to be able to see all the ugly and be there anyway. Friends hold hands. Friends embrace you when the world shakes you to the core. Friends don't see mistakes as faults. They see mistakes as reflections of all the parts of themselves that they hope someone will love anyway. Friends fix things; they don't break them.

"Friends don't hold grudges. Friends know they're not competing with anyone else for your love and trust. Friends don't get jealous. That's what lovers do. You said we were friends."

Jesus ... worst attempt at "I love you" ever.

I rest my free hand on my baby bump. "I've had the worst luck with men. And now, I'm pregnant with someone else's baby. When we met, I was in the process of trying to evict Jimmy, my ex-boyfriend."

Shep flinches slightly. I think he just realized "my friend" with boyfriend issues was, in fact, me.

"I couldn't tell you about the baby, and I was incredibly embarrassed about my situation with Jimmy. And you weren't supposed to be in my life. Yet, there you were. A desperately needed moment of reprieve. A moment of peace. A breath. Shep, you made it easier to breathe. Then you made claim to my heart piece by piece. It happened slowly at first, nearly undetectable. Then in Santa Monica you just ... took the whole damn thing in one afternoon. Then..." I shake my head "...Jimmy's mom died. You decided we couldn't be friends. And things fell apart. Friends pretend to be strong even when they're not. They're experts at putting on a brave face for each other. I needed your brave face ... but you walked away."

I point to myself. "But I didn't. I saw what you needed. You needed an out. So I put on *my* brave face and gave it to you. I was the better friend." I quickly brush away a tear. "You ..." Pulling in a wobbly breath, I shake my head. "You are a terrible friend."

But I love you. God ... I love you so much.

Some people dance around the truth. I just performed an entire recital of theatrics, saying everything but the truth.

Maybe we'll never be real.

Except for a few dogs whining and making an occasional bark, the store is quiet. The "confessing my love" speech just went way off the rails in front of the dog world.

I know it's only a few seconds, but in my head and my heart it feels like eternity. Shep drops his gaze from me to the customer at the counter and says, "Did you find everything you were looking for?"

With plenty of eyes still on me, I tuck my chin, pivot, and leave Wag Your Tail. Now I know the answer. I won't spend another second of my life wondering.

CHAPTER
Thirty-Nine

OVER THE NEXT WEEK, I force myself to stick to a routine. Work. Crochet. Exercise. Walk Cersei. Repeat. Repeat. Repeat. If I don't schedule in time to think about Shep, I won't. Well, that's not true, but the goal is eventually to no longer think about him.

When I get home on a Friday, the first thing I notice is the missing urn on the coffee table. I make my way toward the bedrooms, peeking inside Jimmy's room and turning on the light. Everything's gone.

"Cersei?" She's not here either. Jimmy must have her.

I check my phone. No messages. When I call him, he answers on the third ring.

"Hey," he says.

"Hey. I'm home. All your stuff is gone. So is Cersei. Either we were robbed and the robbers didn't take anything of mine except my dog, or ..."

"I moved out."

I laugh a little. "Okay. You said it would be another week or two since there was a delay with the carpet."

"Check your security camera footage."

"Why?" I make my way to the kitchen.

"Just check it."

401

"Okay. I'll check it."

"And Sophie?"

"Yeah?"

"I'm not mad."

"Mad?"

"You deserve someone like that."

"Like ... what?"

He's being so cryptic.

"Someone who kicks the *squatter* to the curb because no one is going to take advantage of the woman he loves. You deserve *that* kind of love. I should have loved you like that. And I don't have Cersei. He must have taken her." Jimmy disconnects the call.

I stare at the screen for a few seconds. "What are you talking about?" I mumble to myself while bringing up the security footage from inside and outside of the house. "Oh my god ..." It's Shep and some other guy. I rewind further to them arriving at my house in Shep's car. They go to the door. Jimmy answers. They drag him out of the house. Jimmy fights back, but he's outnumbered. Cersei barks, but she doesn't attack anyone. Wow ... she's not a good watch dog.

Words are spewed, but there's no audio. After a long exchange and Jimmy getting punched in the face twice, Shep's friend stays outside with Jimmy while Shep makes multiple trips in and out of the house with Jimmy's stuff.

With a final shove for good measure, they release Jimmy and he sprints toward the house which insti- gates another altercation. Jimmy catches a few more blows to his face. Then Shep stomps into the house and grabs the urn, returning to Jimmy and shoving it into his chest as he points toward the street. I speed up the video as Jimmy loads his stuff into the back of his mom's old car and drives off. Shep and his friend tidy up the house, take Cersei, and leave.

It's not good for me to be angry. Can I talk myself out of this level of anger? Probably not. He has my dog. What is wrong with him?

Grabbing my keys, I drive to Shep's house, taking slow, deep breaths the whole way. This poor baby.

When I knock on the door, dogs bark. It's so loud. He must have Julia and George too. It's *a lot* of barking.

"Just a sec," Shep yells from the other side of the door.

I unclench my jaw and my fists. My anger won't easily dissipate.

The door opens, and it's just him and Cersei. She comes to me, and I bend down to pet her, keeping my gaze on Shep the whole time. He's wearing the same tee and jeans he had on in the video footage.

"What the hell have you done?"

Sliding his hands into his pockets, he leans against the doorframe. "You'll have to be more specific."

Baby. Baby. Baby.

In my calmest voice possible, I steady my shaky words. "You beat up Jimmy, kicked him out of *my* house, and stole my dog."

"Whoa ..." His head juts backward, eyes narrowed. "I didn't steal your dog. I wasn't sure when you'd be

403

home, so I brought her here to feed her dinner. She's been on a walk and played with the pack."

Standing to my full height, I tip my chin up. "You. Beat. Up. Jimmy."

"I removed him from your home a lot faster than the legal system was doing it. You're welcome."

"Why? I didn't ask you to do that. He was planning on leaving in a week or two."

"Oh. I'll tell you why, but I want to get the wording correct. Come in." He disappears into the house, and I'm forced to follow him.

Gathered on the other side of his sliding doors to the backyard there are five dogs.

"Why do you have all of those dogs?"

Shep ignores me. He's too busy unfolding a piece of paper. "The security footage at the shop doesn't have audio, but the dog camera that's right by the door has it, so I was able to replay everything and write down what you said." He smooths out the wrinkled piece of paper using the edge of his counter before studying it.

"W-why .... why would you do that?"

He glances at me quickly. "So I didn't miss anything." Returning his gaze to the paper, he clears his throat. "There's a lot here, but I tried to prioritize. So ... let's see." He mumbles a bit, "I'm a terrible friend ... uh ... let's see ... a weasel ... um ... there's the list of things I didn't live up to ... this, that, okay... where is it? Oh, here. Friends fix things. And then ...." He narrows his eyes, scanning the page again. "Right here. 'When we met, I was in the process of trying to evict Jimmy, my ex-boyfriend.'" Shep eyes me with confidence in his posture. "Done. I fixed that for you. It felt most pressing. You're welcome."

I've got nothing. Not one word. Barely a blink.

"Oh ..." He gestures toward the pack of dogs behind the doors. "Instead of binge drinking or hooking up with a string of bad decisions or eating loads of shitty food, I've been adopting dogs from the shelter. It's getting out of hand. I might need to find a new vice. I think this list will help." He holds up the piece of paper.

"I'm going to continue to make my way through it. I fear some things will require some decoding. Other things are painfully blunt. I'm a little competitive, so as you can imagine, I'm going to do whatever it takes not to be a terrible friend."

He pockets his hands and lifts his shoulders into a big shrug before dropping them with a loud exhale. "I'm sorry, Sophie." He deflates a fraction. It's an unexpected surrender. "If you can give your sister and her husband a baby ... if you can put your life on hold for nine months, I can put on a brave face for you. I can hold your hand. I can be strong for you even on the days I'm not feeling all that strong myself."

Emotion shoots through me, tingling my skin and burning my eyes. A lump forms in my throat and makes it hard to breathe and nearly impossible to speak.

"I'm going to step up and be more so you never have to feel like *less*. I'm going to look at you like my friend, Sophie, the woman I admire for her ability to give freely, to love unconditionally. I'm done feeling sorry for myself because Millie's baby is not mine. Your baby is not mine. This isn't about me, and I will try my best to remember that."

He blurs behind my tears.

I swear this baby is the *one* thing I've managed to get right in my life. I'm so not worthy of this man.

"Shep, my life isn't on hold." I rest a hand on my belly. "This is my life. This baby is and always will be a part of my life."

He nods slowly, deep concentration wrinkling his handsome face. "Want to walk the pack with me sometime?"

I wipe my tears and smile. "Yeah. That would be great."

"I'm golfing Saturday morning. You up for that?"

Sniffling, I continue to nod as my grin doubles. "Yeah."

His lips twist while averting his gaze for a few seconds. "Jimmy had to go. I won't apologize for that."

"I know," I whisper.

Jimmy was going to go. I feel certain of that. But maybe Jimmy needed to learn his own lesson, one I couldn't teach him. What he did to me was wrong, regardless of my pregnancy status. And I'm not sure that means what Shep did to him was "right," but it was big. Really big. Knight in shining armor *big*.

"Thank you. Maybe I should have trusted you with my ugly truth. I might need a copy of that speech. I could probably learn a few things too." I give him a slight shrug and half smile. "But I loved, I *needed* Shep World, a perfect slice of happiness. The greatest destination on Earth."

"Shep World ..." He chuckles and shakes his head. "I get it. Feeling weak is embarrassing. Trust me ... I get it."

I can't imagine Shep ever feeling weak. "Is that why you had to take a friend to help beat up my ex?"

"Shut it, Sophie." He narrows his eyes, but his lips pull into a beaming smile.

CHAPTER *FORTY*

SHEP

OVER THE FOLLOWING MONTHS, I download every self-help audiobook that I can find. I'm fairly certain a therapist would tell me I have some sort of unresolved feelings from Millie lying to me. Months of betrayal. All the times we "made love" and I thought (I hoped) we were making a baby, and she knew we weren't. She wasn't making love to me. She was fucking me.

I told myself I would never make love to another woman. I would fuck them before they fucked me. Turns out, with Sophie, I may have fucked myself.

Figures.

"Where are you?" Sophie asks as I stare into the distance long after we've both teed off.

She's messing with my head. Her bare legs in that skirt or shorts thingy that she wears ... well, they taunt me. It hugs her perfect ass. And her sleeveless tee molds her seven-month baby belly. She's not swollen. She's not lost her ability to kick my ass on the golf course. If anything, I'm more attracted to her now than ever before, which sucks because we're friends. We haven't done the best friend thing since Santa Monica. It's all … really messing with my head.

"I'm uh … thinking about your birthing classes. Those start next week. Right?"

"Yeah." She swings her little ass toward the golf cart. "Why?"

"Do you need a partner?"

"You mean another partner? No. Chloe *and* Mason will be there. Were you going to offer?"

I shrug. Returning my club to my bag. "Yeah. I thought it would be the nice thing to do."

"It would be a little weird. I think it's assumed that one's birthing class partner will be in the delivery room. And if you think I'm letting you be in the delivery room with me, you are living on another planet, buddy. I'm still not sure how I feel about Mason being in there. I know … I just know he's not going to stay by my head. He's going to see ten centimeters of my vagina."

I can't hide my grin, so I cough into my fist. It's never enough. I will never get enough of Sophie Ryan. My sun. Always the brightest star. Warm and comforting. I miss her when she's not with me. And every day, she's the first thought in my head, my sunrise.

"It's not funny, Shep." She grimaces, holding the side of her belly as she climbs into the cart.

"What's wrong?"

She shakes her head. "I'm just getting kicked in the ribs. No big deal."

I stare at her belly. I love her belly. I love *her*. I

really *really* need to tell her that, but I don't want it to stress her out if she's not ready to deal with a pregnancy and me falling in love with her. "Can I ... would it be weird if I uh ... felt the baby kick?"

She lifts her brown eyes to mine and smiles. Without saying anything, she takes my hand and presses it to the side of her belly by her ribs. It moves. I feel it.

Fuck ... I feel *so* much.

"You're ..." I curl my lips together, second-guessing what I want to say. What I want her to know. "You're amazing, Sophie."

Her lower lip does that little quiver thing. And I know behind her tinted white-framed glasses her eyes are filled with tears. It's been a common occurrence lately. She blames it on the hormones.

"And if I ever introduce you to Howie, you have to promise not to tell him that I like you more than him."

"Stop it." She coughs a nervous laugh, sliding her fingers behind her glasses to wipe her eyes.

"I will never stop."

✳✳✳✳✳

OVER THE FOLLOWING WEEKS, I find any excuse to be with Sophie, even when she calls it quits on golfing because she's so close to her due date.

When she answers her door, just after nine at night, my pack and I greet her with a bouquet of pink flowers. I also find any excuse to bring her flowers.

Anything with echinacea, her favorite, but hard to find sometimes.

Just because is my favorite excuse for bringing her flowers.

"I think I'm done walking." Her lower lip juts out, so does her belly and popped out navel where there's a two-inch gap between her black hip hugging cotton shorts and white tank top that I don't think is an actual maternity top. Her royal blue-framed glasses are low on her nose.

"Are you in labor?"

Sophie shakes her head, hair a little matted on one side like she's been napping on that side.

"Then we walk."

"Shep ..." She pouts a little more. "The flowers are beautiful, but I don't deserve them."

"You do. Let's walk."

"I'm too fat or..." she cringes "...bloated to walk tonight."

I hand her the flowers and push her glasses up her nose. "You're pregnant."

"I'm gross."

"You're beautiful."

She rolls her eyes and pivots. "I'll give you a day pass from friend code. You can fold up that piece of paper and burn it. Complimenting me at this point is too laughable."

"Whoa, whoa, whoa ..." I follow her inside the house and get Cersei's leash on her. "What happened to perky Sophie? The one who was glowing because she knew her pregnancy was the world's most generous gift? I'm pretty sure I saw that Sophie a few days ago."

"She got a good look in the mirror." Tears fill her eyes.

I try not to laugh. She's pregnant. She knows that's all this is. *Man ... pregnancy hormones are no joke.*

"Look ..." Her lower lip quivers as she pulls down the waist of her shorts an inch.

"What am I looking at?"

She runs her fingers over an area. "Stretch marks." When she blinks, several tears escape.

I honestly can't see what she's pointing to, so I hunch down in front of her. There are a few purplish squiggly lines. "Sophie—"

"Don't." She sniffles. "Don't say anything. I don't want you to say anything. It won't make me feel better. And I know ... I know it's stupid, they're just stretch marks, but ..." She swallows hard and shrugs.

She's right, my friend code note won't help me. So I do my own thing. I do what feels natural.

"Shep ..." One of her hands threads through my hair when I kiss the purple lines on her lower belly. "What are you doing?" she whispers.

I don't speak because she was right. There are no words to make this better for her in this very moment. So I close my eyes and kiss every inch of her belly. Then I stand.

Her red-eyed gaze lifts to meet mine.

My thumbs brush along her cheeks, erasing the tears. She pulls in a shaky breath.

"Let's walk."

"I can't reach my feet."

I grin, knowing that's not true. "Good thing I can. Sit." I nod to the entry bench.

When she surrenders, I kneel in front of her and slip her white sneakers onto her bare feet and loosely tie them.

Before I stand, she frames my face with her hands. "If I tell you a secret, promise not to tell anyone?" she whispers.

I nod once, resting my hands on her bare legs.

"Sometimes when we're together ... walking the dogs, golfing, eating lunch ... I pretend..." she blinks, averting her gaze "...that this baby inside of me is ..." After a few breaths, she looks at me. "Ours."

Her confession hits me pretty hard. Now ... now is when I need to review that piece of paper before I say the wrong thing.

On a nervous laugh, she lifts a shoulder. "That's stupid, right? Because we're just friends."

Yes. Sophie is my friend. A friend who I love. She's taken up residence in my head and all four chambers of my heart. And my competitive friend doesn't often show me her vulnerable side. Even if it's the hormones, I'll take it. I'll take this vulnerability of hers and let it open the door for me to have my own vulnerable moment.

"It's not stupid. Imagination is never stupid." I peel

her hands from my face, keeping ahold of one as I stand and pull her to her feet too. "We walk."

As we head out the door, I hold the leashes in one hand and keep hers in my other hand.

"Did I guilt you into staying my friend? Has it been hard on you? Watching me, watching Millie with her pregnancy? And be honest. I can handle the truth," she says.

As I guide the pack and my favorite friend down the driveway, I contemplate how to answer her in truly the most honest way. "It's been, uh ... a mix of relief and hope."

"How so?"

"When I see Millie, I feel relieved. I think about what it could have been like had she gotten pregnant when we were 'trying.' A baby she didn't really want. Her desperately wanting to have her own career ... I would have done whatever it took to make things work. But I don't think it would have been enough. I think we would have turned into Howie and Caroline. And that sucks. But when I see you, I have hope. You've made me a believer in patience. I don't know what's in my future, but in the present, what serves me best, what makes me feel like I have purpose is taking care of the people who are in my life now. My family and my *friends.*"

"Shep?"

"Yeah?"

"Not to change the subject, but I've wanted to ask

you something. The answer doesn't matter. It really doesn't. I'm just curious."

"Ask away."

"Are you rich?"

I chuckle. "Is that a deep, philosophical question? Or are you inquiring about my bank account and investments?"

"The latter."

"Why?"

She stares at her feet as we cross the street. "Because I've been trying to really figure you out since the day we met, and it feels like one of the final pieces to the puzzle."

"I don't know how I feel about you solving me."

She giggles. "I'm not sure that's possible, but I think I've earned full disclosure since I've told you my deepest, darkest secrets."

On the other side of the street, I stop, letting the dogs gather around a street signpost, sniffing until their hearts are content. Facing Sophie, I step as close to her as her belly will allow. "Are you sure you've shared *all* your secrets?"

She smirks. "Just about."

"So you're keeping a few?"

"How rich are you, Shep? How ridiculous was it of me to worry about you paying for things? All the times I worried about you losing your job because of the way you talked to Marta? All of the sleepless nights I spent fretting over my attraction to yet another guy who might be on the road to being broke and homeless?"

"Enough. I have enough."

"That's a terrible answer."

I sigh. "I loaned money to a lot of people before Millie asked for a divorce. Family and close friends borrowed money to buy homes, cars, pet stores, things like that. Maybe I get paid back; maybe I don't."

"You gave money away so Millie couldn't take half of everything?"

I shrug. "Your words, not mine."

Sophie narrows her eyes. "Did you loan your dad money for the car you drive?"

I nod.

"The Mustang?"

I nod.

"Your house?"

I nod.

Her lips twist. "The house in Sedona."

I nod.

"Shep, what job did you have before you quit to work on your marriage?"

"Developed video games."

Her brows lift a fraction. "Are you joking?"

I shake my head. "This dyslexic kid wasn't the fastest reader, but I had other self-acquired skills."

"I've never seen you play a game in all the months I've known you."

"I don't do it anymore."

"And you made a lot of money doing it?"

"I did."

With several slow nods, she gives me a little "huh" and pulls my hand to keep walking.

When we return to her house, I toss the bags of poop in her garbage and meet her inside with the dogs.

As I hang up Cersei's leash and she toes off her sneakers, I wait for her to quiz me further on my net worth. She doesn't.

"Want to watch a movie? Or is it too late?" I ask.

"Both. It's too late, and I want to watch a movie."

I grin and head toward the sofa as the pack gather around the water bowl.

"In bed. I need like ten pillows to get comfortable enough to watch a movie." She rests one hand on her lower back and makes her cute little waddle toward her bedroom.

The pack and I follow.

"No." She gives Cersei a stern headshake when she goes to jump onto the bed. Cersei sulks off to find a spot on the floor with the other dogs.

"What are we watching?" she asks, collapsing onto the bed, grabbing pillows for her back, under her head, between her knees, another between her ankles, and another to hug.

I watch her, a little mesmerized.

"Sometimes I pretend this baby inside of me is ... ours."

"Your choice," I say, grabbing the remote and handing it to her while I lie next to her.

She turns on *The World's Most Extraordinary Homes*.

"This isn't a movie."

"I know," she says. "But Piers Taylor has the most soothing voice when he goes full-on architect nerd."

"Nerds do it for you?"

"Mm-hmm ..." She closes her eyes.

I slip off her glasses and set them on the night-stand. "If you're going to sleep, maybe I should go home."

"No," she mumbles in a sleepy voice. "Stay."

"I'll stay for one episode." I slide my arms around her, spooning her and her pillows to me, burying my nose in her hair. My fingers trace the skin where she has those faint purple stretch marks.

"Stay as long as you want," she says on a long yawn.

"Sophie, that's how you end up with men who refuse to leave."

Her body vibrates with a soft giggle.

CHAPTER
Forty-One

SOPHIE

"I HATE YOU. And I mean only love by that statement," Jules says.

I laugh, bare belly catching sun by her pool, a week from my due date. "You're giving me pool access before your kids get out of school. You can hate me for ... whatever reason."

"You're cute. You're basically ready to pop out a baby and you look cute. It's not fair."

Chuckling some more, I sip my lemonade. "I'm sure this doesn't matter, but I feel fat. I mean, beautiful too, but fat. So fat. And I've been avoiding Shep because some days I feel gross. And don't you dare tell Chloe I said that. She's a freakin' wreck right now. She comes by my house every day. Texts me hourly. And loses it if she can't see my location on her Find My Friends."

"She's just really excited."

I sigh. "I know."

"And Shep ... how's that going? Are you slaying the whole friends thing?"

"Totally. Except when my hormones get the best of me and he witnesses me crying over stretch marks."

"Oh dear. How did that go?"

He kissed them.

I told him I sometimes pretend the baby is ours.

Then he held me in bed ... for the whole night.

"Fine. He'd never be anything but kind to me."

"Is he dating? I mean. If you're not having sex with him, someone should be. Right?"

"Don't know. Don't care."

"Liar."

I frown. "He's been there, Jules. Like really been there. He rubs my back. Massages my feet. Cooks me dinner. Brings me flowers. Takes Cersei on pack walks before it gets too hot outside. He came over and cleaned my bathrooms the other day. But that's it. I mean, it's not like I expect him to be all horny for a nine-month pregnant woman carrying a baby that's not his. But I thought when we patched things up that something *more* might come from it. I was wrong. We are friends. Just friends. He stayed the night! We watched a show. I fell asleep. And in the morning, he was next to me fully clothed."

She clears her throat. "Do I get to say 'I told you so?'"

"You told me what?"

"I told you he would not feel comfortable pursuing you after he found out about your pregnancy, *unless* you gave him the green light."

"I spilled my guts that day at the shop. He has actual footage, and he wrote everything down."

"Sophie! Gah! That was a friendship speech. I'm sure it was beautiful and epic. You gave me the highlights, and the common theme in the speech was friendship."

"Not true. I told him that he took my heart piece by piece and then he took the whole thing when we went to Santa Monica."

"Well, it probably got lost in the *friendship* speech. If someone gave you a five-minute speech on how ugly you are but they said the word pretty just once, where do you think your focus would be?"

"Duh, on the pretty. I'd be saying 'Hold up! Did you say I'm pretty?'"

"Congratulations on your astuteness. But Shep might need it put to him a little differently."

"Different how?"

"Oh, I don't know. Maybe 'Shep, I love you. I want you to plant your dick in me from now until eternity. What do you say?'"

I giggle. "I'm not saying that."

She shrugs. "Fine. Skip the 'I love you' part. I honestly think he'll interpret the other part as a declaration of your undying love for him."

Biting the inside of my cheek, I stare at the empty floaty in the pool.

"Sophie, the best time to tell someone how you feel about them is now. When you have kids of your own, you'll find that out quite quickly. You won't let them go

JEWEL E. ANN

from one room to the next without reminding them how much you love them. Life's too unpredictable and sometimes painfully unforgiving. Shep could get in a car accident on his way home from work today. Don't let anything go unsaid."

She's thinking of her brother. The things she left unsaid.

"Calvin is the reason I went to optometry school."

"What?" She lowers her sunglasses to look at me.

"I had a crush on him. The most incurable crush ever. And I was so afraid to tell you. I'm not even sure why. I think I wanted to be able to talk about guys with you, but I knew you'd never let me tell you how hot I thought your brother was."

"Sophie Ryan ..."

I grin. "I had no clue what I wanted to do in life, but following Calvin seemed like as good an idea as any."

"Huh." She leans back and rolls her head toward me. "I can't believe you're just now telling me this."

"Well, my dearest friend, Jules, just told me that it's not a good idea to leave anything unsaid. I fear I have a lot of catching up to do with a lot of people."

"That Jules friend of yours is so smart."

I nod. "She is."

"What time are your parents coming?"

"Mom is coming tomorrow. Dad and Taryn are coming the following day. And then it officially begins. The wait. And you know what that means. I will go two weeks late. Everyone will be here, staring at me, watching me every second. It's going to be the worst."

"Your doctor won't let you go two weeks late."

"I hope not. She's awfully chill. I can see her letting me go until the baby comes out a toddler."

*****

AFTER LEAVING JULES'S HOUSE, I stop by the grocery store to restock since Dad and Taryn will be staying with me until the baby's born. Mom's staying with Chloe and Mason until the birth and for a week after the birth.

As I walk around the store, I feel some growing discomfort. Pain in my lower abdomen. A little twinge on my right side. Aisle by aisle, it increases in intensity.

I'm a week early. This isn't labor. Is it? Mom went nearly two weeks late with both Chloe and me, but when she did go into labor, it happened very quickly. And that thought is what makes me pull my phone out of my purse.

"I was just going to call you," Chloe says, answering on the first ring. "Is everything okay?"

"Don't freak out, but—"

"OH MY GOSH! OH MY GOSH! MASON! IT'S TIME! Are you okay? Is everything okay. We'll head to your house right now to get you."

It's impossible not to laugh a little, but at the same time I cringe because these have to be contractions I'm having. And they are close together. Chloe's excitement once again reaffirms that I've done something truly good with my life.

"I'm ..." I lean onto the shopping cart and take a few breaths. "I'm at the grocery store."

"Which store?"

"Trader Joe's ... Lincoln Village."

"We're already in the car. Don't hang up. Stay on the line."

Again, I laugh and cringe at the same time.

Abandoning my cart, I waddle to my car, stopping to bend forward and rest my hands on my knees when a contraction hits.

"Breathe, Sophie. Slow in. Slow out." Chloe's managed to calm herself down and be the soothing voice I need.

When I collapse into the passenger seat of my car, I put her on speaker and text Shep.

Me: I'm in labor. Can you go to my house and get my bag and the baby blanket? Can you take care of Cersei?
Shep: On it! Breathe, Sophie xo

"I'm texting Mom and Dad. I don't think they'll make it, so I'm going to tell them not to try," Chloe says. "Are you breathing?"

"Uh-huh ..." This hurts way more than I anticipated. "Oh ... shit ..." I reach between my legs.

"Oh shit what? What happened?" Panic resurrects in Chloe's voice.

"My water broke."

"That's fine. Totally fine. Just don't push. Don't you dare push."

"Chloe, I ..." I stutter, frozen in pain as another contraction grips me. It hurts. This has gone zero to a hundred quickly. Too quickly.

I try to focus on something besides the pain as I wait. When they arrive, Mason helps me into the back of their minivan and speeds off toward the hospital.

Everything blurs upon our arrival. It feels like a calm chaos. I don't see straight; the pain is so intense.

"I heard you want to push." Dr. Munson moseys into the room as the nurse helps her slide into a gown and gloves.

"Y-yeah ..." I grimace, and Chloe squeezes my hand harder than I'm squeezing hers.

Dr. Munson checks me. "Nice, Sophie. You're doing amazing. And when you want to push, I want you to listen to your body and push."

"I need s-something for the p-pain ..."

Dr. Munson chuckles. "Sorry, Sophie. This baby is ready to come into the world now. And you're going to do it just fine without anything for the pain."

My next breath is completely robbed by the urge to push.

I don't have time to stop, to think, or really do much careful listening to my body. I just push with every contraction until the familiar cry of a baby fills the room.

"It's a boy!" Chloe yells, kissing my head and my cheek over and over again as tears flood her cheeks.

"Thank you," she whispers repeatedly. "Soph ... oh my god ... th-thank you."

She cuts the cord. Then she and Mason follow the nurse to the other side of the room where they check over the baby while Dr. Munson tends to me.

"You know," Dr. Munson says as she presses on my tummy, "I truly believe there's a special place in heaven for women like you."

I stare at Chloe as the nurse swaddles the baby and places him in his mother's arms. He is not my child. He is my nephew. Chloe's egg. Mason's sperm. And I will be in his life for as long as I live. But still, right now, I feel empty. This isn't a surprise. I should have expected this. We were counseled on this beforehand. It's just not something one can truly prepare for, like I couldn't really imagine what it would feel like to push a baby out of my body until it was happening.

It hurt more than I imagined.

And this emptiness hurts more than I imagined as well.

"Evan, meet your amazing Aunt Sophie," Chloe says as she hands me my nephew. "But I think you already know her quite well." She winks.

I inspect his little nose and tiny fingers at his mouth.

After a while, Mason leaves the room to call his parents and ours while Chloe falls in love with her son. I get acquainted with a breast pump. We agreed I'd pump as long as it was sustainable. Of course, I had no idea it would be this "fun." And by fun, I mean I feel like a barnyard animal.

"If Mason walks in here while I'm doing this, I will never be able to look him in the eye again. As is, I know he snuck a peek at his baby coming out of my vagina."

Chloe snorts while swaying back and forth with Evan in her arms. She's a natural. I know this loneliness, this emptiness, will not last long. I have too many wonderful people in my life to fill it.

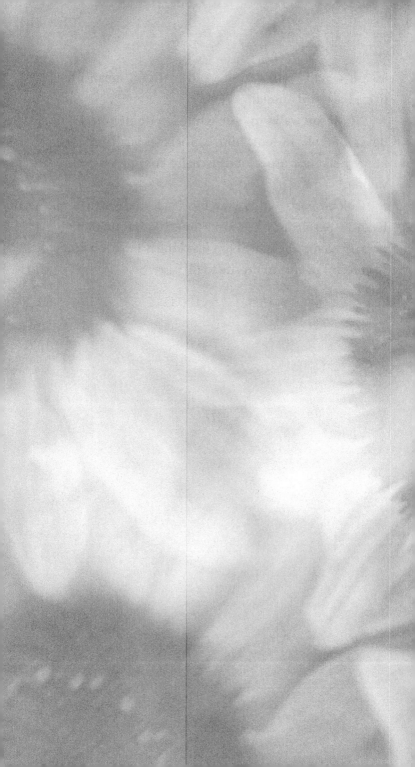

YESTERDAY, Shep dropped off my bag and the baby blanket that I crocheted, but I was asleep. Nobody woke me, so he left because he needed to return to his pack of dogs and my Cersei.

Me: Hi

I accidentally press send on the text to Shep instead of finishing what I was going to say. He texts back before I can finish.

Shep: Fine. Thank you.

I snort and quickly cover my mouth because Chloe's in the chair sleeping while Mason paces the room with Evan in his arms.

Me: I'm being discharged. Want to pick me up and take me to my abandoned car in the Trader Joe's parking lot? If you're not busy. If you are, don't worry about it. I'll have Mason take me or see if Jules can do it.
Shep: Sophie?
Me: What?
Shep: I've been in the waiting room since six this morning.

"What?" I whisper to myself, staring at the screen. Already dressed, I ease off the side of the bed.

"Where are you going?" Mason whispers.

"Waiting room. Be right back. Tell the nurse I didn't jump ship."

I make a snail's trek toward the waiting room. Shep's nowhere in sight because he's hidden behind a huge bouquet of pink flowers. He sets them on a table and meets me halfway.

"I have a sanitary napkin, roughly the size of Cape Cod, in my sweatpants. My belly is wrapped like a mummy to splint my insides back in place. And my boobs are going to quadruple in size and start leaking in the next forty-eight hours."

Shep's eyebrows inch up his forehead.

I shrug. "So I realize this is probably not the best time to say this, but it's the only time that we're guaranteed so—"

"I love you," he says.

I'm ... speechless. And unprepared to hear this from him. And quite frankly, I'm a little perturbed. *He stole my line!*

"Take it back," I say.

"What?" He chuckles.

I cross my arms over my chest. "Take it back. I was talking, and you interrupted me. That's rude. So you have to take it back."

He mirrors my stance, crossing his arms over his chest. "I'll do no such thing."

I shove him.

His eyes widen.

"Did you just *shove* me?"

"Take. It. Back."

His stupid, kissable lips bend into an obnoxious smile. "Why?"

"Because I wanted to love you first."

"Well, I hate to break it to you, but if you just came to this conclusion, then you don't get to call dibs on 'first' because after a lot of self-reflection, I'm pretty sure you had me the day you spilled your iced coffee all over my store. I loved you first. Can you handle that?"

I roll my eyes. "Don't you worry about what I can or cannot handle. I just pushed a seven-pound human out of my body with nothing for the pain, and my boobs make magical milk."

Shep fights his grin.

"Do you want to meet my nephew?" I bail on the conversation.

His relinquishes one hundred percent of that grin. It's blinding. "Maybe in a minute."

"In a minute?"

"Yeah. I have something to do first."

"What's that?" I cock my head to the side.

"I'm going to kiss you. And I'm also going to cop a feel of your boobs before they start leaking."

"You're not—"

He smashes his mouth to mine. And as promised, his hand cups my boob over my T-shirt.

✳✳✳✳

THREE WEEKS and five days later ...

"What's in the bag?" I ask when Shep arrives home from work about thirty minutes after me.

Home.

I did it again. I've let a man basically move in with me. Every day, more of his stuff appears at my house. Every night, he's in my bed. So far, he's kept his job at the pet store, and he showers daily.

"Nothing much." He sets the bag on the counter and pulls me into his arms. "Hi." He grins while brushing his lips over mine.

"Fine. Thank you," I murmur.

He kisses me. It's a little more intense than this morning's goodbye kiss. It's a little more intense than he's kissed me since ... I'd say Santa Monica.

"I ..." I break the kiss. "I'm a..." I give him a little chuckle "...little sensitive in uh ... areas. I just pumped."

A wolfish grin steals his face. It doesn't help my situation. "Sensitive? Or aroused?"

With another chuckle, the nervous kind meant to hide my embarrassment, I take a few steps backward. "Um ... how was the shop today? Busy?"

Shep eyes me like a hunter, moving in on me slowly as I continue to retreat until I hit the edge of the counter, gripping the edge with both hands as I swallow hard. "I miss my *best* friend," he says, while ducking his head and kissing along my jaw to my neck.

"Uh ..." I wet my lips and close my eyes. "It's only been—"

"Three weeks five days ... almost six days," he mumbles over my skin, licking and teasing it with his teeth as his hand snakes up my shirt.

"Shep!" I yelp when his thumb dips into the cup of my bra and grazes my nipple, my very sensitive, recently-stimulated-by-a-breast-pump nipple. "S-six ... w-weeks ..." I stutter as he kisses along my shoulder, one hand sliding the strap down my arm while his other hand drives me insane with more nipple stimulation than is bearable.

"*Four* to six," he murmurs. "We're close enough."

"Shep." I have weak resistance despite my self-consciousness about my lactating breasts and postpartum situation down below.

"I could still spot ..." Spotting is not a sexy subject, but Shep doesn't seem to care.

"You're not. I haven't seen any pads in the trash."

I giggle because I told him about Jimmy and the tampons.

He kisses me and my legs get a little wobbly. "If you're not ready, then we wait." He kisses me again. "Are you ready?"

I'm hyper stimulated. Over the past week, I've been getting, yes, *aroused* when pumping my breasts. It doesn't help that the tiniest of kisses gives Shep an erection that he can't fully hide from me.

We have no baby keeping us awake at night.

I'm back to work and feeling great.

And neither one of us has had sex in months and months.

We've had *nothing* to do with our free time other than think about sex.

I cup him over his jeans, and that's my answer to his question.

"Lube," he says on a moan, while dropping his head to my shoulder and rocking his pelvis into my touch. "I ..." His breaths quicken as my fingers unbutton and unzip his jeans. "I bought ... a bottle of ... lube. I-in the bag." He's unraveling right here, right in front of me in the kitchen.

Lube. Shep bought lube. I bite my lips to hide my grin in case he glances up at me. Only the guy who carries around a piece of paper with the codes of friendship would do his homework to know that lube is suggested for postpartum sex the first time.

However, I'm not the sleep deprived mom who hasn't showered in days and smells like sour milk. I'm the recovering surrogate with sex on the brain and a confusing relationship with a breast pump. I take his hand and guide it down the front of my leggings and into my panties.

"Fuuuck ..." He smashes his lips to mine, spurred on by discovering that I don't need a drop of lube. I'm seconds away from losing it, and I think he's right with me. I'm not sure we'll get our clothes off before one of us orgasms.

We manage to discard our shirts before leaving the

kitchen. My bra gets shoved to my waist midway to the bedroom as he stops to suck and bite my nipples.

Je ... sus ... I'm losing it ...

When we reach the bed, he yanks my leggings and panties down my legs, I manage to kick them off one foot but not the other. So they remain tangled around that ankle while Shep makes a clumsy, incredibly impatient effort at pulling his jeans and briefs down, but he only gets them halfway to his knees before he's pinning me to the bed and sliding into me.

"Ohmygod ohmygod ohmygod ..." I bite his shoulder while my heart sprints—the pulsating *whoosh* in my ears, the palpation along my skin. I'm done. Just like that. I come the second he's inside of me, and he follows suit less than a minute later.

We remain still, a pile of limp limbs and tangled clothes, our breaths slowing down, and one of the dogs whining at the door. My fingers tease Shep's hair, my lips at his ear. "I love you and ... I think you should move in with me."

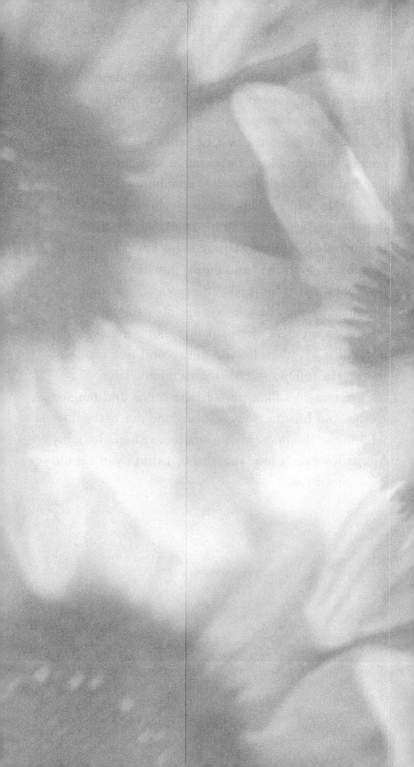

EPiLoGue

"I BEAT YOU." Shep replaces the flag on the eighteenth hole. Even at sixty, he's still sexy and cocky as hell.

"You sure did." I drag my putter to the cart with my good hand. I had surgery on my left wrist several weeks ago. Today, I'm golfing with one arm.

When he hops into the cart, he grins, sliding my glasses up my nose. "Best friends."

I roll my eyes, but there's no way I can keep from smiling.

When we get to the clubhouse bar, Shep grabs my good wrist and gives it a tug. "Midwesterner alert," he says under his breath.

When I spy Deb and Tony at a table in the far corner by the window, I hook my finger through his belt loop and give it a tug. "What's it been? A year or two since we've seen them?"

"Let's eat at home."

I chuckle. "I think Tony had knee replacement surgery last year. Let's go say hi."

"Woman, what is wrong with you?" Shep protests as I drag him toward their table.

"Just living the dream, babe. Golfing every day and sipping cold drinks with friends."

"Well, what on earth do my old eyes see?" Deb lights up as we approach their table.

"You're sucking my old shriveled up balls later," he whispers in my ear before putting on a fake smile and greeting our old friends.

I snort, cupping my hand over my mouth for a second while taking a seat next to Deb. "Hey, how have you guys been?"

Tony pulls out the chair next to him so Shep can have a seat. "We've been pretty good, thanks. You?"

I hold up my arm. "I had surgery on my wrist a few weeks ago, but I'm doing good." I'm good with embracing my age and limitations. And it's two o'clock on a regular ole Tuesday, and we have nothing better to do than catch up with friends.

"We finally got away after babysitting grandkids for the better part of last year," Deb says.

"Oh? How many do you have?" I ask.

Shep kicks my foot under the table, which only feeds my desire to catch up on everything with our chatty friends.

"Six. Can you believe it?" Tony says. "What about you guys? Have you added any since the last time we saw you?"

"We have four grandchildren," Shep says despite his stubborn reluctancy to engage in endless conversation. He's too proud of his family not to brag. "Laramie just got married, so I'm sure we'll be adding to that number soon."

"You have four kids, right?" Deb asks.

I start to speak, but Shep's on it. As long as we stay on the topic of our family, he'll talk all day like ... dare I say a Midwesterner?

"Five." Shep puffs out his chest. "Three girls and twin boys. They're all very close in age. Sophie just couldn't stay off me."

Tony barks a laugh, and Deb tries to control her sniggering, but she fails. I keep my gaze on my husband, my mouth turned up into a knowing grin. We did have our kids close together. Fourteen months after giving birth to my nephew, Evan, Shep and I welcomed our first girl. I'll never forget the day I told him that I was pregnant, that he was going to be a dad.

"I think you should hire another employee," I said while Shep restocked the glass case with dog treats like cookies, biscuits, and small cakes.

"I don't need another employee," he mumbled as I inspected the new display of dog toys.

A couple and their beagle slid past me and smiled.

"You do if you're going to get a different job."

He glanced up, a single eyebrow lifted. "I don't want another job."

I shrug. "You do."

He scoffed, closing the glass case. "And what job could I possibly like better than this one?"

"Dad."

"Dad?" He glanced around. "Whose dad? What dad? Babe, what are you talking about?" He chuckled.

I borrowed the phrase from the great squatter, Jimmy, "I think you'll crush the stay-at-home dad gig. Don't you?"

The couple with their dog set several items on the register counter. Just as Shep started to ask for their phone number, his lips parted, and his unblinking gaze slowly lifted to mine.

"Are you ... pregnant?" he said, barely a whisper. Just the possibility seemed to steal his breath.

Digging my teeth into my lower lip, I nodded.

And only my very best friend could infuse the worst joke ever into that moment. "Is it ... mine?"

I giggled and nodded again.

"Go. Go ..." He threw the couple's items into a bag. "They're ... uh free. On the house. I ... I'm going to be a dad!"

The couple smiled, taking the bag he shoved toward them before Shep jumped the whole counter and took me in his arms. My feet lifted off the floor as he kissed me and twirled me and kissed me some more. It wasn't until he finally set me back on my feet that I realized the tears on my cheeks weren't just mine, they were his too. Just another magnificent day in Shep World.

Our house has been filled with kids and dogs and so much love. And while Jimmy thought he would crush the stay-at-home-dad gig, Shep proved to be the master at that role. He kept the pet store but rarely took a shift unless someone was sick. He had kids to raise, dogs to train, and best friend code to follow.

To this day, he still has that wrinkled piece of paper that he occasionally pulls out of a drawer and reads with his reading glasses. Then he glances up at me while I'm crocheting something, and he says, "I still can't believe you said all these words when you only meant to say three."

I hold his gaze for a few moments. Even our stare-offs are competitive. He waits. And I surrender. I no longer care to fight with him; I only fight for him. "I love you."

The End

ACKNOWLEDGMENTS

For a rom-com, this was a painful labor of love. From storyline, to controversial dialogue, a million blurb revisions, and book cover dilemmas ... this project challenged me more than I ever could have imagined. I'm thrilled to say I'm overjoyed with the end result, and I want to thank my village who helped me get to the end.

To my family, thank you for keeping smiles on your faces while I had repeated breakdowns.

Jenn, thank you for holding my hand through every step of this, for listening, for encouraging, for being honest, for weathering the storm of changes with me.

Thank you, Nina, for long talks, brutal honesty, and top secret confessions about life and the hoops of fire we jump through to navigate the ever-changing world of publishing. You and your team at Valentine PR are superb!

To my beta readers and proofreading team (Leslie, Kambra, Monique, Amy, Sian, Jenn, Shauna, and

Bethany), you are the reason this book exists. Without your feedback and hard work, I might have let this one die on my computer. I'm so glad you helped me find my way back to all the good words, even if half of them were typos.

A big thank you to Max, my editor and publicist, for always finding time to read my manuscripts while working tirelessly with Kate to get my stories out to the world. I think this will be an exciting year!

To my awesome cover designers, Jenn and Estella, thank you for two beautiful covers for this story.

Finally, to my promotional teams of loyal readers and ALL the amazing influencers who have taken a chance on me, your generosity and creativity bring me to tears with every book release. I'm so honored to have you in my life. It is and always will be surreal.

ALSO BY JEWEL E. ANN

Jack & Jill Series

End of Day

Middle of Knight

Dawn of Forever

One (*standalone*)

Out of Love (*standalone*)

Holding You Series

Holding You

Releasing Me

Transcend Series

Transcend

Epoch

Fortuity (*standalone*)

The Life Series

The Life That Mattered

The Life You Stole

Receive a FREE book and stay informed of new releases, sales, and exclusive stories:

Mailing List

https://www.jeweleann.com/free-booksubscribe

ABOUT THE AUTHOR

Jewel is a free-spirited romance junkie with a quirky sense of humor.

With 10 years of flossing lectures under her belt, she took early retirement from her dental hygiene career to stay home with her three awesome boys and manage the family business.

After her best friend of nearly 30 years suggested a few books from the Contemporary Romance genre, Jewel was hooked. Devouring two and three books a week but still craving more, she decided to practice sustainable reading, AKA writing.

When she's not donning her cape and saving the planet one tree at a time, she enjoys yoga with friends, good food with family, rock climbing with her kids, watching How I Met Your Mother reruns, and of course...heart-wrenching, tear-jerking, panty-scorching novels.

www.jeweleann.com